"God bless the day that Walter Mosley created Easy Rawlins!"
—The Washington Post Book World

National acclaim for Walter Mosley's collection of Easy Rawlins stories

Six Easy Pieces

"Easy Rawlins remains [Mosley's] most popular, entertaining, and influential creation. . . . *Six Easy Pieces* balances suspects, false starts, and red herrings with unforgettable descriptions of life before civil rights."

—USA Today

"At their core, these stories are parables about the meaning of manhood. . . . The solutions to the crimes bring the revelation of passion gone tragically wrong, the pathos of friends protecting friends, lovers protecting lovers, mothers protecting sons."

—The Washington Post Book World

"A Christmas and birthday present rolled into one. . . . Mosley throws a lucky seven with this rock-solid addition to the Easy Rawlins series."

—Library Journal (starred review)

"Mosley's clean prose belies the complexity of his characters and their predicaments. Even when Easy must examine his own mysteries—who he is and how much freedom he can live with—Mosley delivers existential angst in the most entertaining disguise."

—San Francisco Chronicle

A Red Death

"Fascinating and vividly rendered . . . exotic and believable, filled with memorable and morally complex situations."

—*The Wall Street Journal*

"Exhilaratingly original."

—*Philadelphia Inquirer*

White Butterfly

"Rawlins . . . might be the best American character to appear in quite some time."

—*Entertainment Weekly*

"Compelling. . . . In all of American fiction, only Richard Wright treats America's race problem more savagely."

—*Village Voice Literary Supplement*

Black Betty

"Detective fiction at its best—bold, breathtaking, and brutal."

—*Chicago Sun-Times*

"As always, Mosley's grip on character is compelling."

—*People*

A Little Yellow Dog

"Easy Rawlins [is] one of the most distinctive voices in crime fiction."

—*Seattle Times*

"[A] well-energized and crafty volume."

—*The New York Times Book Review*

ALSO BY WALTER MOSLEY

FICTION

Gone Fishin'
Devil in a Blue Dress
A Red Death
White Butterfly
Black Betty
A Little Yellow Dog
Always Outnumbered, Always Outgunned
Bad Boy Brawly Brown
Walkin' the Dog
Fearless Jones
Blue Light
RL's Dream
Futureland

NONFICTION

Workin' on the Chain Gang

WALTER MOSLEY

SIX EASY PIECES

EASY RAWLINS STORIES

WASHINGTON SQUARE PRESS

New York   London   Toronto   Sydney   Singapore

FOR WALTER BERNSTEIN

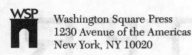 Washington Square Press
1230 Avenue of the Americas
New York, NY 10020

ISBN 978-0-7434-4254-1

First Washington Square Press trade paperback edition October 2003

10 9

"Smoke" first published in the 2002 Washington Square Press edition of
Gone Fishin'.

"Crimson Stain" first published in the 2002 Washington Square Press edition of
Devil in a Blue Dress.

"Silver Lining" first published in the 2002 Washington Square Press edition of *A
Red Death*.

"Lavender" first published in the 2002 Washington Square Press edition of *White
Butterfly*.

"Gator Green" first published in the 2002 Washington Square Press edition of
Black Betty.

"Gray-Eyed Death" first published in the 2002 Washington Square Press edition
of *A Little Yellow Dog*.

For information regarding special discounts for bulk purchases,
please contact Simon & Schuster Special Sales at 1-800-456-6798 or
business@simonandschuster.com.

CONTENTS

CONTENTS

SMOKE

E ASY," SHE SAID, and then the phone rang. Or maybe it was the other way around. Maybe the phone rang, and then Bonnie called my name.

Bright sun shone in the window, and the skies were clear as far as I could see. There was a beautiful woman of the Caribbean lying next to me. From the living room, early morning cartoons were squeaking softly while Feather giggled as quietly as she could. Somewhere below the blue skies, Jesus was hammering away, building a single mast sail that he intended to navigate toward some deep unknown dream.

It was one of the most perfect mornings of my life. I had a steady job, a nice house with a garden in the backyard, and a loving family.

But I was nowhere near happy.

The phone rang again.

"Easy," Bonnie said.

"I hear it."

"Daddy, phone," Feather yelled from her TV post.

Her dog, Frenchie, growled in anger just to hear her say something to me.

Jesus stopped his hammering.

The phone rang again.

"Honey," Bonnie insisted.

I almost said something sharp, but instead I grabbed the receiver off the night table.

"Yeah?"

"Ezekiel?"

Ezekiel is my given name but I never use it. So when that deep voice came out of the phone, I stalled a moment, wondering if it was asking for someone else.

"Ezekiel?" the voice said again.

"Who is this?"

"I'm lookin' for Raymond," the near-bass voice said.

"Mouse is dead."

I sat up, pulling the blankets from Bonnie's side of the bed. She didn't reach for the sheets to cover her naked body. I liked that. I might have even smiled.

"Oh no," the voice assured me. "He ain't dead."

"What?"

"No." The voice was almost an echo. There was a click and I knew that the connection had been broken.

"Easy?" Bonnie said.

I put the phone back into its cradle.

"Easy, who was it?"

Bonnie pressed her warm body against my back. The memory of Raymond's death brought about the slight nausea of guilt. Add that to the heat of the woman I loved and I had to pull away. I went to the window.

Down in the backyard I saw the frame of Jesus's small boat on orange crates and sawhorses in the middle of the lawn.

"It was . . . a woman I think. Deep voice."

"What did she want?"

"Mouse."

"Oh. She didn't know he was dead," Bonnie said in that way she had of making everything okay with just a few words.

"She said he was alive."

"What?"

"I don't think she *knew*. It was more like she was certain that he couldn't be dead."

"That's just the way people think about him," Bonnie said.

"No. It was something else."

"What do you mean?"

I went back to the bed and took Bonnie's hands in mine. "Do you have to leave today?" I asked her.

"Sorry."

Jesus's hammer started its monotonous beat again.

Feather turned up the volume on Crusader Rabbit now that she knew we were awake.

"I know you got to go," I said. "But . . ."

"What?"

"I dreamt about my father last night."

She reached out and touched my cheek with her palm. Bonnie had work-woman hands, not callused, but hard from a long life of doing for herself and others.

"What did he say?" she asked me.

That was her superstitious streak. She believed that the dead could speak through dreams.

"He didn't say a thing," I said. "Just sat there in a chair on a raft in the water. I called out to him four or five times before he looked up. But just then the current started pullin' the raft

downstream. I think he saw me but before he could say anything he was too far away."

Bonnie took my head in her arms and held on tight. I didn't
try to pull away.

WE SAT DOWN TO BREAKFAST at nine o'clock, two hours
after I was supposed to be at work. Jesus had taken Feather to
school. After that he was going to work four hours as a box boy
at Tolucca Market on Robertson. In the late afternoon he'd
come back home and read to me from *Treasure Island.* That
was our deal: he'd read out loud to me for forty-five minutes
and then discuss what he had read for three quarters of an
hour more. He did that every day, and I agreed to let him drop
out of high school.

Jesus wasn't interested in a public school education, and
there was nothing I could do to light a fire under him. He was
smart about things he cared for. He knew everything about
grocery stores because of his job. He worked there and did
gardening around our neighborhood to afford his boat
dreams. He liked carpentry and running. He loved to cook
and explore the beaches up and down the coast around L.A.

"What are you thinking about?" Bonnie asked.

We were holding hands under the table like schoolchildren
going steady.

"Juice," I said. "He's doin' pretty good."

"Then why do you look so sad?"

"I don't know. Maybe it's that phone call."

Bonnie leaned closer and squeezed my hand. "I'm going to
be gone longer than usual," she said.

"How long?"

"Maybe three or four weeks. Air France is having a special junket around western Africa with black political leaders and some European corporate heads. They need a French-speaking black stewardess who can also speak English. They'll need me on call for special flights."

"Oh. Yeah." It felt like she was punishing me for feeling bad.

"I told you that I'd have to be gone sometimes," she said sweetly.

"That's okay," I said. "Just don't go believin' it when one'a those men says that he wants to make you his queen."

HUNDREDS OF CHILDREN were assembled in front of Sojourner Truth Junior High School when I arrived—three and a half hours late.

"Mr. Rawlins," Archie "Ace" Muldoon said, greeting me on the granite stair of the main building. Short and balding, the little white man doffed his White Sox baseball cap in deference to his boss—me.

"Hey, Ace. What's happenin' here?"

"Fire in the metal shop bungalow."

"But that's down on the lower campus. Why they wanna evacuate up here?"

"Mr. Newgate." That's all he needed to say. Our principal, Hiram Newgate, was the source of all discord and wasted energy.

"Rawlins, I want to talk to you," Newgate said from the entrance hall. It was as if Archie conjured him up by saying his name.

"What about, Hiram?" I called back.

Newgate's lip curled into a snarl at my disrespectful tone.

He was tall and scarecrow-thin with cheekbones that were almost as high as his eyes. He would have been ugly if he didn't have perfect grooming, bright white and immaculate teeth, and clothes bought only in the finest Beverly Hills stores. That day he was wearing a shark-gray jacket and slender-cut black slacks.

He was looking good but I had outdone him. I was dressed in one of my best suits; off-white linen with felt buff shoes, brown argyle socks and tan shirt that I kept open at the collar due to the nature of my job,which was supervising senior head custodian.

I liked dressing up because of my background, which was poor and secondhand. But it also gave me a secret pleasure to see Newgate look me up and down, comparing my clothes to his.

"Where have you been?" the jade-eyed principal asked me.

I shrugged, not having enough respect for the man to lie.

"That's not an acceptable answer."

"What's the fire report, Archie?" I asked my custodian.

"Fire captain's down in the yard," the small man said.

"Mr. Rawlins," Principal Newgate sputtered. "I'm speaking to you."

"Sorry, Hiram," I said as I walked away. "But I'm late and there's going to be a lot of paperwork around this fire."

"What?" he exclaimed. He probably said a lot more, but I touched Archie's arm and we went quickly toward the stairway that led down to the lower campus.

*   *   *

THE METAL SHOP bungalow was slightly scorched when the firemen arrived. They had reduced the building to splinters by the time they were through.

It was a strange vision for me. A burnt and shattered building surrounded by white men dressed in red. They were all young and grinning. Outside the nearby chain-link fence were dozens of men and women among the displaced students—all of them black or brown—staring wide-eyed at the demolition. I could feel my heart thumping and my hands getting hot.

A fireman approached us. He was hatless and haggard, no older than I, but he looked to be ready for retirement. He was making his way toward us with a deliberate and tired gait.

"You the principal?" the old-looking fireman asked. His gray pupils were watery, almost white.

"No," I said. "My name is Rawlins. I'm the plant supervisor."

"Where's the principal?"

"Mosta the kids're on the upper campus. He's makin' like a general on his horse up there, keepin' the troops from deserting."

That got a laugh from the fire captain. He reached out to shake my hand.

"Gregson," he said. "I'm the shift commander. Looks like you got a problem here."

I glanced at the poor colored people looking in at those uniformed marauders. I wondered if Gregson and I saw the same problems.

"It's arson," the fireman continued. "We found a scorched gasoline can under the building. It's a pretty sophisticated incendiary smoke bomb."

"They set it off with people in there?"

"Weren't you here?" Gregson asked me.

"I was late today."

"Oh. Well, somebody pulled the fire alarm and then set off the device, or maybe they set it off and then pulled the alarm. Maybe someone else saw the smoke but I doubt it; the people in the classroom hadn't even seen it yet. They pulled the alarm on the wall of the janitors' bungalow."

I BORROWED SOME LINED PAPER and a pencil from one of the students, through the fence, and took down all the information: Gregson's phone number, the police number to call to give information to the arson squad, and the names and numbers of the forms I had to fill out. He told me that an inspector would show up in the afternoon. All the while the firemen prowled around the shattered building, using their axes just in case some embers still burned.

I went up to Principal Newgate's office after that. I detested the man but he was still my boss.

"I'll buzz him, Mr. Rawlins," Kathy Langer said.

Everything about her was brown except for her skin: eyes, hair, dress, and shoes. She was a young white woman, a new transfer to Truth. Hiram's secretaries were always new, because they never lasted very long. He was always complaining about how they filed or typed. The last one left because he yelled at her for forgetting to put three sugar cubes into his coffee.

"It's Mr. Rawlins," she said into the phone. Then she looked up at me and said, "Just a minute. He's finishing a call." She smiled when she saw me looking at her drab clothes. It was the kind of smile that had gotten many young black men hung down South.

"Police?"

"No," she said as she inclined her head, showing me her throat. "Some guy who's been calling. I think it's personal business."

A moment later the buzzer sounded and she said, "You can go in now."

I hadn't been in Newgate's office for a few weeks and was surprised at the change in decor. I suppose the shock showed on my face.

"What?" Newgate said. He was sitting behind a beat-up ash-blond desk.

"What happened to all your fancy furniture?"

When Newgate became principal, he had brought expensive ebony wood and teak furniture with him. Along with the carpeting, his office had looked like a rich man's den. Now the floors were bare, the desk looked to be due for disposal, and his books and papers were in stacks along the walls.

"I bought a new house," he said. "I took the furniture for the living room."

"Why didn't you tell me? I coulda come up with a decent desk and some shelves." I knew the answer to my question before I finished asking it. He didn't want to ask me for anything. I was too uppity and confident for him to request my help. It's not that he had a problem with my color; Newgate wanted everybody to treat him like the master.

"What do you have on the fire?" he asked.

"Arson."

The principal paled visibly. "While the students were in

class? They could have been killed." He was talking to himself more than to me. "That's, that's horrible."

"I don't think anybody coulda been killed," I said. "Fire captain told me that even though they used a gasoline can it was pretty much just a smoke bomb."

"A kid's prank?"

"Naw. He said the bomb was very professional-looking."

Newgate and I stared at each other for a moment. "What do you think, Mr. Rawlins?"

What I thought was that Hiram Newgate had never asked me what I thought about anything. But what I said was, "I hope that it's just a one-time thing. Not some kind of craziness."

"What do you mean?"

"I wish I knew."

"Well," he said, still shaken. "I'm sure that it's just some kid with a problem. If he does something like this again we'll find him."

"I hope you're right."

"I have a doctor's appointment at noon so I'll be out midday. If the police come you give them what they need."

THE REST OF THE DAY was pretty noneventful. No more fires or fire alarms. No plumbing or electrical disasters. It was actually a good day because Newgate wasn't around looking into everybody's business. He bothered the teachers as much as he did the custodial staff. He often walked into classrooms unannounced to make surprise evaluations. That might have been a good idea, but Newgate was rude and rough. He loved Truth more than anyone, but not a soul there cared for him.

❖   ❖   ❖

THAT AFTERNOON I was out inspecting the lower yard when First Wentworth called me. First was a small boy, thirteen at the time. Like many of the young children, he spent his summers hanging around the schoolyard, taking advantage of the facilities we offered for daycare. He played caroms and tetherball from ten, when the playground opened, until two, when it closed. After that I let him work with me, moving desks out of the classrooms so that my custodians could strip the floors and seal them for the new school year.

"Mr. Rawlins," he called from halfway down the eighty-seven stairs leading to the upper, older, campus. At least I think he said my name. I just heard his voice and saw him running down the granite steps.

While he ran I continued my inspection, looking into the trash cans on the yard. In one can I found a beaded white sweater that some child had discarded. It was a nice sweater, one hundred percent cotton. It represented a few days' labor out of a poor woman's pay, I knew. But clothes for children are like skin on snakes: to be shed now and then, allowing the new child to emerge.

"Mr. Rawlins," First said when he reached me.

I put the sweater under my arm. "Hey, Number One."

"I don't know what he was doin' over there." First was talking as if we were already in the middle of a conversation. "But I saw him."

"Who?"

"That white man."

"What white man?"

"The one who put that thing under Mr. Sutton's classroom."

"What thing?"

"A big red can," the boy said. "I don't know why."

"Why didn't you say anything before this?" I asked.

"I forgot that I saw'im. But then later Mr. Weston said that the school might burn down."

I could have asked him why he came to me, but I knew the answer. I was the only black person on the campus who had any authority. Most of the children came to me with their problems because bill collectors, policemen, and angry store owners were the only white people in their daily lives.

"And it was a white man?" I asked First.

He nodded, looking at my feet.

"Was he wearin' a suit?"

"Uh-uh. Just some pants and a green windbreaker."

"Have you seen him around here before?" I asked. "Does he work here sometimes?"

First shook his head. "No. I mean I seen'im but he don't work here."

"Where'd you see him?"

"Wit' Cousin."

"Who's that?"

"It's a boy, a man. You know."

"A young man?"

"Uh-huh, he used to go here. But he graduated an' dropped out." First looked up at me. "Am I in trouble?"

"No, Number One. You did all right. You might have to tell somebody else about it. But don't worry right now. Don't you have a class to go to?"

"Yeah. History-geography."

"You better go then."

I watched the child, who was so willing to rely on my strength, run up all those eighty-odd stairs without a falter.

I CALLED THE POLICE STATION and asked for Sergeant Andre Brown. When he wasn't there, I talked to another policeman; I forget his name. I forget because he was of no help. He told me to come in the next afternoon and file a report. When I said that I thought it might be more important than that, he hung up.

Then I called the fire department. Gregson was out on a call. When I told the operator why I was calling, he told me to call the police.

"ALL I KNOW IS that his nickname was Cousin," I said to Laini Trellmore, Sojourner Truth's registrar.

"Cousin. Hm," the elderly woman said to herself. She looked closer to seventy-five than the age she gave, which was sixty-one. I wasn't the only one to suspect that under her duties as record keeper, Miss Trellmore had altered her date of birth to keep her job past the age of forced retirement.

She frowned.

"Oh yes. I remember now. Douglas Hardy. Oh yes. Trouble from the first day to the last. He was sixteen years old and still in the ninth grade. Oooo. The kind of boy who's always grinning and nodding and you know he just did something bad."

"You got an address for his family in the files?"

THE HARDY FAMILY lived on Whithers Court off of Avalon. It was a dead-end street that had once been nice. Neat little

single-family homes built for working people in a cul-de-sac.
But the houses had all been bought up by a real estate syndi-
cate called Investors Group West. They raised the rent as
much as the market would bear. The turnover in tenants had a
harmful influence on the upkeep of the dwellings and the
street. Barren lawns and walls with the paint peeling off were
the norm.

The Hardys' home was secured by a screen door frame that
had no screen. There was loud cowboy music blaring from
inside. I looked for a doorbell but there was none. I knocked
on the door, but my knuckles were no match for the yodeling
cowboy.

I pulled the door open and took a tentative step inside. It
was that step, uninvited into the house of people who were
strangers to me, that was the first step outside the bounds of
the straight and narrow life that I pretended to. The room
had a gritty look to it. Dust on the blanket-covered sofa and
dust on the painted wood floor. The only decoration was a
paper calendar hung by a nail on the far wall. It had a large
picture of Jesus, his bleeding Valentine's heart protruding
from his chest, over a small booklet of months. There was no
sign of life.

I considered calling out, but I would have had to shout to
be heard over the warbling cowboy, and anything that loud
might alarm any occupants of that tinderbox home.

I turned off the radio.

"What the hell is goin' on?" someone said from beyond a
doorway that led to the kitchen.

A short brown woman hustled in. She was wearing a shapeless blue shift that had white butterflies all over it. The neck of

the dress had been stretched out, one side sagging open over her left shoulder.

"Who the hell are you?" she asked, squinting and scowling so that I could see the red gums of her almost toothless maw.

"Ezekiel," I said, remembering the morning caller.

"What the hell do you want?"

"I'm lookin' for Cousin."

Her nose twitched as if she were tied to a post and a mosquito were trying to bite her nose.

"Rinaldo!"

I heard a man grunt somewhere in the house. The heavy pounding of footsteps followed and soon a man, not as short as the woman but not as tall as I, came through the doorway. He was wearing only boxer shorts and a yellow T-shirt. His nose, chin, and forehead jutted out from the face as if his head were meant to be used as an axe. His eyes seemed insane, but I put that down to him getting rousted by the woman's scream.

"What, Momma?"

"This man lookin' for Cousin."

"The hell are you?" Rinaldo asked me.

"Cousin's in trouble," I said.

"The fuck he is," Rinaldo said.

"Watch your language, boy," Toothless Mama said.

"The hell are you?" Rinaldo asked again. He balled his fists and levered his shoulders to show off a ripple of strength.

"He knows a man who tried to burn down the junior high school," I said. "Somebody saw them together—"

"Who?" the woman asked.

Ignoring her, I kept on talking to Hatchet Face. ". . . if I don't see me some Cousin I'm just gonna give the police this address and let you shake your shoulders at them."

Rinaldo's eyes got crazier as he woke up. He seemed torn between attack and flight. He was fifteen years my junior, but I felt that I could take him. It was Mama who scared me. She was the kind of woman who kept a straight razor close at hand.

"Cousin didn't start that fire," Mama said.

"How would you know?"

"He was here with us."

"Where is he now?"

Mama and Rinaldo exchanged glances. They were afraid of the police. They had good reason to be. All black people had good reason to be. But I didn't care.

"Tell me or I'll go right down to the precinct," I said.

"He live on Hooper," Rinaldo said. He blurted out an address.

"Okay," I said, and I took a step backward. "I'ma go over there. If somebody calls him and warns him off I'm sendin' the cops here to you."

Rinaldo gave his mother a sharp look. Maybe he wondered if he should try to kill me. I took another step back. Before they could decide on an action, I was out of the door and on the way to my car. Rinaldo came out to watch me drive off.

"WHO IS IT?" a voice asked after I knocked.

"Are you Cousin?" I asked.

There was a pause, and then, "Yeah?"

"I'm John Lowry. Rinaldo sent me."

When he opened the door, I punched him in the face. It was a good solid punch. It felt good but it was a stupid thing to do. I didn't know who else was in the room. That crouching, slack-jawed man might have been a middleweight contender. He could have had an iron jaw and a pistol in his pocket. But I hit him because I knew that he had something to do with the fire at my school, because Mama and Rinaldo set my teeth on edge, because the police didn't seem to care what I did, and because my best friend was dead.

Cousin fell flat on his back.

The room was painted a garish pink and there was no furniture except for a single mattress no thicker than a country quilt.

"Get up," I said.

"What I do to you, mister?" he whined.

"Why you try'n burn down the school?"

"I didn't burn nuthin'." Cousin got to his feet.

He was an old twenty. Not smart or mature, just old. Like he had lived forty years in half the time but hadn't learned a thing.

I knocked him down again.

"Hey, man!" he yelled.

"Who's the white man you were with?"

"What white man?"

"You want me to kick you?" I moved my right foot backward in a threatening motion.

"What you want from me?"

"The man put that bomb under the metal shop at Truth."

Cousin's skin was a deep, lusterless brown. His jaw was swelling up. He passed his hand over his head from fear that I'd mussed his hair.

"You the law?"

"I work for the school."

"Man named Lund."

"Lund?"

"Uh-huh."

"How you spell it?"

"I'on't know, man."

"What do you know?" I asked in disgust.

"Roke Williams. Roke run a crap game down Alameda. Lund work for the man sell him p'otection."

I DROVE TO A SMALL BUILDING on Pico and Rimpau. All the way I was wondering why a man in organized crime would be setting a bomb at a Negro junior high school. I wondered but I wasn't afraid—and that was a problem. If you go up against men in organized crime, you should at least have the sense to be afraid.

There was a weathered sign above the front door of the building. If you looked closely you could make out the word HETTLEMANN and, a little farther down, RINGS. I had no idea what the building used to be. Now it was a series of sales and service offices rented out to various firms and individuals. On the fourth floor was a block of offices run by a man named Zane. They did bookkeeping and financial statements for small businesses.

The three flights of stairs was nothing for me. For the past few months I had cut down to ten cigarettes a day and I was used to the vast stairway at Truth.

When I opened the door on the fourth floor, I came into a small room where Anatole Zane sat. Zane, by his own estima-tion was a ". . . manager, receptionist, janitor, and delivery boy . . ." for his quirky accounting firm. He hired nonprofessionals who were good with numbers and parceled out tasks that he took in for cut-rate prices.

Jackson Blue was his most prized employee.

"Mr. Rawlins." Zane smiled at me. He got his large body out of the chair and shook my hand. "It's so good to see you again."

Zane did my year-end taxes. I owned three apartment buildings around Watts and had the sense to know that a professional would do a better job with the government than I ever could. I had introduced the modest bookkeeper to the cowardly, brilliant, and untrustworthy Jackson Blue.

"Good to see you too, Anatole."

"Jackson's in his office doing a spreadsheet on the Morgans."

"Thanks."

I went through the door behind Zane's small desk. There I entered a hall so narrow that I imagined the fat manager might get stuck trying to make it from one end to the other.

I knocked on the third door down.

"Yeah?"

"Police!"

I heard the screech of a chair on the floor and three quick steps across the room. Then there was a moment of silence.

After that, a quavering voice: "Easy?"

A door down the hall opened up. A bespectacled Asian man stuck his head out. When I turned in his direction, he jumped back and slammed the door.

"Come on, Jackson," I said loudly. "Open up."

The door I had knocked on opened.

If coyotes were black, Jackson Blue would have been their king. He was small and quick. His eyes saw more than most, and his mind was the finest I had ever encountered. But for all that, Jackson was as much a fool as Douglas "Cousin" Hardy. He was a sneak thief, an unredeemable liar, and dumb as a post when it came to discerning motivations of the human heart.

"What the fuck you mean scarin' me like that, Easy?"

"You at work, Jackson," I said, walking into his office. "This ain't no bookie operation. You not gonna get busted."

Jackson slammed his door.

"Shut up, man. Don't be talkin' like that where they might hear you."

I sat in a red leather chair that was left over from the previous tenants. Jackson had nice furniture and a fairly large office. He had a window too, but the only view was a partially plastered brick wall.

"How you doin', Jackson?"

"Fine. Till you showed up."

He crossed the room, giving me a wide berth, and settled in the chair behind his secondhand mahogany desk. He avoided physical closeness because he didn't know why I was there. Jackson had betrayed and cheated so many people that he was always on guard against attack.

"What you doin'?" I asked.

He held up what looked like a hand-typed manual. It had a cheap blue cover with IBM and BAL scrawled in red across the bottom.

Jackson smiled.

"What is it?"

"The key code to the binary language of machines."

"Say what?"

"Computers, Easy. The wave of the future right here in my hand."

"You gonna boost 'em or what?"

"You got a wallet in your pocket, right, man?"

"Yeah."

"You got some money in there?"

"What you gettin' at?"

"You might even have a Bank Americard, am I right?"

"Yes."

"One day all your money gonna be in this language here." He waved the manual again. "One day I'ma push a button and all the millionaires' chips gonna fall inta my wagon."

Jackson grinned from ear to ear. I wanted to slap him, but it wouldn't have made a difference. Here he was the smartest man you could imagine, and all he could think about was theft.

"Roke Williams," I said.

"Niggah was born in the alley and he gonna die in one too. Right down there offa Alameda."

"Who runs him?"

"Was a dude named Pirelli, but he got circulatory problems."

"Heart attack?"

"Kinda like. A bullet through the heart. Now it's a man named Haas. He's a slick bita business run his people outta the Exchequer on Melrose."

"How about a man named Lund?"

Jackson squinted and brought his long thumbs together. "No. Don't know no Lund. What's this all about, Easy?"

I told Jackson about the smoke bomb and Cousin.

When I finished he said, "So? What do you care about all that, man? It ain't your house."

"It's my job."

"Your job is to make sure that the toilets don't smell and that the trash cans is emptied. You not no bomb squad."

I remember trying to dismiss Jackson's argument as some kind of cowardly advice, but even then there was a grain of truth that made it through.

"Maybe not," I said. "But I'm in it now."

"You better bring some backup you wanna tango with Haas."

That reminded me of Mouse. He had been my backup since I was a teenager in Fifth Ward, Houston, Texas. Mouse was crazy, but he was always on my side.

"I got a call this mornin', Jackson. It was a woman with a deep bass voice—"

"She ask you about Mouse?"

"How you know that?"

"She called me too. Three days ago. Said she was lookin' for Raymond."

"What you say?"

Jackson became wary again. He scratched the back of his neck with his left hand and looked off to his left. When he saw that there was no escape route, he turned back to me. "I don't want no trouble now, Easy."

"Trouble's over, man. Mouse is dead."

"Like you once told me: you don't know that."

"I saw him. He wasn't breathin' and his eyes were wide. That bullet opened him up like a busted piñata."

"But you didn't go to no funeral."

"Etta carried the body outta the hospital. You know how much she loved him. She probably put him in the ground herself."

Jackson wrung his hands.

"What did you tell that woman?" I asked.

"Nuthin'. I didn't tell her a thing."

"Okay," I said. "What didn't you say?"

"You cain't tell nobody I told, Easy."

"Fine."

"A girl named Etheline, Etheline Teaman."

"What about her?"

"I met her a few weeks back and we started talkin' shit. I told her 'bout some'a the crazy stuff Mouse done did. You know, just talkin' jive. She told me that just before she left Richmond she met a gray-eyed, light-skinned brother named Ray. She said he got in a fight one night, and even though he was small, he put down this big dude with a chair, a bottle, and his knee. She didn't even know Mouse, man. She only moved here from Richmond six months ago."

"Where is this girl?"

"Piney's."

"A prostitute?"

"So what? You ain't askin' her to take care'a your kids. She said that she knew a man might be him. That's what you asked me."

"Why didn't you call me about this, Jackson?"

"If Mouse is alive and don't want nobody to know, then I don't need to say a word."

It was Jackson's long silence that bothered me. He turned

into a loudmouth braggart after just one beer. For him to have kept quiet about his suspicions meant that something in what he heard made him fear that Mouse was really alive.

And Mouse was a man to fear. He was deadly to begin with, and his heart was unrestrained by any feelings of guilt or morality.

"What you gonna do, Easy?"

"Go out and buy me a tie."

I STOPPED AT THE May Company downtown and bought an orange silk tie. It had blue veins running through it and a yellow kite veering to the side as if it had broken its string.

I knotted my tie using the rearview mirror and then drove off to Melrose Avenue.

The Exchequer hotel and bar was a small building wedged between a lamp store and a hospital for the elderly. Lined out on the sidewalk were the aged inmates of that old folks' prison. They sat in wheelchairs and on benches, looking out over Melrose as if it were the river Styx. I turned my head now and again as I passed them, thinking that one day, if I made it through this life, I would end up like them: discarded and broken at the side of the road.

There was one child-sized woman wearing a thin blue robe over blue pajamas. Her sagging, colorless eyes caught mine.

"Mister," she mouthed. Then she waved.

"Yeah, honey?" I crouched down in front of her.

"When you were a boy you were so beautiful," she whispered.

I smiled, wondering if my boyhood was showing in my face.

"Just like your mother," she said.

"You knew my mother?" I asked. Maybe she thought some black maid in the old days was my relation.

"Oh yes," she said, her voice getting stronger. "You're my grandson—Lymon."

Her eyes, when I first saw them, were beyond despair, verging on that stare that a dying man has when all hope of life is gone. I had seen many men during the war, shot up and dying, whose eyes had given up hope. But now the old lady's eyes overflowed with delight—her white grandson, me, filling their field of vision.

She reached out a hand and I took it. She leaned forward and I accepted the kiss on my cheek. I kissed her gray head and stood up.

"I'll come back a little later, Granny," I said. Then I walked off to meet with a gangster.

THE HOTEL LOBBY WAS SMALL and simple. Not elegant or tawdry, but plain. The registration desk could have been a bell captain's station. The rug would have to be changed in a year or less. The only outstanding features were the light fixtures set high up on the walls. They were in the form of nude women finished in shiny gold leaf. Above their heads they held big white globes of light.

"Help you?" the small man behind the desk asked. He was white and bald, about my age—which was mid-forties at the time. His eyes, nose, mouth, and ears were all too small for his small head. His miniature features showed disapproval and distrust of my presence. I couldn't blame him. How often did white people see black men in fancy suits in 1964?

"Lookin' for Mr. Haas," I said.

"Who are you?"

"You don't need to know my name, man."

The desk clerk ran his tongue up under his lower lip and looked over at a doorless doorway. He nodded toward the dark maw and I went.

"WHAT'S UP, ROCHESTER?" a white man with big ears asked me. He was standing at the bar.

"Could be your ticket," I said.

While he considered my words, I took a step closer to get within arm's distance, so that if he decided to go for a weapon, I could stop him before he stopped me.

"Fuck you," he said.

"Now that's better," I replied. "Are you Mr. Haas?"

"Who wants to know?"

"Ray," I said. "Ray Alexander. I need to talk some business with the man."

"Wait here."

Big Ears wore an ugly, copper-colored iridescent suit. As he shimmered away from me into the gloom of the bar, I wondered if I had gone crazy somehow without warning. Jackson Blue was right; I was way out of my prescribed world there at the Exchequer.

I had fallen back into bad habits.

"Can I help you?"

It was yet another white man, this time a bartender. His words offered help, but his tone was asking me to leave.

"Mr. Haas," I said, pointing toward the gloom.

A shimmering copper mass was emerging. Big Ears came up to me. "Come on."

*   *   *

IT WAS POSSIBLY the darkest room I had ever been in that wasn't intended for sleep. A man sat at a table under an intolerably weak red light. His suit was dark and his hair was perfect. Even though he was seated, I could tell that he was a small man. The only thing remarkable about his face were the eyebrows; they were thick and combed.

"Alexander?" he said.

I took a seat across from him without being bidden. "Mr. Alexander," I said.

His lips protruded a quarter inch; maybe he smiled. "I've heard of you," he ventured.

"I got a proposition. You wanna hear it?"

Ghostly hands rose from the table, giving his assent.

"There's a group of wealthy colored businessmen, from pimps to real estate agents, who wanna start a regular poker game. It's gonna float down around South L.A., some places I got lined up."

"So? Am I invited to play?"

"Five thousand dollars against thirty percent of the house."

Haas grinned. He had tiny teeth.

"You want I should just turn it over right now? Maybe you want me to lie down on the floor and let you walk on me too."

Haas's voice had become like steel. I would have been afraid, but because I was using Mouse's name, there was no fear in me.

"I'd be happy to walk on you if you let me, but I figure you got the sense to check me out first."

The grin fled. It was replaced by a twitch in the gangster's left eye.

"I don't do penny-ante shit, Mr. Alexander. You want to have a card game it's nothin' to me." He adjusted his shoulders like James Cagney in *Public Enemy*.

"Okay," I said. I stood up.

"But I know a guy."

I said nothing.

"Emile Lund," Haas continued. "He eats breakfast in Tito's Diner on Temple. He likes the cards. But he doesn't throw money around."

"Neither do I," I said, or maybe it was Raymond who said it and I was just his mouthpiece in that dark dark room way outside the limit of the law.

The old folks were gone when I emerged from the hotel. I missed seeing the old lady. I remember thinking that that old woman would probably be dead before I thought of her again.

FEATHER WAS ASLEEP in front of a plate with a half-eaten hot dog and a pile of baked beans on it. *Astro Boy*, her favorite cartoon, was playing on the TV. Jesus was in the backyard, hammering sporadically. I picked up my adopted daughter and kissed her. She smiled with her eyes still closed and said, "Daddy."

"How you know who it is?" I asked playfully. "You too lazy to open your eyes."

"I know your smell," she said.

"You have hot dogs?"

"Uh-huh."

"What you do at school all day?"

At first she denied that anything had happened or been learned at Carthay Circle elementary school. But after a while she woke up and remembered a bird that flew in her classroom window and how Trisha Berkshaw said that her father could lift a hundred pounds up over his head.

"Nobody better tickle him when he's doin' that," I said, and we both laughed.

Feather told me what her homework assignment was, and I set her up at the dinette table to get to work on her studies. Then I went outside to see Jesus.

He was rubbing oil into the timbers of his sailboat's frame.

"How's it goin', Popeye?" I asked.

"Sinbad," he said.

"Why you finishin' it before it's finished?"

"To make it waterproof inside and out," he said. "That's what the book says to do. That way if water gets inside it won't rot."

His face was the color of a medium tea; his features were closer to the Mayans than to me. He had deeper roots than the American Constitution in our soil. Neither of my children were of my blood, but that didn't make me love them less. Jesus was a mute victim of sex abuse when I found him. Feather's own grandfather had killed her mother in a parking lot.

"I got a lot to do the next few days, son," I said. "Could you keep close to home for Feather?"

"Can I have a friend come over?"

"Who?"

"Cindy Needham."

"Your girlfriend?"

Jesus turned his attention back to the frame. He could still be a mute when he wanted to be.

*   *   *

I MIGHT HAVE CLOSED my eyes sometime during the night, but I certainly didn't fall asleep. I kept seeing Raymond in that alley, again and again, being shot down while saving my life. At just about the same time John F. Kennedy was assassinated, but I never mourned our slain president. The last time I saw Mouse, his lifeless body was being taken to the hospital with a blanket covering his wounds.

TITO'S WAS A RECTANGULAR BUILDING raised high on cinder blocks. The inside had one long counter with two tables at the far end. Only one of the tables had an occupant. I would have bet the .38-caliber pistol in my pocket that that man was Emile Lund.

More than anything he looked like an evolved fish. There were wrinkles that went across his forehead and down along his balding temples. His eyes bulged slightly and his small mouth had pouting, sensual lips. His chin was almost nonexistent, and his hands were big. His shoulders were massive, so even though he looked like a cartoon, I doubted if anyone treated him that way.

The fish-man had been making notes in a small journal, but when I opened the door he looked up. He kept his eyes on me until I was standing at his table.

"Lund?" I asked. "I'm Alexander."

"Do I know you?"

"You wanna talk business or you wanna talk shit?" I said.

He laughed and held his big fins out in a gesture of apology.

"Come on, man. Don't be so sensitive. Sit down," Lund

said. "I know your rep. You're a man who makes money. And it's money makes my car go."

"Mona," Lund said to the woman behind the counter.

She was wearing a tight black dress that probably looked good on her twenty years before. Now it was just silly, like her brittle blond-dyed hair, her deep red lipstick, and all the putty pressed into the lines of her face and neck.

She waited for a bit, just to show that she didn't jump the minute someone called her name, and then walked over to our table. "Yeah?" the waitress said.

"What's your pleasure, Mr. Alexander?" Lund inquired.

"Scrambled eggs with raw onions on 'em, and a bottle of Tabasco sauce on the side." It was Mouse's favorite breakfast.

The waitress went away to pass my order on to the cook. Lund made a final note in his small journal, and then put the book away in a breast pocket.

"So, Mr. Alexander," he said. "You wanna play cards."

"I'm gonna play cards," I assured him. "I need a little seed money and some insurance against Roke Williams and the cops."

"From what I hear about you, you never buy insurance," the fish said.

"Man gets older he gets a little more conservative, smarter—you know."

The fish smiled at me, tending more toward shark than sardine. I took it in stride. After all, I wasn't the moderate custodian/landlord Easy Rawlins, I was the crazy killer Raymond Alexander. I was dangerous. I was bad. Nobody and nothing scared me.

The waitress came over with my eggs. I doused them with the hot sauce and shoveled them down.

"When do I get to see your game?" Lund asked me.

"Tonight if you want."

"Where?"

"We got a garage over on Florence." I took a slip of paper from my pocket and put it on the table. "That's the address."

"What time?"

"Nine-thirty would be too early. But anytime after that." My eggs were gone. I never liked raw onions and eggs before but I loved them right then. "You could sit in if you wanted to."

"Maybe so," he said. "Maybe so."

I WENT FROM TITO'S to the 77th Precinct.

Sergeant Andre Brown was in his small office. He was the highest-ranking black policeman in the station. And we had developed a sort of friendship.

Earlier that year there had been a gang killing of a student from Truth, and rumblings about bad blood between the gangs. I was able to point Brown in the direction of some bad eggs, making it possible for him to break up the trouble before it flared into a war.

Brown was in his thirties, tall and thin, with a thick mustache and a surprising deep laugh. He was a very clean man. Perfect nails and skin. His office had every book in place and every file in order. His graduation ring was from UCLA.

"Mr. Rawlins," he greeted me.

"Sergeant," I said. "How are you?"

"Fine. Just fine. I hear you had some problems at the school."

"Yeah." I sat down and stretched out my legs across his small office. "Yeah. That's kinda why I'm here."

Brown stood up and closed his door. This was something he'd never done before.

"Before you say anything," he said, "I have something to discuss with you."

"Okay. Shoot."

"The captain took me aside a few weeks ago and we had a talk about you."

"Yeah?"

"He told me to watch out for you. He said that you've been involved in some criminal activity and that you have been known to keep company with a hard-core criminal element." He looked at me, indicating that it was my turn to speak.

"I don't know what he said, but I'm no criminal, and I haven't been involved in any crimes," I said. That wasn't completely true, but it was close enough for Brown and I knew it. "It's true that I've known some pretty bad men, women too. If you go out your door down here you're likely to meet some bad folks, cain't help that. But what your captain might have meant is that I used to be in the business of doing favors."

"What kind of favors?"

"People, black people, got all kinds of difficulties, you know that. A kid gets mixed up with the wrong crowd, a car goes missing. Calling the police, many times, just makes something bad that much worse. In that kinda situation I would come in and give a little push. Nothing criminal. Nothing bad."

"Like an unlicensed private detective."

"Exactly like that. But you know I've been outta that business since coming to work at Truth."

Brown smoothed out one side of his mustache with a long

slender finger while he peered into my eyes. "Okay," he said at last. "All right. What can I do for you?"

That was my first experience with the second half of the twentieth century; the first time a man, black or white, holding a professional office, had given me the benefit of the doubt. He wasn't running a scam. He wasn't trying to get back at the police department. He simply saw my value and believed in my character.

"Have the kids in the gangs been messin' 'round wit' numbers or some other kinda gamblin'?" I asked.

"Not that I know of. I'm pretty sure not. Last group of kids I busted didn't have five dollars between them. Why?"

"I might know who set that smoke bomb at Truth."

"Who?"

"I won't be sure till tomorrow morning," I said. "The minute I know I'll turn it over to you."

Andre leaned forward in his chair. He was considering pushing me but decided against it. "Okay," he said.

We shook hands as equals, and I went off feeling like a new man. I was walking tall and flush with pride. But in spite of all that I wasn't even certain of my own name.

I WENT HOME to make sure that Feather and Jesus were okay, and then I made it back down to Florence. Bernard's Automotive Repair was managed by my oldest L.A. friend, Primo. He lived in the first house I ever owned. I still owned the house, and Primo never paid me a dime, so it was easy to get his keys to the garage for the night.

I unlocked the side door and turned on the radio in the mechanics' office. I switched on the office light and left the rest of the garage in darkness. Then I set myself up in a corner to the left of the door. Between my knees I had a baseball bat. On my lap was the .38. That was eight-fifteen.

IN THE DARK I HAD TIME to ponder my situation. There I was, waiting for more trouble than most citizens ever know. I had taken on Mouse's name and I was acting like him. It felt good, way too good. I expected Emile Lund to come in that door and see the light and hear the music. He'd be with one or two henchmen, but I had the element of surprise. I was a fool, I knew I was a fool, and still I didn't care.

Raymond Alexander had been the largest part of my history. My parents were both gone before I was nine. My relatives treated me like a beast of burden, so I ran from them. I fought a war for men who called me nigger. The police stopped me on the street for the crime of walking. Raymond was the only one who respected me and cared for me and was willing to throw his lot in with mine, no matter the odds.

I was sitting in that drafty corner because I didn't want Mouse to be dead. Somehow by using his name I felt that I was making a tribute, even a eulogy, to his meaning in my life.

THE IRIDESCENT GREEN HANDS on my watch said 11:03 when the door cracked open. Lund walked in alone. That worried me. If he'd come with a friend, it would have meant that he was cautious. A cautious man is more likely to be reasonable when facing a baseball bat and a pistol.

Lund was wearing jeans and a windbreaker, further proof that he was the man who bombed my classroom. I let him take two steps before pressing the gun barrel against the back of his neck.

"Hold it right there, man," I said in a husky, threatening tone.

Lund grunted and spun around, pushing my gun hand to the side. While he was concentrated on trying to disarm me, I hit him in the head with the bat. It was glancing blow and merely slowed him down. I hit him on the nose with the butt of my pistol, and he slowed a bit more. Fear was working its way into my gut because I realized that even though I was using Raymond's name, I'd never be able to inflict the kind of pain that he dished out. I pushed the angry gangster and he fell hard.

"Hold still, fool," I said.

But he ignored me and reached under the windbreaker. He was disoriented, so it was easy for me to kick the pistol out of his hand. He tried to crawl toward the gun, so I kicked him in the ribs. By this time I was getting sick. Nothing seemed to stop Lund. He struggled up to his knees and spat as if that would hold me off long enough for him to get his bearings. Blood was cascading from his nostrils, a high wheeze coming from his throat.

"Stop!" I yelled, but he got up on one foot.

I realized that I could either kill this man or run from him, but that I'd never subdue his spirit. He reminded me of a welterweight I'd seen, Carmen Basilio. That man would take punishment for twelve rounds or more, but he'd always come back, and in the last minutes he'd always win because his opponent was exhausted from waling away at the Italian boxer.

I unleashed a right uppercut that lifted Lund to his feet. Then I hit him with a straight left hand. Mouse would have hit him with the bat, repeatedly. I knew then that I would have to honor my friend in some other way.

Lund was unconscious, or nearly so. His eyes were half open and he was muttering something. I searched him and came up with his black book. I didn't think that it would help me much, but it was all I could get from him.

As I was going out of the door, Lund had gained his feet. He was still wobbly, searching the floor for his gun. I hurried out to the street.

DRIVING UP CENTRAL, I pondered my foolish actions. I thought that I'd just flash a gun at the gangster and he'd give me anything I wanted. I forgot about the dark alleys I'd once traveled. Hard men didn't get that way by turning over. Lund would have died before he bowed down to me.

I SAT UP IN MY LIVING ROOM, flipping through the pages of Lund's journal. There were multiple entries on every page. Each entry consisted of a name and a two- or three-letter code. At the bottom of each entry there was a date and a dollar amount. Roke Williams had several entries. He was paying Lund at least fifteen hundred dollars a month. Roke must have been making three times that amount. I knew that the gambler lived in a one-room apartment with the toilet down the hall. He made more in a month than most workingmen made in a year, and still he lived like a hermit crab.

One man, Vren Lassiter, had a special notation. In parentheses under his name were the initials "SchP." Lassiter had a

minus sign next to his dollar amount. He owed over six thousand dollars.

It wasn't until I was undressed and in the bed, under the
covers and almost asleep, that the initials made sense to me.

That was three A.M.

THE DRIVE FROM MY HOUSE near Fairfax and Pico down
to Truth was only twenty-five minutes at three in the morning.
Before four I was in the registrar's office looking up the faculty
records.

HE WAS LIVING in an apartment building on San Pedro. It
was a turquoise and plaster affair, designed to be ugly so that
the tenants would know that they were poor.

I knocked on the door of apartment 3G. No one answered.
I jiggled the knob and it turned.

He had lied about the furniture. He didn't use it for the
new place. His big ebony desk wouldn't have fit through the
front door. Hiram Newgate sold everything to pay Vren
Lassiter's debt and now he was dead, slumped over on the thin
cushions of a cheap couch, a .22-caliber bullet in his left temple, the pistol still in his hand.

I looked around the house. Photographs were spread
across the card table in a nook that was supposed to be a
dinette. The pictures were of two men, Hiram and a younger,
sandy-headed man. They were arm-in-arm, holding hands. In
one picture Hiram was laughing out loud.

I searched around for some kind of note, but there was
none. I did find a letter though. It was from Lassiter. In it Vren
beseeched his good friend to understand that he couldn't help

making bets. He tried to kick the habit but he couldn't. And if Hiram didn't help, they'd probably kill him.

I figured that Newgate went to Lund and took on the debt, that Lund threatened the school because he figured out that Truth was more important to Hiram than his own life. Newgate had earned his own private abbreviation: SchP, School Principal.

I put the letter back into the desk and went to the front door. I turned to look one last time, to make sure that there was nothing I left behind. His eyes glittered as if they had moved. I came up to him and stared into those orbs. He was still alive. Paralyzed, but still alive. He saw me, knew me.

"It's gonna be all right, Principal Newgate," I said. I touched his cheek and nodded.

I made the anonymous call to the police from his phone and left. I was out of the neighborhood before the sirens came.

I WAITED TWO WEEKS before going to the 77th Precinct.

"Where'd you get this?" Andre Brown asked me at Leah's Doughnut and Coffee Shop three blocks down from the precinct. In his hand he held Emile Lund's notebook.

"Found it."

"If you found it, how would you know who it belongs to? His name's not in it anywhere."

"I guessed. I'm a good guesser, Officer."

"These are his clients?" Brown asked. He was becoming wary of me.

"Yeah. I guess."

Officer Brown studied me. He was a good study. Nine

times out of eleven he would come up with the solution to his inquiry—but not that morning.

"I hear they brought your principal back home yesterday," he said. "Some friend of his took him in?"

"Guy named Vren."

"That's an awful thing. Shoot yourself in the head and end up paralyzed for life."

I took a deep breath.

"What does this book have to do with the fire?" Andre asked.

"He's the one set the smoke bomb."

"How do you know that?"

"Read the book."

THAT NIGHT Feather sang us a song she'd learned in school. It was about a sailor lost at sea. He fought sea serpents and snake people and terrible storms. But at the end of the journey, he found a sunny land. And to his surprise, that sunny shore was the home he'd left long long ago.

"I learned it for Juice, Daddy," she said. "'Cause'a when he's in that boat he can sing it and then he could find his way back here."

"Me too, baby," I said. "Me too."

CRIMSON STAIN

E THELINE," SHE SAID, repeating the name I'd asked for.

"Yeah," I said. "Etheline Teaman. I heard from my friend that she works here."

"Who is your friend?" the short, nearly bald black woman asked. She was wearing a stained, pink satin robe that I barely glimpsed through the crack of the door.

"Jackson Blue," I said.

"Jackson." She smiled, surprising me with a mouthful of healthy teeth. "You his friend? What's your name?"

"Easy."

"Easy Rawlins?" she exclaimed, throwing the door open wide and spreading her arms to embrace me. "Hey, baby. It's good to meet you."

I put one hand on her shoulder and looked around to the street, making sure that no one saw me hugging a woman, no matter how short and bald, in the doorway of Piney's brothel.

"Come on in, baby," the woman said. "My name is Moms. I bet Jackson told you 'bout me."

She backed away from the entrance, offering me entrée. I didn't want to be seen entering that doorway either, but I had no choice. Etheline Teaman had a story to tell and I needed to hear it.

The front door opened on a large room that was furnished with seven couches and at least the same number of stuffed chairs. It reminded me of a place I'd been twenty-five years earlier, in the now defunct town of Pariah, Texas. That was the home of a pious white woman—no prostitutes or whiskey there.

"Have a seat, baby," Moms said, waving her hand toward the empty sofas.

It was a plush waiting room where, at night, women waited for men instead of trains.

"Whiskey?" Moms asked.

"No," I said, but I almost said yes.

"Beer?"

"So, Moms. Is Etheline here?"

"Don't be in such a rush, baby," she said. "Sit'own, sit'own."

I staked out a perch on a faded blue sofa. Moms settled across from me on a bright yellow chair. She smiled and shook her head with real pleasure.

"Jackson talk about you so much I feel like we're old friends," she said. "You and that crazy friend'a yours—that Mouse."

Just the mention of his name caused a pang of guilt in my intestines. I shifted in my chair, remembering his bloody corpse lying across the front lawn of EttaMae Harris's home. It was this image that brought me to the Compton brothel.

I cleared my throat and said, "Yeah, I been knowin' Jackson since he was a boy down in Fifth Ward in Houston."

"Oh, honey," Moms sang. "I remember Fifth Ward. The cops would leave down there on Saturday sunset and come back Sunday mornin' to count the dead."

"That's the truth," I replied, falling into the rhythm of her speech. "The only law down there back then was survival of the fittest."

"An' the way Jackson tells it," Moms added, "the fittest was that man Mouse and you was the fittest's friend."

It was my turn to throw in a line but I didn't.

Moms picked up on my reluctance and nodded. "Jackson said you was all broke up when your friend died last year. When you lose somebody from when you were comin' up it's always hard."

I didn't even know the madam's Christian name but still she had me ready to cry.

"That's why I'm here," I said, after clearing my throat. "You know I never went to a funeral or anything like that for Raymond. His wife took him out of the hospital and neither one of them was ever seen again. I know he's dead. I saw him. But Etheline met somebody who sounded a lot like him a few months ago, up in Richmond. I just wanted to ask her a couple'a questions. I mean, I know he's dead, but at least if I asked her there wouldn't be any question in my mind."

Moms shook her head again and smiled sadly. She felt sorry for me, and that made me angry. I didn't need her pity.

"So is Etheline here?"

"No, darlin'," she said. "She moved on. Left one mornin' 'fore anybody else was up. That's almost four weeks ago now."

"Where'd she go?"

Another woman entered the room. She wore a man's white dress shirt and nothing else. All the buttons except the bottom one were undone. Her lush figure peeked out with each step. She was maybe eighteen and certain that any man who saw her would pay for her time.

When she sneered at me, I understood her pride.

"Inez," Moms said. "You know where Etheline got to?"

A man came stumbling out from the doorway behind Inez. He was fat, in overalls and a white T-shirt. "Bye, Inez," he said as he went around the sofas, toward the door.

"Bye," she said. But she wasn't looking at him. Her eyes were on me.

"Well?" Moms asked.

"What?" Inez's sneer turned into a frown at Moms's insistence.

"Do you know where Etheline has got to?"

"Uh-uh. She just left. You know that. Didn't say nuthin' to nobody." Inez kept her gaze on me.

"Well," Moms said. "That's all, Easy. If Inez don't know where she is, then nobody do."

"You wanna come on back to my room?" Inez asked, sneering again.

She undid the one button and lifted the tails of the shirt so I could see what she was offering. For a moment I forgot about Etheline and Mouse and why I was there. Inez was the color of pure chocolate. But if chocolate looked like her I'd have weighed a ton. She was young, as I said, and untouched by gravity or other earthly concerns.

"How much?" I asked.

"Thirty dollars up front," Moms said, no longer pitying or even friendly.

I handed the money over and followed the woman-child down a short hallway.

"You got thirty minutes, Easy," Moms called at my back.

At the end of the hallway we came to a right turn that became another, longer passage. Inez stopped at the fourth door down.

Her room was done up in reds and oranges. It smelled of

cigarette smoke, sex, lubricant, and vanilla incense. Inez let her shirt drop to the floor and sneered at me.

I closed the door.

"You shy?" she asked.

I scanned the room. There were no closets. The bed was just a big mattress on box springs. There was no frame that someone could hide under.

"How do you want me?" Inez asked.

"On a desert island for the rest of my life," I said.

There was a bench at the foot of her bed. It was covered with an orange and cream Indian cloth that had elephants parading around the edges. I took a seat and gestured for Inez to sit on the bed. She mistook my meaning and got down on her knees before me.

"No-no, baby. On the bed, sit on the bed." I lifted her by the elbows and gently guided her to sit.

"How you gonna fuck me like that?"

"I need to find Etheline."

"I already told you. She left. She didn't say where she was goin'."

"What did she say before she left?"

"What do you mean?" Inez was getting a little nervous. She covered her breasts under crossed arms.

"Did she have any friends? Was there some neighborhood she lived in before she came here?"

"You family to her?"

"She might know something about a friend'a mine. I want to ask her about him."

"You paid thirty dollars to hear about where she lived before here?"

"I'll give you twenty more if I like what I hear."

I hadn't noticed how large her eyes were until then. When

she put her arms down I saw that her nipples had become erect. They were long and pointed upwards. This also reminded me of my long-ago visit to Pariah.

"I don't know," Inez said. "She had a regular customer name of Cedric. And, and she went to . . . yeah, she went to The Winter Baptist Church. Yeah." Inez smiled, sure that she had earned her twenty dollars.

"What was Cedric's last name?"

The girl put one hand to her chin and the other to her ear. She pumped the heel of her left foot on the floor.

"Don't tell me now," she said. "I know it. We'd be sittin' on the purple couch after dinnertime, waitin' for the men. Shawna would be playin' solitaire and then, and when Cedric came Etheline always smiled like she really meant it. She always saw him first and said, 'Hi, Cedric,' and Moms would say, 'Good evenin', Mr. Boughman.' Moms always calls a man in a suit mister. That's just the way she is." Inez grinned at her own good memory. She had a space between her front teeth. I might have fallen in love right then if another woman didn't hold my heart.

"What kinda suit?" I asked.

"All different kinds."

"Black man?"

"We don't cater to white here at Piney's," Inez said.

I stood up and took out my wallet, giving Inez four five-dollar bills. "You supposed to walk me out?" I asked.

"You don't want me?"

"Don't get me wrong, honey," I said. "I don't even remember the last time I've seen a girl lovely as you. You might be the prettiest girl ever. But I got a woman. She's away right now but I feel like she's right here with me. You know what I mean?"

"Yeah," Inez whispered. "I know."

＊　　　＊　　　＊

IT WAS STILL EARLY when I left Piney's, about noon. I drove up toward Watts thinking that I should have been at work instead of in the company of naked women. Whorehouses and prostitutes belonged in my past. I had a job and a family to worry about. And as much as I missed him, Mouse, Raymond Alexander, was dead.

But just his name mentioned on the phone ten days earlier had thrown me out of my domestic orbit. He was on my mind every morning. He was in my dreams. Jackson Blue had told me that Etheline talked about a man who might have resembled Mouse. I kept from seeking her out for seven days, but that morning I couldn't hold back.

Maybe if Bonnie wasn't off being a stewardess in Africa and Europe, things would have been different. If she were home, I'd be too, home with my Mexican son and my mixed-race daughter. Home with my Caribbean common-law wife. Either at home or at work, making sure the custodians at Sojourner Truth Junior High School were picking up the vast lower yard and clearing away the mess that children make.

But there was no one to stop me. Bonnie was gone, little Feather was at Carthay Circle Elementary, and Jesus had left early in the morning to study the designs of sailboats at Santa Monica pier.

I was living out the dream of emancipation—a free man in America, desperate for someone to rein me in.

WINTER BAPTIST CHURCH was just a holy-roller storefront when I came to Los Angeles in 1946. Medgar Winters was minister, deacon, treasurer, and pianist all rolled into one. He preached a fiery gospel that filled his small house of worship with black women from the Deep South. These women were drawn to the good reverend because he spoke in terms of country wisdom, not like a city slicker.

By 1956 Medgar had bought up the whole block around 98th and Hooper. He'd moved his congregation to the old market on the corner and turned the storefront into a Baptist elementary school.

In 1962 he bought the old Parmeter's department store across the street and made that his church. Parmeter's space seated over a thousand people, but every Sunday it was standing-room-only because Medgar was still a fireball, and black women were still migrating from the South.

That February, 1964, Medgar was sixty-one and still going strong. He might have been the richest black man in Los Angeles, but he still wore homemade suits and shined his own shoes every morning. The old market had become the school, and the storefront was now the church business office.

I got to the business office a few minutes shy of one o'clock.

The woman sitting behind the long desk at the back of the room was over sixty. She wore glasses with white frames and a green blouse with a pink sweater draped over her shoulders. Six of eight fingers had gold rings on them and, when she opened her mouth, you could see that three of her teeth were edged in gold. She was buxom but otherwise slender. She seemed unhappy to see me, but maybe that was her reaction to anyone coming in the door.

"Hi," I said. "My name is Rawlins. I'm looking for someone."

She peered over the rim of her spectacles but didn't say a word.

"She's one of your congregation."

Again the silent treatment.

"Etheline Teaman," I said as a final effort.

"We don't give out information on our members, Rawlins," she said.

"I understand, ma'am. That makes sense. You don't know who I could be or what I'm after."

The woman's eyes tightened a little, trying to divine if there was some kind of threat in my words.

"But," I continued, "I have a serious problem. I'm very upset. You see, my cousin, Raymond, moved up to Oakland last year to work for these people clearin' forest up north of San Francisco. Nine months ago his mother gets a letter sayin' that there was an accident, that Raymond fell into the Russian River where they were movin' logs, and he was lost. You can imagine the grief she must have felt. Here some white man writes her a letter sayin' that her blood was gone and there wasn't even a body for her to cry over and put in the ground with a few words from her minister."

The woman behind the desk gave a little. Maybe she had a son or nephew.

"A few weeks ago I found out that a woman here in your congregation had seen Raymond at some services up in Richmond. She might know him, something about how he died. You know my auntie would love to hear anything."

"I'm sorry—" the church bureaucrat said, but I cut her off.

"Now I know you can't break the rules, but maybe you could give her a note from me. Then if she wants to she can give me a call."

"I guess that would be okay. I mean it wouldn't be breaking any rules."

"Can I use a piece of your note paper?"

My note was simple. I told her my name and number, saying that I needed some information, that my friend Jackson Blue suggested I talk to her. I also added that I didn't want to bother her at church and that I would pay her expenses if there was trouble with making time to meet me. The church lady frowned momentarily when she read it over, but then she seemed to accept it.

"I'll try and get it to her by Sunday, Mr. Rawlins," she said. "I sure will."

I COOKED DINNER that night. Fried chicken, macaroni with real yellow cheddar, collard greens, and unsweetened lemonade. The lemonade was for Jesus, who didn't like anything sweet. Feather put sugar in hers and mixed it happily as we sat at the dinette table.

"When Bonnie comin' home, Daddy?" she asked.

"Two or three weeks still. You know she got a heavy schedule for a month and then she can stay with us for a long time."

"Then can we go to Knott's Berry Farm?"

"Uh-huh."

"And, and the tar pits again?"

"You bet."

"I wish she was home already so we could go this weekend," Feather said.

"I'll take you Saturday if you want, baby sister," Jesus said.

He was working on his fourth piece of chicken. I didn't use a batter on my chicken the way many Southerners did. I just dredged it in flour seasoned with salt, pepper, and garlic powder. That way the skin got crispy and you didn't have to feel like you had to eat through bread to get to the meat.

"We can all go," I said. "I mean, Bonnie's fun, but the three of us can still have fun together too."

"Oh boy!" Feather shouted.

Jesus, who rarely smiled, always did so when his little sister was happy. He'd gotten a haircut that day. The straight black hairs stood up like bristles on his tea-brown head.

"How's the boat comin'?" I asked my adopted son.

"Good."

"You work on it today?"

"Yeah."

"How much did you get done?"

"I don't know."

Jesus was seventeen. He'd dropped out that school year and spent his days building a single-mast sailboat. I asked him many times what he planned to do with that boat, but he didn't seem to know.

"How was work today?" I asked him.

"Okay. They need you to sign a letter saying that I can work when I'm supposed to be in school."

"Okay. You go down to Santa Monica?"

"I saw this guy," Jesus said, his voice suddenly full of emotion. "He was fixing a sail. Sewin' it. He told me that a long time ago people from Europe and Africa on the sea in between them had big colored sails with pictures on them."

"The Phoenicians," I said. "The Athenians too, I bet."

"Are there pictures?" Jesus asked.

"In the library."

The light dimmed a little in his eyes. Jesus was always adrift around too many books.

"That's okay, honey," I said. "I'll go with you. I'll find the book and sit there while you read it to me. That'll be our lessons for the next couple'a weeks."

Since Jesus dropped out of school I had a reading session with him every day for an hour and a half. He'd read to me out loud for forty-five minutes and then we'd talk, or he'd write about what he'd read for another forty-five. If either of us missed a day, we had to make it up on the weekend.

After hearing about books on sails, Jesus sat up straight and made conversation. He was a good boy. At seventeen he was a better man than I.

I WENT TO WORK on Friday. We had no principal since Hiram Newgate's attempted suicide. He was now bedridden, mostly paralyzed. I checked out the work of my custodians. I had to get on Mrs. Plates, because she didn't empty the big cans in the main hall of the Language Arts building.

"I'm just a woman, Mr. Rawlins," she complained. "You cain't expect me to lift them big heavy things."

One year before I arrived at Truth, a man came on the campus without any business. Mrs. Plates asked him to leave, and he cursed at her. A fistfight ensued, and the man had to be taken away in an ambulance. Helen Plates was stronger than most of the men who worked for me. But I couldn't say that to her. She was a woman, and therefore had to be treated more delicately.

"Well," I said. "I'll tell you what. I'll get Ace to empty your cans, and then you can do all his toilets."

"Toilets!"

"Yeah. No heavy liftin' in toilets."

"Mr. Rawlins, you know three little cans ain't worf two floors of toilets."

"I know," I said. "But Ace got to come all the way up to the upper campus to unload them things for you."

Helen sighed heavily. "Okay," she said. "I'll empty the cans. But if I hurt my back, the school board gonna have to pay my disability."

＊   ＊   ＊

SATURDAY THE KIDS and I went to the tar pits and the art museum. I found a book on ancient sailboats that Jesus and I read that night. On Sunday we went to the marina, where Jesus pointed out all kinds of boats to Feather and me.

THE CALL CAME a little before nine o'clock Sunday night.

"Mr. Rawlins?" a young woman's voice asked.

"Who is this?"

"Etheline Teaman."

"Oh. Hello, Miss Teaman. Thank you for calling."

"I didn't understand your note," she said. But she did. She was insinuating that she didn't want me to put her business out there at the church.

"You know my friend—Jackson Blue," I said.

"Um. I don't think I know anybody with that name."

"Oh, yeah," I said. "You know him. He used to come and see you at Piney's."

"What do want from me, Mr. Rawlins?" Her voice had turned cold.

"Before you left Richmond and came down here, you met a man named Ray."

"What if I did?"

"Did he have gray eyes?"

"I don't know. Maybe. They were light, I remember that."

"Did he have a last name?"

"If he did I don't know it."

"How about a nickname?"

"Some people used to call him Mr. Slick 'cause he was always so well dressed."

"Where was he from?"

"I don't know." She was getting tired of my questions.

"Did he have a Southern accent?"

"Maybe. But not real deep like country or somethin' like that."

"Listen, Etheline," I said. "I'm tryin' to find out if this man you knew was my friend. Can you describe him?"

"Hell," she said. "I could show you a picture if that would get you to leave me alone."

"A photograph?" I asked.

"Uh-huh. I got it in my trunk, with all the rest'a my letters and stuff."

"Honey, I sure would like to see that."

"You said somethin' in that note you gave to Miss Bristol about money?"

"I'll give you a hundred dollars just to have a look at that photograph."

I could have offered twenty; that was a lot of money. But I wanted to pay what the picture was worth to me. I guess it was a little superstition on my part. I felt that if I tried to skimp on the value of her gift, somehow things would turn out bad.

She gave me an address on Hedly, a small street between downtown and south L.A.

Feather and Jesus were both asleep by then. Feather was only eight and needed her rest. Jesus was an early riser, intent on finishing his boat.

I WAS NERVOUS on the ride over. In my mind I knew that Mouse was dead, but in my heart I had never accepted it. The attending nurse said that he had no pulse minutes before EttaMae came and carried him out of the emergency room bed. But I could never find EttaMae after that, and some deep part of me still held out hope.

I pulled up in front of the house near ten. There was a light on on the front porch and another behind a drawn shade inside the house. The house looked nice enough, but night-time is kind on the eyes. I walked up on the front porch feeling all right. Going to Piney's had made me feel that I was slipping back into the street life, that I had lost my grip on being a citizen. But going to see Etheline, a reformed, church-going prostitute, was almost a normal thing.

I knocked.

I knocked again. Maybe she was in the bathroom.

I found a button and pushed it. I could hear the buzzer through the door. That jangling noise got under my scalp and I felt a moment of fear.

I tried the knob. It was locked but the door wasn't fully closed. The dead bolt was keeping it open. That couldn't have been good. I went inside, hoping for a reasonable explanation. I didn't have to go far. She was there in the entranceway, wear-ing her cream colored church suit, a crimson stain over her heart. The knife was on the floor next to her body. She'd been a beauty in life, I could see that. But now her pretty face was hardening into clay.

I went around the house, looking for the trunk she'd men-tioned. I found it at the foot of her bed. Someone else had already been there. The trunk was open, and all of its contents were strewn across the bed. There were no photographs, not a one.

I went back into the door where Etheline lay dead. I pulled up a chair from the living room and sat there next to her. I didn't sit there long, maybe five minutes.

The problem was simple. I had asked the church lady, Miss Bristol, to give Etheline a note with my name and num-ber on it. She'd given the note to the girl at church that day, and now Etheline was dead. There was a good chance that the police would come to see me, trying to place me at the scene of the crime. If I called them right then, they'd come over and I'd become the prime suspect. No matter how innocent or law-abiding I was, they'd take me to jail and beat me until I confessed. That was a foregone conclusion—at least in my mind.

My other choice was to drive home and go to bed. If the police called me, I'd tell them that I didn't know a thing. If someone saw my license plate parked out in front of her house, I could say I dropped by but no one answered the door.

The first way was the honest, law-abiding way, the kind of life I craved. But the second way was smarter. Leaving that poor dead girl was the wise choice for a black man down at the bottom of the food chain. I walked out of that front door, wiped the doorknob clean, and, though I didn't realize it at the time, drove off into a new period in my life.

THE POLICE DIDN'T CALL me the next day or the day after that. I read about the murder in the *Sentinel*, L.A.'s black newspaper. They reported that Etheline AnnaMaria Teaman was found dead in her foyer by a neighbor who came by to drive her to work at her new job at Douglas Aircraft. The murder weapon was found at the scene. Theft seemed to be the motive. As of yet, there were no suspects in the crime.

It seemed a strange coincidence that she was murdered between the time she called me and the time I arrived. If Raymond was alive, maybe he had something to do with her, more than she let on. After all, why would she have had a photograph of a man that she'd only seen a couple of times in a bar?

I didn't think that Mouse would have killed that girl. It isn't that he was above killing women. But in the times I knew him, he would more likely seduce a girl or threaten her. He got no pleasure out of killing people who couldn't fight back.

But maybe he'd changed. Or maybe he was in trouble.

I pulled out the phone book and began looking for Cedric or C. Boughman. I was lucky that day. The only Cedric Boughman lived on 101st Street.

The address took me to a small house at the far end of a deep lot in the heart of Watts. Instead of a lawn, Boughman's yard had corn and tomatoes, huge fans of collard greens, and rows of carrots. Near the house there was a wire enclosure where eight hens clucked and pecked. They set up a loud din of protest as I reached the front door.

A small woman, somewhere near fifty, appeared in the shadowy screen. Caramel-colored and delicate, she wore glasses with very thick lenses. She stared at me for a moment before saying anything.

"Yes?" she asked.

"Hi. My name is Rawlins. I'm lookin' for Cedric."

"He ain't doin' too well today, Mr. Rawlins," the woman said sadly. "Been sittin' back there for almost a week just shakin' his head and sobbin'."

"What's wrong?"

"He won't say," she replied. "But it must be some girl. Young men pour their whole heart and soul out for just one kiss. It takes a while to get back on your feet after somethin' like that."

"He's been like that a whole week?" I asked.

"Just about. He ain't eat hardly a thing, and you know, he won't even put on his pants."

"He don't even go to work?"

The woman smiled when I mentioned work. "You know he work for the church," she said happily. "Stay home with his mother and make her proud down at Winter Baptist. He's the youngest deacon they ever had."

"And the church don't mind him stayin' home?" I asked.

"God bless Minister Winters," she said, closing her eyes in reverence. "He sent a man down here to tell us that Cedric could take off all the time he needed to."

"He's a good man," I said. "Almost a saint."

The woman took in a deep breath and smiled as if she had just inhaled God. "He was me and Mr. Boughman's savior when we come out here from Arkansas. Every Sunday we'd go to that little chapel and hear about how the Lord was testin' us, makin' us stronger and better for our kids." The feeling in her face, the curl of her lip, was ecstatic. "There was always apple pies and pork sandwiches after the sermon so even if you hadn't eaten all week, at least that one day your body would be satisfied along with your spirit. Mr. Boughman used to say to me, 'Celia, the Lord put that man on earth to save the poor black man.'"

"Do you think I could see Cedric a minute, Mrs. Boughman?"

"Oh, I don't know."

"He might be able to help me find out what happened to my cousin," I said. "You see, my cousin, Ray, died in a logging accident. Cedric might know somebody who talked to him before he died."

Mrs. Boughman peered at me as if trying to puzzle out what I was saying.

"Maybe helpin' somebody else will help Cedric throw off his blues," I suggested.

This argument won Celia over. She pushed the door open and pointed the way. When I walked in, I caught a whiff of her perfume, simple rose water.

The house had a low ceiling that gave the feeling it was

sinking into the earth. There were no windows except on the front wall, and these were covered with thick, floor-length drapes. There were pictures and plaster statues of saints and Jesus on every wall and surface. The air was stagnant as if it were the ether of an ancient tomb that had just been cracked open after six thousand years.

I went through the living room into a long hallway.

"Keep goin'," Celia Boughman said at my back. "It's all the way at the end."

It was a very long hall. The house looked small from outside, especially because the yard was so deep, but that hallway was long enough to be a building of its own. When I finally came to the end, I found a half-open door. Inside, Italian opera music was playing.

"Cedric," I called. "Cedric."

No answer.

I pushed the door open. He was sitting on a piano stool, wearing only blue striped boxers, supporting his big head with the long fingers of his left hand.

"Cedric Boughman," I said, trying to sound like a parent wanting their child to know it was time to pay attention.

It worked. He looked up at me. A sob came from his chest.

"What?" he said.

"My name's Rawlins," I said. "Easy Rawlins. I'm lookin' for a friend'a mine—Raymond Alexander."

"I don't know him," Cedric said. He let his head back down into the basket of fingers. He was thin and quite a bit darker than his mother.

"Maybe not, but I think Etheline Teaman did."

When I mentioned her name, Cedric not only looked up, but got to his feet. It was like he was a puppet, and my words were the strings that gave him life.

"What about Etheline?"

"I think she knew Raymond up in Richmond."

"Is that where she is? In Virginia?"

"No, man. Richmond, California. Etheline told me that she had a picture of Raymond. Did you ever see it?"

"She had lots of pictures. Lots of 'em. She took snapshots of everybody she knew with that little Brownie camera of hers."

Cedric stumbled over to a cluttered desk and sifted around, looking for something. He found a small photograph and handed it to me. It was a picture of him and the young woman that I first saw as a corpse. They were standing side by side, but there was something wrong. I realized that it wasn't Etheline standing there next to Cedric, but her reflection in a full-length mirror. She was taking the picture with a camera held at waist level in her left hand. They were standing next to each other, and at the same time gazing across a distance into one another's eyes.

"That's some picture," I said. "She's good."

"She's real smart," Cedric agreed. "She's going be a real magazine photographer one day. And she's an artist too. This is only half of the picture. After we took this one, she made me take the picture of her with me in the mirror. She has that one in her photo book. I told mama that I wanted to get them both blown up and put 'em on either side of my room. Then it'd be like us lookin' at each other and takin' pictures of each other too."

"You gonna do that?" I asked, to pull him further out of his shell.

"Mama didn't like it. She said it looked wrong to her. I think she's afraid that I'll move out or somethin'."

"When's the last time you saw Etheline?" I asked.

"A week ago today," he said, as if he were talking about the creation of the world.

"Where'd you see her?"

"At the church," he said, the sadness back in his tone and demeanor. "At the church."

"Winter Baptist?"

"Yes sir. She told me that we should be friends. She had spoken to Reverend Winters and decided to be by herself for a while. She said that, that . . ."

"You haven't seen her since then?"

"No."

"She ever talk to you about Raymond? A little brother with gray eyes and light skin."

"I don't know. I don't think so," he said. "Have you talked to her?"

I tried to read his eyes, to see if he was crazy or lying or being sincere. But the pain of his broken heart hid the truth from me.

"Just on the phone," I said gently. "To ask her if she heard from my friend."

The music had been soft during our talk. But now a powerful soprano was professing some deep emotion—love or hate, I couldn't tell which.

CELIA BOUGHMAN was leaning over the wire chicken coop when I came out of the house. By the time I'd come up to her, she'd grabbed one of the frantic hens by the throat.

"Mrs. Boughman?"

"Yes, son?" She held the chicken up and tested it for plumpness.

"Has your son been at home all the time for the past week?"

"Yes he has. Haven't left his room except to go to the toilet. Haven't even bathed."

"Have you been here all that time?"

"Except Monday. Monday's my shoppin' day. I have Willard, the boy down the street, drive me to the store and I buy all I need till the next week."

"How about Sunday?" I asked. "Didn't you go to church?"

"No. Cedric was so sad, I felt bad leavin' him to go to the church that he loved. No. I stayed here and made him dinner."

With that she took the chicken by its head and spun the body around like a child's noisemaker. She grabbed the neck and twisted it until the head came off of the body, and then dropped them both on the ground. The body jumped up and started running in circles. It bumped into my leg and then headed off in the opposite direction.

"Did Cedric talk to you?" Celia asked pleasantly.

"Yes he did."

"Oh that's good. Maybe he's gettin' over his broken heart."

The chicken ran into me again. This time she fell over and lay there on the ground, kicking in the air.

"Thank you, Mrs. Boughman," I said. "I'm sorry to have bothered you."

"You want to stay for dinner, Mr. Rawlins? We're havin' fried chicken."

"No thanks," I said. "I just had chicken the other night."

I ENTERED the department store that had become a church at sunset. Two men in dark suits saw me from up near the pulpit. They headed my way.

"Hold it right there," one of the men said. If he were standing behind me, I would have worried that there was a rifle aimed at my back.

The front of the church was half a lot away, so I waited patiently. They were deep brown men with frowns on their faces.

"Can I help you?" said one of the men. His big belly protruded so far that it created a cavern in the chest area of his suit.

"Lookin' for the reverend," I said.

"He ain't here," the other man said. He had small fleshy bumps all over his face and hands.

"That's funny," I said. "A man over in the office just told me that he was here, gettin' ready for the Wednesday night meetin'."

"Well he ain't," Bumpy said.

"That's too bad—for him," I replied.

"What's that supposed to mean?" the fat man asked.

"It means that I got a problem in my pocket that he needs to know about. He needs it bad."

"What you sayin', man?"

"You just tell the minister that Easy Rawlins wants to talk to him about something of paramount concern. I'll be sittin' in this chair right here till you get back."

Fatso took the message, and Bumpy waited with me. I sat there looking around Winter Baptist. It didn't feel like a church then, but I knew when the organ started playing and the minister was in his groove that a holy light would shine in. I had friends who didn't believe in Heaven or its Host, but still they never missed a Sunday sermon at Winter Baptist.

Birds were chirping from somewhere up around the ceiling. They had come into the church and set up their nests. I thought that the minister probably left them there to make that sacred space seem something like the Garden of Eden.

"Do I know you?" a gravelly voice asked.

He had come in from behind me, probably hoping to see if he knew me and my implied threat.

"No, sir," I said, rising to my feet. "My name's Easy Rawlins."

"What do you want?" Reverend Winters looked more country than usual that evening. He wore blue jeans and a checkered red work shirt. The brown leather of his shoes was old and worn out. You could see the impression of his baby toes on the outer edges. A pair of shoes like that might have outlasted a marriage.

"Can we talk privately for a moment, Reverend Winters?"

The minister made a gesture with his head, and Bumpy started patting me down. I didn't like it, but I didn't lay him out either. Bumpy grunted and Winters motioned toward the other side of the room.

We walked together, under the scrutiny of his private guards.

"Well?" he asked me. "Let's get this over with. I got a sermon to deliver in just an hour and a half."

Winters wasn't tall or striking, neither was he delicate or particularly strong. His chin was subpar, and the top of his head was almost large enough to indicate a whole new species of man. His skin had the color and luster of dark honey standing on the windowsill. But it was his voice that set him apart from mortal men. As I said, it was raspy, but it was also rich and commanding. His voice alone made you want to go along with whatever words he was making. It was very disconcerting, but other things bothered me more.

"Cedric Boughman and Etheline Teaman," I said.

That brought the minister up short. He seemed to be studying his own reflection in my eyes.

"This some kinda blackmail or somethin'?" he whispered.

"Never did like that word," I said. "And you don't have nuthin' I want, except maybe the truth."

"Fuck you." The words shocked me. For some reason I never expected a man of God to be coarse in that way. But the shock went deeper than that. It was like a slap in my face, making me aware of my situation.

"Somebody stole somethin' from Etheline," I said. "An album of photographs."

"How the hell would you know that?"

"I got my ways, Brother Winters. Believe me. Someone stole her photograph album."

"So what?"

"Do you know where it is?"

"Why would I?"

"Etheline was a prostitute not a month ago," I said. "She had a regular, a man in your employ name of Cedric Boughman. She also attended your church. She got special instructions from you—in person. Now Cedric is cryin' in his bedroom and you sendin' him his salary until he's fit to come back to work."

"This is a Christian institution, Mr. Rawlins. We don't turn away lost sheep. We don't persecute a man when he loses someone he cares for."

"That sounds good, but it's a lie. Cedric is either crazy or he don't even know that Etheline is dead."

"What does that have to do with me?"

"I don't know what's goin' on," I said. "I don't know who killed Etheline or why. All I know is that there's a picture I need to see lost somewhere, and I intend to find it. I will keep on asking questions until I do find it."

"Easy," the minister said. "That's your Christian name?"

"Ezekiel."

"Good name. Where you from, Ezekiel?"

"Texas mostly. I was born in Louisiana."

"New Orleans?"

"New Iberia."

"Country, huh? Like me."

Just that quickly, Winters had gotten the upper hand. If we were boxing, I would have been the tomato can from Podunk, and he would have been Archie Moore.

"You know country is plain and simple," the minister said. "A country man does what he does, day in and day out. If the year is good then his wife got a few extra pounds on her. If it's bad he works a little harder. That's all."

I would have bet that those words were destined for that evening's sermon.

"Brother Boughman is in charge of school administration. He's a good boy, but young. He gave in to temptation. He had congress with the devil, but what he found in that devil's pit was a lost angel. He talked her into coming to church. Then he talked her into leaving that house of sin. And when she did that, he sent her here to me."

"Then you told her to leave him and come to you," I said. "Then somebody stabbed her in the heart."

The minister winced. "I been workin' hard for more'n eighteen years, Brother Rawlins. Eighteen years on the front lines against Satan and his crew. I work every day, all day. I've pulled men out of the bottle and the needle out of young women's arms. I teach black chirren to love themselves and I give old women a place to feel like they make a difference. I work hard and I get tired sometimes."

"Was Etheline a rest stop?" I asked.

"I loved her." His voice lost its power. I almost believed

him. "She was like a gift from God. At first it was just a physical thing. She had learned how to make men melt and holler.
Some days she would come up into my rooms and I'd tell her
to leave. But she would push my protests aside and grab hold
of my spirit. She would stay with me deep into the night, lis-
tenin' to all the weak things that I could never say to anyone in
the congregation. I had to be strong for them, but with her I
could let down. I could be that country boy."

"Are you married, Reverend Winters?"

"Yes, son. Yes I am."

"So all that love was secret and stolen," I said. "Dangerous
for a man in your position."

"What you gettin' at?"

"Did she take a snapshot of you, Reverend? Did she have a
picture of the two'a you together?"

"What if she did?"

"Well," I said. "Some might say that a picture like that
would be like Joshua at Jericho: It could bring down these
walls."

"And you think I would hurt that girl from fear of somebody findin' out about us?"

"It wouldn't be the first time somethin' like that happened.
Did you write to her?"

He didn't answer the question, but his face admitted the
indiscretion.

"It's like I said in the beginning, Reverend Winters. I didn't
know the girl. She's not my concern. But I need to see that
photograph. And I will have it. So if you know where I should
look, it might be very helpful to your cause."

The minister took a seat then. He looked down at his old
comfortable shoes for succor, but even they couldn't help him.

"You're wrong in this, Mr. Rawlins. I had nothing to do

with that girl's death. I loved her. And even though she broke it off with me, I would have never hurt her. Never."

"She broke up with you too?"

He nodded and held his head the same way Cedric had done.

"When?" I asked.

"On Sunday, right after service. She left me a note, said that she would only bring me grief, that she had to make a new life where no one knew her and no one could hurt the ones she loved."

The minister lowered his head and grieved. I stayed quiet for a minute or two.

"Did she have any friends other than Cedric?" I asked.

"My secretary," Winters whispered. "Lena McCoy. Lena helped Etheline to get on her feet when she came to us. She got her a job at Douglas where her husband works."

"If you tell me how to get in touch with her, maybe I can figure this stuff out without causing you grief."

"You okay, Reverend Winters?" Bumpy asked. He and the fat man had come to investigate their pastor's obvious dismay.

"Okay, Reggie," Winters said. He stood up to meet his followers. "Mr. Rawlins is gonna need Lena's phone number. Call her up and tell her to help him all she can."

Bumpy didn't like it, but he was a soldier in the army of the Lord. The commander and chief had spoken, so all he could do was heed and obey.

ON MY DRIVE HOME I wondered at the sequence of recent events. Etheline broke up with Reverend Winters the same Sunday that she heard from me. If she had read my note first, then it could have been the reason she was getting ready to leave. She wrote to Winters, she called me—maybe she got in touch with somebody else. And if my note was the reason she was burning her bridges, then it could have also been the cause of her death.

That is, if the minister was telling the truth. There was no way for me to know what Medgar Winters really felt or knew. The only thing that I was sure of was that if I had caused that girl's death, I would make sure that the killer didn't have a happy ending either.

JESUS HAD MADE DINNER and eaten with Feather by the time I'd gotten home. He made hamburger patties with tomato soup and baked potatoes. She was asleep and he was in the backyard, under electric light, working on his small boat.

Moths of all shapes and sizes flitted around in the halo of light. Jesus was working a plane across a plank of wood that he intended for one of the benches of his boat. I came up to him, took the other plank, and began work on it. After forty-five minutes we'd finished leveling the seats. Then we stained and sealed them. No more than a dozen words passed between us in two and a half hours. We had the kind of kinship that didn't need many words.

THE NEXT MORNING I made Feather's lunchbox and drove her to school. She was happy to spend the time with me, and it was joy in my heart to talk to her. She was missing Bonnie, and so was I.

"How come you miss Bonnie, Daddy?"

"I don't know," I said. "Lots of reasons, I guess. Mostly I just like seeing her in the morning. Why do you miss her?"

"Because," she said, "because when Bonnie's home it's two boys and two girls."

❖   ❖   ❖

I CALLED LENA McCOY from the custodians' bungalow on the lower campus of Sojourner Truth junior high.

"Hello," a man's voice answered.

"Lena McCoy, please," I said.

"Who is this?"

"Mr. Rawlins."

"What do you want with my wife, Mr. Rawlins?"

"I had a meeting with Reverend Winters yesterday. I asked him some questions that he couldn't answer, and he suggested I ask Lena."

"Do you know what time it is?" Mr. McCoy asked.

"Yes sir, I do," I said. "Eight o'clock in the morning, workin' man's time. Time to get up and out of the bed. Time to go out and earn that daily bread."

"What questions do you have for my wife?"

"It has to do with church activities, Mr. McCoy. This isn't any scam. I'm not tryin' to put somethin' over on you. I don't want any money or anything. Just a little information about the church."

"Why can't you—"

Mr. McCoy cut off what he was saying and mumbled something to someone in the room with him. At one point he raised his voice, but I couldn't make out the words. I could hear the phone jostling around, and then a woman came on the line.

"Yes? Who is this?" the woman asked.

"Lena McCoy?"

"Yes?"

"My name is Easy Rawlins. Reverend Winters—"

"Oh, oh yes, Mr. Rawlins. Deacon Latrell told me about you. I'd be happy to talk to you, but I'm late for work as it is. Could you meet me at the church later today?"

"Sure. What time?"

"How about four? That would be good for me. I have to go with the minister to an interfaith dinner at six."

"Four'll be fine."

WHEN I ENTERED the church that afternoon, I ran into a small, elderly man wearing overalls and pushing a broom.

"Afternoon, brother," the older custodian hailed.

"Afternoon," I replied. "I'm supposed to be meetin' a Lena McCoy."

"You wanna go all the way to the pulpit and turn right. You'll see a green door, it opens onto a stairwell. Take the stairs two flights up. Go in that do' and you'll see a woman."

"Mrs. McCoy?"

"Naw. That's Mrs. Daniels. She'll show you to Lena."

"Thank you," I said.

"Nuthin' to it."

As I walked toward the pulpit, I could hear the swish of the janitor's broom on the concrete floor. It was a comforting sound, reminding me of my job at Truth. It felt like a long-ago fond memory, even though I had just come from work.

I needed Bonnie even more than I let on.

"MR. RAWLINS?" Mrs. Daniels said, repeating my name. "I don't have no Rawlins on the minister's schedule today."

"I'm here to speak to Mrs. McCoy," I said.

The church receptionist was round and pleasant-looking, but she didn't like me much. "Is this church business?" she asked.

"Yes, ma'am," I said.

She stared at me a moment too long.

"Listen, lady. I have important business with your minister's assistant. If I walk outta here, it will be you who has to answer for it."

I'd lost another opportunity at making a friend. The receptionist waved her hand toward a door behind her.

I knocked, and woman's voice said, "Come in."

I entered, coming upon a medium-sized black woman who was sitting behind an oak desk in the middle of a large, sunny room.

"Mr. Rawlins?"

The room had a plain pine floor with bookcases against the wall behind the desk. There was a baby avocado tree in a terra cotta pot next to one window.

"Mrs. McCoy?"

The woman got from behind the desk and went to a door between the bookcases. She opened this door and turned back to me.

"Come with me, please," she said.

That half-turn told me a lot about Mrs. McCoy—the woman. She was around thirty-five, but still had the bloom of youth to her face and figure. It was a nice figure, but her deep green dress played it down. The color of the dress also blunted the richness of her dark skin. She wore makeup like an older woman might have, with little color or accentuation. But the sinuous motion of her turn revealed the sensual woman that lived underneath her clamped-down style. She was at home in her body, dancing with just that little turn.

We came into a room that was even simpler than the assistant's office. The minister's office had a plain floor with no bookcases at all. There was a podium holding a large Bible next to the window, and a simple painting of the face of a white Christ hung on the far wall. He didn't even have a desk, just a table with two chairs pulled up to it. The only means of comfort in the room was a wide-bed couch pressed into the corner.

"This is Reverend Winters's office," she said. "No one will bother us in here."

She took one of the chairs at the table, and I sat in the other.

"What can I do to help you, Mr. Rawlins?"

"Your husband was unhappy to hear me on the phone this morning," I said. I decided to find out a little bit more about the woman before hearing what she had to say about Etheline.

Lena looked down and then back again. "Foster is old-fashioned," she said. "He doesn't like gentlemen unknown to him calling me on the telephone."

"You'd think Reverend Winters would have known that and had me call you at the office."

"He has so much on his mind," Lena said. Her face took on a soft glow when talking about her boss. Even the severe makeup couldn't hide the feeling she had for him.

"Did he tell you why I was here?"

"Yes. It's about that poor young girl."

"Dead girl," I said.

Tears appeared in the luscious woman's eyes. She nodded and looked down again. Lena McCoy was so full of love and compassion that any man would be drawn to her. It's not that she was beautiful, not even pretty, really. But there was something physical there, and caring. If there was music in a room and I saw Lena McCoy, I would have asked her to dance, even though I didn't like dancing.

"I have some hard questions to ask you about Etheline, Lena. And I want you to answer them."

She nodded again.

"She was having an affair with your boss, right?"

"Yes."

"Right here in this room."

Her assent was a simple movement of her head, like a bird makes when warbling softly.

"What did you think about that?"

"I was happy for him."

"Happy?"

"Yes. Medgar gives of himself like some kind of saint. He meets fifty people in this room every day. And they're all askin' for somethin'. They want money or a soapbox or for him to travel fifty miles to talk to a roomful'a people who don't even care. They cry on his shoulder. They confess their sins. And he takes it all in, Mr. Rawlins. Twelve hours every day, seven days a week."

"And Etheline was different?"

"The first day she came here, she brought homemade brownies and a bunch of little white flowers. Medgar had those daisies in a glass of water for two weeks. I finally had to throw them out."

"Why did she meet the minister?" I asked.

"To apologize. To apologize for her sins. To ask him if she was worthy to be in his congregation."

"You heard this?"

"Medgar tells me everything." It was the first hint of pride in Lena's tone.

"Everything?"

"Yes."

"He tell you when they became lovers?"

"He didn't need to, but he did. After the first time I would sneak her in through the side door so that no one else would know."

"You helped him cheat on his wife?"

"His wife helps herself to everything he has. They been married since before he came to Los Angeles. You know he seems the same, but inside he's changed. He's gotten bigger. Mrs. Winters changed on the outside. She wears nice clothes and drives a big car. But on the inside she's hungry and jealous. She ain't never so much as brought him a cupcake on his birthday."

"What happened when Lena broke it off with the reverend?"

"He cried," she said. "He put his head on my shoulder and cried like a child."

"Was he angry?"

"He knew that they'd have to stop one day. He knew it was wrong what he did. But you know sometimes a man is weak."

"Do you know Cedric Boughman?"

"Sure I do. He brought Etheline to Medgar's attention."

"Do you think that Cedric might have harmed Etheline?"

"Why would he?"

"Because she left him for your boss."

"But she left Medgar to go back with Cedric."

"What?"

"Didn't the minister tell you?" She was really surprised. "Etheline left him a note Sunday after services. She said that she was going away with Cedric, back up to the Bay Area where she was from."

"Then why did Winters keep paying Cedric?"

"He did that before Etheline left him, and he would have done it for any of his inner circle. He's a good man."

"Are you in love with Reverend Winters?" I asked.

She could have been a wild night creature frozen in my headlights.

"Are you?" I insisted.

"What does a question like that have to do with anything?"

"I don't know. If you were in love with him, you might wanna protect him, you might be mad that he was with another woman. I mean if he needed love, why not come to you?"

"I'm a married woman, Mr. Rawlins."

"He's a married man. Maybe that's why your husband gets so mad when a man calls you. Mad 'cause he feel another man nearby."

"I would never cheat on my husband," Lena said. "The minister is the whole world to me, but I'd never cross that line."

"And what about him? How did you feel about him crossin' over into sin?"

"Men are weak, Mr. Rawlins. They're strong of arm but frail in their hearts. They need forgiveness more than women do."

"How about Etheline?" I asked. "She's a woman. Did you forgive her?"

"Etheline was just a child. People had been usin' her all her life. She didn't know any better. Is there anything else?"

I shook my head.

Lena got up from her chair gracefully but she stumbled at the door.

WHEN I WAS HALFWAY through the pews, Bumpy and Fatso picked up my trail. They followed me across the wide church and into the side parking lot. The lot was full when I got there, so my car was parked in the alley.

They followed me back there.

I wasn't worried. When I got to my car, I bent down to tie my shoe. I also got the .25-caliber pistol out of the elastic band of my sock. The deacons were twenty feet away from me. I could see that the hollow-chested one had found himself a lead pipe.

I palmed the pistol, stood up, and smiled. That smirk stopped them dead in their tracks. If they had been hyenas or wild dogs, they would have had their noses in the air, sniffing for danger. Something was different. The prey had gained confidence. The rules of the game had suddenly changed.

I unlocked my car door and opened it, but I didn't climb in. I just stood there, daring the deacons to approach. They watched me, waiting for a sign. When I finally got in, Bumpy took a tentative step forward. I pointed my pistol at him, and he took two steps and one skip back.

After that they let me drive off unmolested.

IT WAS ABOUT FIVE when I got back home. The phone was ringing when I got to the front door, but whoever it was, they'd hung up before I got to the receiver. Feather and Jesus were in the backyard. I sat in my reading chair thinking about the last week.

Whorehouses and sinful ministers were nothing new to me. Even murder was an old friend, like Mouse. But for years I had been getting up and going to work, putting my paycheck into the bank. Paying my bills by check instead of cash. I was a member of the PTA. I had slept in my own bed every single night from Christmas to Christmas.

I followed the same routes every day, but all of a sudden I seemed to be lost. It was like I was a young man again, every morning leading me to someplace I never would have suspected. I wasn't enjoying myself, though. I didn't want to lose my way. But I had to find out about Mouse. I had to be sure whether he was dead or alive.

❖   ❖   ❖

FEATHER AND JESUS came inside around six.

"Mail, Daddy," Feather said when she saw me.

Jesus went to the console TV and grabbed a brown envelope that I'd failed to notice.

"What's that?" I asked my son.

He shrugged his shoulders and said, "It was on the front
step when we got home."

He dumped the paper envelope on my lap and then went
into the kitchen to make ready for dinner.

When I ripped the seam open, a sweet scent escaped. It
was a black photo album. The cover was worn and stained,
but the pages were all intact. I turned the pages, looking at all
the Kodak snapshots neatly held by little paper divots built
into the black leaves. Six pictures on each side of each page.
Pictures of men, some of women. One woman appeared
again and again. Etheline had been beautiful when she was
alive.

"Who's that, Daddy?" Feather leaned against my forearm
and pointed, pressing her finger against Etheline's dress.

"A pretty lady."

"Uh-huh. She a friend'a yours?"

"L'il bit."

"Is she gonna go to Knott's Berry Farm with us?"

"No. She wanted me to look at this picture book and see if
there was a picture of Uncle Raymond in it. You remember
what Uncle Raymond looked like?"

"He looked funny," she said, snickering.

She climbed onto my lap and the little yellow dog growled,
peeking out from behind the drapes. There were over fifty
pages of photographs in the bulging album. Feather made up
stories about who the men were and what their relationship
was to Etheline.

There were two pictures of Inez with men. She was lovely in those pictures. The thought crossed my mind that I could be with her for just thirty dollars.

"That one look like Uncle Raymond," Feather said.

It did. A smallish man, not much taller than Etheline, with light eyes and *good* hair. If you had described Mouse to a police sketch artist, he might have drawn this man's picture—but it wasn't Raymond. His face was too round, his jaw too sharp. He was smiling, but it wasn't the contagious kind of smile that Mouse had. It was just some mortal man, not the angel of death, my best friend, Raymond Alexander.

I studied the album for hours after Feather and Jesus went to bed, until I was pretty sure I knew who the murderer was.

I ENTERED THE DEEP LOT on 101st Street at nine-fifteen the next morning. Mrs. Boughman was sweeping the ground with a straw broom. I hadn't seen anyone sweep bare earth since I'd left the South. It wasn't a pleasant memory.

"Good morning, Mr. Rawlins. Cedric went to work this morning," she said proudly.

"He did? That's great. He must be feeling better."

"I'll tell him that you dropped by when he gets home," she said. "You know, it's funny. When you left the other day, he asked me who you were."

"Yeah. I know. How are you, Mrs. Boughman?" I asked in a tone that was less than concerned.

"Fine."

"You know I got a gift and a warning yesterday afternoon."

"I don't know what you mean, Mr. Rawlins."

"One of the deacons from that department store you call a church dropped off an envelope at my doorstep. He left it because I asked for it. But the fact that he left it at my door meant that he knew where I lived; that was the threat."

The elder Boughman shook her head as if nothing I said made sense.

"It was a photograph album," I continued. "A woman named Etheline Teaman had put it together. It was full of snapshots of her and her friends. All the men she ever knew. All of 'em except for two."

If Celia Boughman were thirty feet tall, she would have spun my head like a noisemaker and left my decapitated body to run around that yard bumping up against her leg.

"Missin' is Medgar Winters and Cedric Boughman."

"Cedric," she said, with odd emphasis.

"She called you, didn't she?"

"Who?"

"Etheline. She called you and left a message for Cedric. Or maybe she saw you at church Sunday last, and said something, a little too much. Maybe about wanting to see Cedric. Maybe about taking him on a vacation to Richmond. Whatever it was, you weren't gonna lose your deacon son and he wasn't gonna lose his soul to a whore."

It was when Celia Boughman's mouth fell open that I was sure of my logic.

"You stabbed her through the heart and took the evidence that your son had been so close to her," I said. "And then when you couldn't take it anymore, you brought the picture album and probably a stack of letters to Reverend Winters. You confessed your sins and left him with the evidence. That's how I see it. I saw manila envelopes like the one the book was in at the church, and I could smell the slightest hint of cheap rose water on the pages of that book."

"Don't tell Cedric," she said. "Don't tell him. He wouldn't

understand. He didn't know what a woman like that would do to his life."

She leaned against her broom to keep from falling.

I shook my head and walked away.

"YOU SAY THAT you suspect the woman?" Detective Andre Brown asked me. We were sitting in his office at the 77th Precinct.

I had given him the photo album and told him of my adventures between the whorehouse and church, leaving out my discovery of the murdered girl.

"Yes sir, Detective Brown."

"Because this book was in a manila envelope and you smelled perfume when you first opened it?"

"That's about it."

"That's pretty slim evidence."

"I know."

"So what do you want me to do?" the tall and slender Negro policeman asked. "There weren't any fingerprints on the knife."

"I hope that you can't do anything. There's no court that could judge this crime."

"Then why are you here?"

"Because an innocent young woman was murdered, officer. I owe it to her memory to tell somebody the truth."

SILVER LINING

"**M**RS. MASTERS, I'd like you to meet Mr. Ezekiel Rawlins," Kathy Langer said. "He's our senior head custodian."

I had just entered the secretary's office. Masters was standing there next to Kathy's desk.

"Nice to meet you," I said to the new principal of Sojourner Truth Junior High School. "I hope you're going to like it here at Truth."

"Oh, yes," Ada Masters replied. "I already love it. It's a beautiful school. And it's so good to meet you at last, Mr. Rawlins. Are you feeling better?"

I had missed a few days of work looking for the photograph of a man I might have known. It turned out to be the picture of a stranger. I had squandered my sick days and made a bad impression on the new boss. The worst thing about it was, I didn't give a damn.

"Okay now," I said. "One'a those seventy-two hour viruses. Woke up this morning and it was gone."

Mrs. Masters's pale blue eyes concentrated on me. She was at the midway point between fifty and sixty, petite and well dressed. The gray suit she wore was elegant, made from cashmere. The light gray blouse showing at the V of her jacket had the high sheen of silk. Her sapphire ring was real and her glasses were lined with nacre cut from a single shell. For all that expense her clothes weren't showy; a careless eye might miss the finer touches and think that Masters was dressed according to a city employee's salary.

The secretary, Kathy Langer, was an interesting contrast to her new boss. She was young, pert, and ready to make babies. Her coarse, nut-brown hair was almost shiny, her clothes came from the May Company bargain table or maybe JCPenny's. A vegetarian could have eaten her blunt-toed brown shoes with a clear conscience. Her face wasn't pretty but it was hungry, a thing most working-class men like. And she had a habit of lifting her chin to bare her throat, at least when I was in the room with her.

There I was, a big black man, in the room with two white women who would never meet traveling in their own social circles. It seemed odd to me and I wanted to say something about it. But I didn't think that either one of them would understand or appreciate my views.

"Will you take a walk with me, Mr. Rawlins?" Mrs. Masters asked.

"Easy," I said. "That's the name I go by."

I saw Kathy mouth the name. When she saw me regarding her she smiled and moved her shoulder like a lounging cat getting comfortable in a new corner.

"I'd like you to walk me around the lower campus," Principal Masters said.

WE VISITED SEVERAL CLASSROOMS. The teachers looked wary until they saw Mrs. Masters smile at them and wave. She wasn't like the previous principal, Hiram Newgate, who only dropped in to see what infractions he might find.

We also spent a while in the garden: the biology and agrarian science department of the school. Out there the students grew radishes and studied elementary anatomy.

Finally we came to the custodians' bungalow. The rest of my crew was out working by then so we had the room to ourselves. It was a big rectangular space with a large table down the center of it. Along the walls were shelves crowded with cartons of paper towels, toilet tissue, and boxes filled with bottles of ammonia, window cleaner, and bleach. There were five-gallon cans of wax piled in one corner and an entire wall of pegboard hung with dozens of sets of keys next to the door. The table was strewn with newspapers, overflowing ashtrays, empty paper coffee cups, and plates with half-eaten cakes on them.

"Nice place," Mrs. Masters said. "The kind of place where the job gets done."

"Sorry about the mess. But, you know, if I want 'em to keep the school clean I can't complain about this room until Friday after lunch."

"I understand," she said. "May I have a seat?"

"Please do." I was thinking that Newgate never asked permission for anything. He'd stand up if you didn't offer a seat and nurse a grudge against you from then on.

"Can I get you a cup of coffee?" I asked.

"No thank you. I am very happy that you're back, Mr. Rawlins," she said. "You know the faculty and the students talk a lot about you."

"They do?"

"Yes. It seems that they've come to rely on you for many problems that have nothing to do with the maintenance of the plant. Many of the women teachers, some men too, say that they depend on you for discipline when some of the more aggressive students have problems."

Ada Masters had a mild way about her. She was small and unthreatening. In that manner she had gotten more out of her new charges than harsh-mouthed Newgate ever could.

It was true that students and teachers alike came to me when there was a problem. I was a black man in charge at a black school. No boy student was big enough to challenge me and the parents trusted me more than they did the white teachers. I was well read too. I'd perused every textbook in the school and often found myself instructing the kids on how to do their homework and even how to use the library.

I never neglected my own work, at least not until the past few weeks. It was coming up on the first-year anniversary of the death of my friend, Raymond Alexander. I felt responsible for Raymond's death. He had been trying to steer clear of trouble but he helped me out one last time and got a bullet in the chest. His wife, EttaMae Harris, carried him out of the hospital just before they were about to declare him dead. I'd been looking for him, for his grave if that's where he was, but Etta had disappeared and there were only whispered rumors that Ray hadn't actually died but had gone back to Texas or up to the Bay Area or down in Mexico.

Lately I had been spending afternoons roaming around the city looking for clues about EttaMae or Raymond, who most people knew as Mouse.

I thought that the new principal had walked me around to gently let it drop that I shouldn't miss any more days, but then I realized that she was going to stop me from working outside of the job description for the supervising senior head custodian.

"I wanted to thank you," she said.

I girded myself thinking that this was the soft caress before the slaughtering knife.

". . . for taking such good care of the school."

"Say what?" I said.

"You have been the spine of Sojourner Truth," Mrs. Masters said.

"I have?"

"You know you have. There are paintings of you in the art class, letters from thankful parents on file in the main office. The only negative notices are the job evaluation reports from Principal Newgate. He thought that you were insolent and insubordinate. I suppose that if he had been a better principal some future artist might have drawn him."

"Oh they did," I assured her. "There were quite a few portraits of Principal Newgate that I've had to wash off of the children's rest room walls. If he had found them I would have probably got a transfer letter in there too."

Mrs. Masters's laugh was hushed but hardy. She covered her mouth and leaned forward in her chair. A tear rolled down her cheek.

"Easy?" It was a man's voice.

At the door stood Jackson Blue, himself a living doorway into another dimension of my life.

Mrs. Masters straightened up and wiped the tear from her face.

"You have work to do, Mr. Rawlins," she said. "Come up to the office tomorrow morning and we'll talk about what you think I need to pay attention to here at Truth, as you call it."

She got to her feet and walked to the door. Jackson stepped out of the way and they both made graceful little bows with their heads. When she walked out Jackson closed the door behind her.

"What the hell are you doing here, Jackson? This is my job."

"You walked in on me just a few weeks ago, brother," Jackson replied. "At least I didn't knock at the door and yell out that I was the cops."

He was right. I had pulled that tasteless joke on him.

"So what do you want, man? You know that woman you just chased outta here is my new boss."

Jackson snaked into the chair that Masters had vacated. He clasped his hands together and started rocking to and fro. He was a short man with small bones. His face was slender, sharp, and very dark. He wore black jeans, a black T-shirt, and gray rubber-soled shoes with no socks.

"Well?" I asked.

"It ain't good, man."

"Listen," I said. "If I can't cover it with a mop and a bucket'a soapy water you don't even need to tell me. My street days are over."

"Jewelle MacDonald."

Jackson stared at me with certainty. He knew he had me hooked.

"What about JJ?"

"You remember when you brought me over her house last year, when I was in trouble with them gangsters?"

"Yeah? What about it?"

Jackson's shrug was as damning as a signed confession.

"You and her?" I asked.

Just before Mouse had been shot I brought Jackson to my real estate agent's home in Laurel Canyon. His name was Mofass. Mofass lived with what we called an almost-in-law, Jewelle MacDonald. She was barely more than a third of his age but she loved him and ran his business since emphysema slowed him down.

Jackson had been in trouble because he was competing

with the mob for the numbers game in Watts. He had information I needed so we traded favors: a foolproof hideout for
some names and addresses.

"After it was all over," Jackson said, "I went back up there.
She told me that Equity Realty had a relationship with
another company that manages that apartment I got on
Ozone."

"And then she brought you some groceries?" I asked.

"She was just lettin' stuff off, you know. Then we started
talkin'. She told me that she was brought up a Catholic in
Texas. You know, fish on Fridays an' like that. I told her that
the whole philosophical structure of the Catholic Church was
based on Aristotle hundreds of years before Christ was even
born. You know I said it just to fuck with her head. She just
told me that I was crazy but the next time I saw her she must
have been to the library or something, because she knew
about Plato and Socrates and them, and she wanted me to
explain what I had said."

I sighed. Jackson was winding up into a story. Most other
times I would have cut him off but I let him go on because I
didn't really want him to get to the point. I was in no hurry to
go into the world where men got shot down in the street for
doing their friends a favor.

"So," Jackson continued, "I read her the riot act on
Aristotle, Augustine, and Aquinas. You know, you'n me talked
about all that stuff ten years ago, more."

"Uh-huh," I grunted. "So what?"

"I figured out up at her house that she liked talkin' about
books and shit. But I didn't know that it got her hot. I never
met a black woman who got hot over a man's book knowledge."

I wanted to tell him that he didn't know my girlfriend,
Bonnie Shay, but I thought better of it.

"So what, Jackson? Mofass can't hardly leave the house. I guess if JJ wants a boyfriend, it's okay."

"It's not that, man," Jackson said. "I mean Jewelle made it plain from the start that she ain't never gonna leave Mofass. She wants to be with me. She lets me stay in that apartment and helps me out if I need it. But I cain't call her up at the house or stay with her the whole night because she got to get back up there to the canyon and take care'a him."

"So you're kinda like a married man's girlfriend on the side," I said, cracking a smile in spite of my trepidations.

"Laugh if you want to, man. But once I figure out the binary language of machines I'll be inside them computers and you'll be out in the cold."

"What's the problem, Jackson?"

"Clovis."

Another name, another universe of danger.

"What about her?"

"Really it ain't her. Or maybe it is," Jackson speculated.

"What, Jackson? What you tryin' t'say?"

"Misty Stubbs."

"Who's that?"

"She's Jewelle's half-sister on her dead daddy's side."

"Yeah? So?"

"Jewelle's been writin' to Misty down in Texas all these years since she been up here. She been askin' Misty to come up but the girl got married when she was fifteen and had to stay with her husband. You know, like it should be. Anyway, I guess her and the husband started not gettin' along a while back and Misty finally decided to come out here. We went down to Greyhound and everything but she didn't show up."

"But she said she was comin'?"

"Give us the schedule and everything."

"Did JJ call her house in Dallas?"

"How could she do that, man? Misty was leavin' her husband."

"Maybe Misty changed her mind."

"They closer than full sisters is, Easy. Misty wouldn't do somethin' like that and not say."

"Well what do you want from me?" I said. "Girl got on a bus or she didn't. Maybe her husband stopped her. Maybe she got pulled off somewhere on the road. Either way it's the kinda story you tell to the cops."

"But I didn't say about Clovis yet," Jackson said.

"Okay. Okay. Hit me."

"Clovis come over to the real estate office three days ago. She waltzed right up to Jewelle's desk like they never had no problems. You know Jewelle ain't scared'a Clovis and them no more 'cause she got Jackie and Lorenzo workin' for her. Those boys always go around armed."

I knew Jackie and Lorenzo. They were okay. But Clovis MacDonald, Jewelle's aunt, was deadlier than three men and almost as smart as her niece.

"Clovis was all smilin' and pleasant," Jackson continued. "So Jewelle knew that somethin' was wrong. She axed Clovis why she was there and Clovis said that Jewelle done stoled Mofass's real estate company from her and she wanted a piece of the business back."

Clovis was wrong to have blamed Jewelle. It was really Mofass and I who pushed Clovis out of the business. But the real problem with her memory was that she had taken the business from Mofass in the first place. When Clovis was just a waitress, at a nameless diner we used to frequent, she seduced Mofass and then imprisoned him in her house. Jewelle helped him escape and then she took over the real estate office and turned it into a major concern. At one time I thought that I could be in the property business, but once I saw how good Jewelle was I realized that I would always be a little fish.

"What did Jewelle say?"

"She axed Clovis to leave. Clovis just smiled and put up her hands. But before she left she said, 'I bet you Misty would be happy if you signed me back into the business. I bet you that she'd come hug and kiss you if you did the right thing.'"

I could imagine the chill in that evil woman's smile. Mouse had once asked me if I wanted Clovis dead. He didn't like hurting women but he made allowances now and then. I told him no, but deep in my heart I knew that it would have been the safe move to make.

"What you think about that, Easy?"

"What do you mean what do I think? I don't think anything."

"Come on, man. Clovis knew that Misty came down here. Somehow she fount out and grabbed her."

"You don't know that, Jackson. It could have been just some innocent comment. That's all."

Jackson Blue stood up from his seat with such force that the chair he was in flew five feet backward and crashed to the floor.

"Fuck you, man!" he shouted. "You know better'n that shit!"

I was amazed. I had never seen, nor ever expected to see, Jackson show anger or rage. He was a coward down into his bones and always fled from confrontation.

"What's wrong with you, Jackson?"

"She's up in that house with Mofass now. She cain't eat or sleep or do her job. I axed her to come to you but she wouldn't. She's afraid that you might go against Clovis and get her friend killed. But you know tomorrow afternoon she's gonna go down to Equity and sign half of the business over to Clovis. That's what's wrong."

It was wrong, there was no question about that. And there was no question about what I should do. JJ was a friend of mine. Equity Realty managed my three small apartment buildings in and around Watts. And Clovis was the closest thing I ever had to a true enemy.

"How can she do that, Jackson? Mofass owns the business."

"She got the power of attorney ever since Mofass been sick. She the one wit' the final say."

I looked over at my pegboard of keys. They reminded me of the homemade Christmas ornaments we had when I was a child.

"You know I have to talk to her, Jackson."

"Yeah."

"She's gonna be mad that you came to me."

"I know she will, brother. But what can I do? Clovis be like a cancer once she get in there."

I took a deep breath and wondered if a vengeful supreme deity actually existed. Or maybe it was Hindu karma that had caught me by the tail. Something was pulling me back into the street.

I DROVE UP TO MOFASS'S HOME. It was at the end of an unpaved path two turns off of Laurel Canyon Road. From the driveway of their hidden home you could see the Los Angeles basin. Ragged brown smoke clung to the atmosphere like some kind of evil spirit dancing the dance of the damned.

Jewelle opened the door. She wore a cranberry-colored dress with wide skirts and a tapered waist. The neckline was straight across and low cut. If it wasn't for that frown she would have been captivating.

When I met JJ she was still a child. She was hopeful, filled with life and energy that made you want to laugh and do things for her happiness. Now, though sad, she had the figure and presence to make a man want to change his life for her. That's what Jackson Blue had done. He had gone against everything that came naturally to him in order to bring me to that door.

"What you doin' here, Easy Rawlins?"

"You know why I'm here, girl. 'Cause you need help."

"I don't need your kind of help," she said.

She swung the door in my face. It would have slammed if I hadn't put my foot across the threshold.

Jewelle possessed a powerful spirit. She had stood up to Clovis while still in her teens, saving Mofass from that evil woman's clutches. She had borne the weight of her half-sister's disappearance up until the moment that door would not close; then she fell up against me and cried. I walked her outside toward the sheer cliff that was the marker of their backyard. I held her as we walked because she would have fallen if I hadn't. She was wailing by the time we reached the overhang.

"Tell me about it, baby," I said.

"You shouldn't be here, Easy. You shouldn't."

"I ain't gonna do nuthin' unless you say to, JJ. But you know you got to talk this out."

"They'll kill her."

"Not if it means that Clovis don't get Equity. She'd set loose Satan in the kingdom of heaven if she could just make a dollar and not pay the tax."

It was true and JJ knew it. The woman-child smiled bitterly and pushed away from me.

"I'd give her every dollar I got to keep Misty safe," JJ said.

"Has she told you that she has her?"

"No. Not in so many words. She says that Misty would be happy, that she'd come over and make me a toast if I did the right thing by the MacDonald clan."

"Could she have heard that Misty was supposed to come down here? I mean if she knew that she was supposed to come and didn't, then she could feed you a story and there'd be no way you could find out the truth."

"She had Mr. Sunshine," JJ said with trembling lips.

"Who's that?"

"It's a rag doll, a lion with jade-green eyes. Misty had that thing since before she could even talk. She always kept him with her."

"And Clovis give this doll to you?"

"No. She sent it in the mail. I got it two days ago."

"Any letter?"

"No. Just the doll in a cardboard box."

"You got the box?"

"Uh-huh."

"Let's go see it."

MOFASS AND JEWELLE had a big house. The entrance was like a dais that stood high over a gigantic living room. The back wall of this room was all glass looking out onto the vista of L.A. There was a table and four high-back chairs next to this window. JJ left me in one of these while she went to look for the doll.

I sat back and crossed my legs, appreciating the view in late afternoon. JJ was a real estate whiz kid. She bought and sold buildings around the county and turned a larger profit every year. She was able to lease that house, in a neighborhood most black people didn't even know existed, because she was a valuable asset to the white men she dealt with.

"Mr. Rawlins," a faint but deep voice called.

I turned my head slowly, not wanting to witness the demolition of one of my oldest L.A. friends. Mofass stood there leaning on two thick walking canes, one for each hand. He wore a heavy maroon-colored robe and had leather slippers on his ashen-black feet. He was breathing hard and looked like an old oil tanker that had been shipwrecked and washed up on land. He leaned to the side, sighed, and groaned. His breath was like the wind whistling through the rusted-out hull of the wrecked ship he resembled. His yellowy eyes were fog lamps in the deep night of his face.

"Hey, William," I hailed. "You up and around, huh?"

"Not too much longer. Uh-uh, no."

"You been sayin' that fo' years, man. But I still see you every Christmas."

"It's the tent," he said.

"Oxygen tent?"

"Yeah. JJ got it hooked up over my bed. I gotta gas mask and'a oxygen tank too but I don't use that too much. An hour under the tent and I can be almost normal for fifteen minutes. Then I got to get back there 'fore I run outta air an' cain't walk no more."

The hulking wreck lowered himself in the chair opposite me.

"Where JJ?" he asked suspiciously.

"She went to get something to show me," I said.

Mofass leaned forward in his chair and made a motion that he wanted me to do the same.

"I think she gotta boyfriend, Mr. Rawlins," he whispered.

"Why you say that?"

"She got this pretty young thing named Rosa come up and take care'a me sometimes when she go out. She says she goin' to do business. But I smell her perfume and see them high heels. You know JJ was runnin' around in tennis shoes before Rosa."

"She was a child before, William. She growin' up and wants to dress more like a woman, that's all."

"Sometimes she out late at night, Mr. Rawlins." There were tears in the old man's eyes. "Late. She don't think I know. She thinks I'm asleep, but I ain't. I get up and wander around lookin' for her an' sometimes I cain't find her."

"You ask her where she been?"

"She says that she just run out to pick somethin' up in Hollywood or that she just took a drive, but I know better. You know I got a long-barrel twenty-two pistol right under my pillow. When I get a good breath I'ma go out an' find the motherfucker. Kill him too."

"Uncle Willy," JJ called from across the football field of a living room. "What you doin' up?"

Mofass just stared at his girlfriend. He didn't have enough breath to make himself heard that far away.

She came up to us carrying a small walnut tray with two sodas on it. There was a cardboard box under her arm.

"I brought you a drink," she said to Mofass. "But you weren't in your room."

"Cain't I come out and see my friend?" he complained.

"Sure you can," she replied.

She put down the drinks on the table and began fussing with Mofass's robe. You could see the love those two had for each other. They behaved like people who had been together for decades. Jewelle was barely in her twenties but she had an old soul.

After she had him squared away she handed me the box. "Here it is, Mr. Rawlins."

"What's that?" Mofass asked.

"Piece'a mail come for me at Equity," I said. "Somebody didn't know my address and then JJ opened it by mistake."

"That's why you should be listed," my old property manager chided. His voice was still deep and raspy but it was also feeble, like the distant rumble of a thunderstorm that has almost passed from earshot.

I took out the bear and the paper it was wrapped in. It was just a tattered old doll made of cotton, sewn with hemp, and given green eyes made from glass. It smelled a little like buttermilk. The newspaper the doll was wrapped in was the Dallas *Gazette*, dated two weeks before. The postmark on the box was L.A. three days earlier.

"What is that stuff?" Mofass asked.

"Just a joke, Mo," I said. "Old friend'a mine tellin' me that she's in town."

"Don't . . . seem . . . too . . . funny. . . ." Mofass gasped between each breath. He reached out with his right hand and JJ was there to catch it. She helped him to his feet. I tried to lend a hand but she pushed me off.

"I'll take care of him," she told me.

She put herself under his arm like a human crutch. They made their way across the immense living room and then passed through a door.

While they were gone I considered the box and its contents. I knew a cop who might have been interested but it was slim evidence and there would be no action before the next day when Clovis wanted to close the deal.

I had a pretty clear notion of what to do next but I couldn't begin until JJ returned. So I sat in the window, drinking my cola.

No complex ideas or deep emotions came to me; just the

image of an orphaned child, at the age of eight, on his own and moving fast. He traveled from Louisiana to Houston, and from there to North Africa, Italy, Paris, and finally the Battle of the Bulge. I'd encountered death and destruction from the very start. I came to L.A. to get away from it but death clung to me——he was my oldest friend, my only constant star. I thought about my years trading in *favors* on the streets of L.A. *I'll do for you if you do for me*, was my motto and creed.

Sitting there in that window, looking out over a city that had no idea I was there, made me feel powerful in a funny way. At the Board of Education they told you the kind of broom you needed and the amount of time it would take you to sweep up a classroom or hallway. They took out taxes and retirement funds from your paycheck and told you what days you could take off and how often you could be sick. Everything was preplanned and managed. The paperback rule book was three-hundred-and-forty-seven pages long.

I yearned to be sitting where I was sitting, to be my own man. Loving freedom and loving danger are one and the same thing for most black men. Freedom for us has always been dangerous. Freedom for us has been a crime as far back as our oldest memories. And so whenever we're feeling liberation we know that there's somebody nearby with a rope and a collar, a shotgun and a curse.

That's why I always loved Mouse. He was crazy and a killer and trouble in any circumstances. But he never accepted our slave heritage. He never bowed his head in front of an enemy. "Kill me if you can," he said more than once. "But if you cain't you better know how to run."

"Easy," JJ said.

I hadn't noticed her return in my reverie.

"How is he?"

"Sleepin'. You know he can't be out of that tent more than ten minutes at a time."

"She's in L.A.," I said handing her the doll.

"You think that 'cause'a the postmark?"

"Uh-huh. Yes I do."

"What should I do, Easy?"

"What time you supposed to get together with them tomorrow?"

"Noon."

"Call 'em up. Tell 'em you can't do it before five. Tell 'em Mofass has to get a shot or somethin'."

"Why?"

"To buy me time. I wanna look at Clovis, see what's happenin' at that house of theirs. Do you have a picture of Misty around?"

JJ reached into a fold of her cranberry dress and came out with a faded photograph. The sepia tones revealed a tomboy, with a space between her front teeth, smiling so wide that you wondered if she had ever known sorrow.

I must have grinned when I saw the photo.

"She's the closest person to me in the world," JJ said. It was both a vow and a threat.

Clovis shared a big four-story house with her brothers and sisters on Peters Lane, up in Baldwin Hills. They lived there with various other husbands and wives, and some children.

I parked down the street in a run-down old Ford sedan that I borrowed from my mechanic friend, Primo. I got there at four-thirty in the afternoon.

The MacDonald clan was a filthy lot. They parked their cars on the lawn and kept a ratty old sofa out on the front porch. The paint was peeling off the walls. But even though they lived like sharecroppers I knew they had money in the bank. While Clovis had Mofass under her power she'd siphoned off enough money to buy property under her own name.

At six, the brothers, Fitts and Clavell MacDonald, came out of the house with two dark-skinned women, laughing loudly, probably half drunk already, they climbed into a new Buick and drove off.

As the evening wore on I saw most of the whole ugly tribe. Grover, Tyrone, Renee, Clovis and her husband Duke. There were other men, women, and children who seemed to live there. But there was no one who matched up with Misty's photograph.

I DROVE HOME AT EIGHT O'CLOCK.

Feather had refused to go to bed until I was there. Jesus sat up with her watching some show that was mostly canned laughter.

"Daddy!" my little girl shouted when I came in.

I guess Jesus was worried too. He kissed me, which is something the seventeen-year-old hadn't done in two years. I put Feather to bed and talked with Jesus about his boat for a while.

"I want to go camping with some friends next weekend," he told me.

"Where?"

"Around Santa Cruz."

"Who you goin' with?"

"A girl and some of her friends."

"Who's that?"

"Marlene."

"How old is she?" I asked.

"Eighteen."

"You can get in trouble behind that shit, boy."

Again he was silent. Jesus never argued with me. When he disagreed or got angry he just clammed up.

"White girl?"

"Uh-huh."

"Friends too?"

He nodded.

I stared at my adopted son. He was my child more than blood might have been. For many years he was mute. He had been molested as an infant and young child, sold to men for sex. I took him out of that. For a while I had him living with Primo because I thought that a Mexican child needed a Mexican family. But Jesus wanted to be with me and somehow it just felt right.

I wanted to protect him but telling him no or which way to go would never work. Jesus had a mind of his own and all I could do was make suggestions.

"Be careful," I said, feeling as helpless as I feared he might be.

Jesus smiled and hugged me.

AT ELEVEN-THIRTY I was still up, reading *Anthem* by Ayn Rand in the living room. The little yellow dog had taken up his post at the hallway, guarding Feather's sleeping place from the grim ogre——me. As time had gone by I had begun to appreciate the dog. He came to me, the last living testament of a woman who had been murdered. He hated me because he blamed me for his mistress's death. Now his love was for Feather and he took her protection as his purpose in life. I had grown to respect him for his devotion to my daughter and so our regular standoffs at the door to her room made me smile every evening at bedtime.

The phone rang. I picked it up before it was through the first bell.

"Hello."

"Easy?" she said in a brittle voice.

"Hey, baby. How are you?"

"A little tired," Bonnie Shay said. "I just woke up. They've been running us ragged."

"Where are you?"

"In Paris. For the last ten days we've been in West Africa so I couldn't call."

"The ambassadors and princes been askin' for your number?" I said in a joking voice.

"No. What do those men care about a stewardess?" she said. But there was fraction of a second of delay in her voice.

"Easy?" she asked in the static of long distance.

"What?"

"Is something wrong?"

"No, baby," I said. "I just miss you. I need you here with me."

"Can you hear me smiling?" she asked, and I felt ashamed of my suspicious heart.

"Loud as daybreak," I said.

"How are Feather and Jesus?"

"He's planning some kind of camping trip and she's gettin' bolder every minute."

"Tell them I love them."

"Sure will."

"I love you too, Mr. Rawlins."

"And I love you."

There was another pause. We were too old to profess love back and forth, over and over, and too young to just hang up.

Finally Bonnie said, "I should go."

"I'll hang up first," I suggested.

"Okay."

I LEFT THE HOUSE at four the next morning. The streets were empty and dark. I made good time to the MacDonald residence. The lights were off and four cars were parked on the lawn. I lit up the first of ten Chesterfield cigarettes I allotted for myself per day. I sat back in the smoky haze thinking about how much I loved being a silent watcher.

The dark street looked like a stage after the play is long over and the actors and the audience have gone home. I was thinking about Jesus growing up, and Bonnie so many thousands of miles away. About Mouse being gone from my life, like my dead mother and my father who, in fleeing a lynch mob, also abandoned me.

I imagined my father running into the darkness, his own dark skin blending with the night. A calm came over me as he disappeared because I knew they would never catch him. I knew that he was alive and breathing——somewhere.

"HEY, MISTER!" the old lady shouted. I started awake. The sun was just coming up. Two cars were already gone from the MacDonald lawn. The woman's face on the other side of the glass was pocked and haggard, deep molasses brown and relenting to the pull of gravity.

"What?" I said.

She motioned for me to roll down the window.

I did what she wanted and asked, "What do you want?"

"You watchin' them?" she asked, pointing toward the MacDonald residence.

When you wake up suddenly from a deep sleep, as I just had, part of your mind is still in dreams. And in dreams time is almost meaningless. There are times I've dozed off for just a minute and had dreams that covered an hour or more of activity. That's how it was for me at that moment. I saw the woman, read the lines on her face, deciphered the obvious anger in her tone, and decided that she wasn't mad at me but at those filthy, uncouth MacDonalds. She was also, I surmised in a fraction of a second, a first-degree busybody who had more information on the kidnappers than the police could gather in seven years.

"Yes I am," I replied.

"What they do to you?"

"Stoled my car," I said in good old Fifth Ward lingo.

"Bastids," she spat. "Make the whole neighborhood a pigsty. Noisy and vulgar, I hate 'em."

"The man who stoled my ride was with this girl," I said, showing the angry old woman my photograph of Misty.

"I seen her. Yeah. She was wit' some guest'a theirs. A man drove a old red truck. It had Texas plates on it."

"That's the guy took my car. He asked me could he borrow it. Left me a suitcase to hold. All it had was some underwear and that picture of the girl drove off with him."

"You wanna use my phone to call the cops?" the woman asked.

"I sure do. But first I wanna wait here and make sure he's in there. 'Cause if I call and he ain't there, that old bitch Clovis'll just say they never heard of him."

"You got her ticket, brother," the old woman agreed. "I'm right over there in the white-and-green house. You need somethin' you just come over to me."

"I'll be there," I said. "Just as soon as that man show up. He come here much?"

"Almost every day. In the mornin' too. You probably don't have long to wait."

With that the old lady left for her home. I was sure that she'd be watching but that was all right. If I fell asleep again she'd rouse me to the mysterious Texan's arrival.

HE GOT THERE AT ABOUT EIGHT. The truck was an interesting combination of dull red paint and brown rust, like lichen rolling over a scarlet stone. The black man at the wheel was large with muscle, about thirty. He wore overalls and a T-shirt. I wondered if there was a straw hat on the seat next to him. He drove right up on the lawn and ran to the front door. Antoinette, the prettiest MacDonald next to JJ, ran out to meet him. Antoinette was a healthy girl. Even under her loose one-piece dress you could see her large upstanding breasts. They hugged and kissed, and kissed again. Clovis came out then, talking in a loud voice, though not loud enough for me to make out the words.

Antoinette stood back, seemingly afraid of what was being said. The big Texan was nodding at every word, listening hard. When she was finished he asked something and Clovis yelled something back. The Texan jumped into his truck and took off. I waited a second and followed him.

Clovis and Antoinette didn't seem to notice me.

THE TEXAN LED ME on a long drive through L.A. He took side streets, always headed south. We went down into Compton. We were still in L.A. county, but the houses became sparse and the street was barely covered by asphalt. I had dropped almost two blocks behind the Texas truck because there was hardly any traffic. When I saw the red pickup turn right up ahead, I increased my speed to make sure I didn't lose him.

I turned the corner just in time to see the truck park in the

driveway of a small blue house. I went all the way to the end of
the block, turned the corner, and pulled to the curb.

My heart was racing but not from fear. I was excited by my
proximity to the solution of JJ's dilemma.

Sitting in the car I wondered how to get past the cowboy's
defenses. I needed a distraction.

My first thought was to set the house on fire. There had
recently been a fire at Truth. Everyone always runs out to the
curb when threatened by flame and smoke. But maybe, if
Misty was a hostage in the house—tied up and gagged—
maybe the kidnapper would leave her in there rather than be
implicated in the capital crime of kidnapping.

Two women in pink and blue dresses were making their
way down the street. The one in blue carried a small white
cardboard box about the size of a workman's lunch pail. This
box had cardboard handles that folded out from the top.

I thought about the police. Looking back on it now I realize that I should have called the cops. I could have said that I
saw a woman, bound hand and foot, carried into the house.
But I was never happy about dealing with the city's armed
thugs. Even though the cowboy was probably guilty I couldn't
call the law in on him until I was sure.

The ladies were handing two long rectangular bars to a
woman standing at the front of the house nearest me. When
they came back to the sidewalk I was waiting for them.

"Excuse me, ladies," I said.

The taller one was in the pink dress suit. It was Sunday
attire; all that was missing was a hat. She was tall and dark-
skinned. There was a gold wedding ring on her finger so I supposed that someone had once found her beautiful. I suspected
that that was a long time ago. She had a frown that would give
children nightmares.

"What do you want?" she demanded. It was as if she recognized me as the no-good black sheep of the family and wasn't about to let me get an inch too close.

"Are those church chocolates?"

"Oh yes," said the shorter woman wearing the powder-blue dress. She was dark too. But she was sweet all the way through. "A big grin and big butt on a black woman and you know I be a happy man," my uncle Stanley used to profess. He would have been happy seeing what I saw.

"With almonds?" I asked the friendlier church lady.

"Yes," she said.

"You know I love church candy."

"This ain't no tea party, young man," the lady in pink said. "We're selling these chocolates."

"Hester," the lady in blue complained. "There's no need to be rude."

"I have a house to take care of, Minne Roland," Hester replied. "So now, mister, if you would please move—"

"I would like to buy all of your candies, ladies," I said, reaching for my wallet. "How many have you got left?"

"Almost twenty," Blue Minne replied.

The bars sold for thirty-five cents a piece. I gave them seven dollars and they thanked me. Hester made a grimace that I was sure was meant to be a smile.

I walked off toward the cowboy's house laden with chocolates and high hopes.

THE FRONT DOOR hadn't been used much recently. There were spider webs at the corners and leaves sticking out from underneath the welcome mat. There were stains on the peeling white door left from the last rainstorm three months ago.

I pressed the doorbell. There was no sound from inside.

I knocked on the door.

There came the sound of footsteps. But not the heavy-booted feet of the black cowboy I'd been following. The door whined and cracked as it opened. The short honey-brown woman had a wide smile and smaller eyes than JJ's photograph indicated.

"Hey y'all," she said, greeting me with all the friendliness of the country.

"Hi," I said, widening my eyes in surprise.

Misty took my stare as a compliment; it might have been if it were not for my astonishment at her carefree attitude.

"You sellin' candy?" she asked.

"You bet," I said. "Milk chocolate and almonds for twenty-five cents a bar."

"Misty, who you talkin' too?" The man's voice was hard and serious.

The cowboy appeared in the disheveled room behind the young Texan miss. His skin was rough and brown with the strong aura of drab green emanating from underneath. His eyes were brown too but just barely. This cowboy's ancestors could have well included a rattlesnake or two.

"Anthony Lender," I said, remembering the name of a white private I once went to war with. "Sellin' chocolate."

"What you wanna knock on this door for?" he asked me.

"To sell a pretty young lady somethin' sweet," I said.

Misty smiled at me and the snake pushed her aside.

"It don't look like no one live in here," he said. "Why you wanna come up here?"

"I saw you drive up when I was across the street goin' door to door," I said, stalling for time. "I'm sellin' chocolate to build the house for our minister. It's really good chocolate and cheap . . ."

While I spoke I reached into the box as if I were going to show him just how good my candies were. But instead of chocolate I whipped out my .38 caliber pistol and hit him in the center of his forehead. As the cowboy fell backward I hit him again on the side of the jaw. He fell heavily and I knew that he was no longer conscious. I pulled the door closed behind me and presented the muzzle of my gun to the once smiling face of Misty.

"This gun can shout a lot louder than you," I said. "So I suggest you keep it down and do what I say."

Misty was not only pretty, she was smart. She nodded and glanced at her boyfriend.

"You got some sheets somewhere?" I asked her.

"In the bedroom."

"Show me."

She led me through a doorway into a room so small it would not have been large enough to contain a vain woman's wardrobe. There was a single bed and sheets strewn around it.

"Take that sheet and bring it back out front," I commanded.

She did as I said.

"Now tear it into five long strips," I said handing her my pocket knife.

"We ain't got no money, mister," she said as she worked.

"But you will soon enough won't you, Misty?"

She stopped cutting for a second.

When she was through with the sheets I used the strips to hogtie the cowboy and gag him. When I was through I had Misty sit down on the floor in front of me.

"You gonna rape me?" she asked.

"No."

"What you want wit' me an' Crawford? And how come you know my name?"

"How much they payin'?"

"Who?"

"Clovis and them," I said, falling into the rhythm of the Texan dialect.

Misty was good. She looked like and talked like a hick off the back of a watermelon truck, but she knew how to feint and lie.

"I don't know no Clovis," she said, her voice a fraction softer than it had been before.

"You made the right choice comin' to L.A., girl," I said. "But wrong in goin' in against your half-sister. I know you know Clovis. Clovis is your family too. So now you tell me what's happenin' or I'ma make sure you spend your pretty years in jail for extortion."

"I didn't do nuthin'," she said. "I just been livin' in this shitty house."

"I bet you Clovis owns the deed on this house."

"What if she do?"

"Put that together with Clovis forcing JJ to sign over half her business to her and you got prison stamped all over it."

"You can't prove that."

"Come with me," I said. And we left the tethered cowboy dreaming of money that he would never collect.

"DID YOU PLAN IT from the beginning?" I asked her on the long drive back to Laurel Canyon.

"What?"

"Did you plan to steal your sister's business when you were writin' her from down Texas?"

"No. I didn't even know she had nuthin' when I was down there. She'd just write and say how she lived with this old man Mofass and how they loved each other. She said that he was too sick to work but she loved him anyway so I thought that they was poor."

"So when did you get in with the plan?"

"I left Crawford a note tellin' him that I was comin' up here. He called Clovis an' told her. He wanted her to talk me into comin' back."

"Yeah?" I prodded.

"She told him to get up here and then they all met me at the bus stop in San Diego."

"How they know when you gonna get there?"

"They's on'y one bus a day to L.A. from Dallas."

"But why would you let them turn you against your sister?"

"I told you already."

"Told me what?"

"She lied makin' me think that her an' her boyfriend was poor. She never sent me no money or tried to help me get on my feet. An' she stole Clovis's money in the first place."

"So you wanted to steal it back from her?"

At that question Misty went silent.

For the rest of the ride she stared out of the window.

"WHERE WE GOIN'?" she asked when we turned off onto JJ's road.

"Where you think?"

"You said to the police."

"I figured I'd skip the constabulary and go straight to the judge," I said.

When we got to Mofass's door, I expected to have to pull JJ off of Misty. But there were no fireworks, no waterworks either. JJ grinned when she saw her missing sister. The smile faded when I told her what was what. JJ didn't ask why and Misty offered no excuse.

"Well I guess that's it," JJ said when I was through explaining.

＊　　　＊　　　＊

I TOOK MISTY back down to Compton and dropped her off about six blocks from her hogtied cowboy.

On the way home I thought about JJ. She must have been brokenhearted over her sister's betrayal. Money, I thought, is a harsh master in poor people's lives. It warps us and makes us so hungry that we turn feral and evil. If Misty and JJ had stayed back home in their poor shacks, they would have been friends for fifty years baking pies and raising children side by side.

JESUS HAD BOUGHT a sleeping bag with money he'd saved from work. We sat up late into the night talking about my experiences camping out in France and Germany with the small troop I belonged to.

"Did you kill a lotta Germans?" the bright-eyed boy asked.

"Yes I did."

"Did you hate 'em?"

"I thought I did——at first. But after a while I began to realize that the German soldiers and the white American soldiers felt the same about me. I used my rifle a little less after that."

"How come?"

"Because I didn't really know who it was I wanted to shoot."

"So you didn't kill any more?"

"I didn't kill except if I absolutely had to."

I showed Jesus how to camp so that nobody could see you. I cautioned him to stay low when he heard something in the bushes.

"Be careful out there, son," I said to him. "You know I love you more than anything."

＊　　　＊　　　＊

THE PHONE RANG at two thirty-five.

"Yes," I said, expecting it to be Bonnie.

"Easy," she cried. "Easy, come quick. They're dead. They're all dead."

I filled an empty mayonnaise jar with water and then drove the car I'd borrowed from Primo toward the canyons. At the base of the hills I got out and made mud from the dirt at the side of the road. I smeared the mud on Primo's license plates.

THE DOOR TO THE HOUSE was open. The large living room was strewn with bodies and blood. Clovis was thrown back on the couch so that she was hanging over the backrest. Fitts and Clavell were lying one in front of the other. It seemed as if they had been running at someone but were cut down——first Clavell and then his brother——in the middle of their rush.

Mofass was leaning up against the wall that the brothers had rushed. The .22 caliber pistol was in his hand. JJ was kneeling next to him, trying to pull him up by the arm.

"Damn criminals," Mofass said. I could barely hear him.

"Get up, Uncle Willy," JJ pleaded. "Get up."

"Take her outta here, Mr. Rawlins," he said. His eyes were so blurry and yellow that they seemed to be melting right out of his head.

"What happened?" I asked.

"Ain't no time for questions. Take her outta here."

When I tried to pull JJ to her feet she clutched Mofass's arm. Her grip was brittle though and I manged to pull her away.

"Get his oxygen tank," I told her.

While she ran into the other room I interrogated my real estate manager.

"What happened?"

"They wanted to steal my property," he said. "They wanted to hurt my girl. Fuck that. Fuck that."

"We got to get you outta here, William," I said.

"No, Mr. Rawlins. I got to stay here an' cover up for the cops. They cain't know JJ was in on this."

I didn't know for a fact what he meant. But I had my suspicions.

JJ returned with the oxygen tank and mask. When she held the mask to Mofass's nose and mouth he sighed. He smiled at his child lover and then shook his head for us to go.

I dragged JJ to the car.

"We can't leave him," she said as we were driving away.

"We have to call the police, JJ."

"No. He killed them."

"Tell me what happened."

"I called Clovis after you left. I told her that I decided against lettin' her in the business. She said sumpin' but I just hung up. Then, about two hours ago, they all came over with the contracts for me and Uncle Willy to sign. I told 'em no an' Uncle Willy pretended that he was 'sleep."

"Then what."

"Fitts started twistin' my arm like he used to when I was a kid. I guess I screamed and he slapped me. I fell down and heard this sound like a cap gun. I thought maybe it was my nose bone or sumpin' but then Clovis made this squeakin' sound. I looked up and seen her holdin' her chest and then the crackin' sound happened again and she fell back on the couch. Uncle Willy was standin' at the do' with his pistol in his hand. Fitts and Clavell run at him but Uncle Willy cut 'em down. He used one hand to hold himself up on the wall and the other to shoot."

"We got to get outta here," I said.

"Not without him," JJ said.

"He got his oxygen mask," I reasoned. "When the cops come they'll call it self-defense. But if you're here you might get in trouble."

I CALLED THE POLICE from a phone booth, telling them that I had heard shots from Mofass's home. Then I took JJ down near Jackson Blue's apartment on Ozone Street in Venice.

I parked down the street and called him from a booth.

"JJ's in trouble," I said to the sleepy con man. "If you got a woman in there with you send her away. Take JJ in and make her feel comfortable. If the police ask, you tell 'em she was with you for the night."

"Ain't no woman up in here, Easy. Send her on."

I watched as JJ walked down the block to Jackson's house and then I went home to bed—if not to sleep.

THE MORNING EXAMINER had the triple murder and suicide on the front page. The police, tipped off by an anonymous call, went to the secluded Laurel Canyon home where they found the four corpses. Mofass had given his life for Jewelle.

She returned home that morning and told the police that she'd left early to see her boyfriend. She also informed them that Clovis had been pressing to get back into business with them. The contracts Clovis wanted them to sign seemed to prove the story.

My name was not mentioned. And I have no idea where Misty and Crawford went. Jewelle stayed in her home. Jackson didn't move in but they still see each other.

I went back to work the next day wondering how long it would be before my past showed up and put me into an early grave.

LAVENDER

IT WAS A TUESDAY MORNING, about a quarter past eleven. The little yellow dog hid in among the folds of the drapes, peeking out now and then to see if I was still in the reclining living room chair. Each time he caught sight of me, he bared his teeth and then slowly withdrew into the pale green fabric.

The room smelled of lavender and cigarette smoke.

The ticking of the wind-up clock, which I had carried all the way from France after my discharge, was the only sound except for the occasional passing car. The clock was encased in a fine dark wood, its numerals wrought in pale pink metal—copper and tin most probably.

The cars on Genesee sounded like the rushing of wind.

I flicked my cigarette in the ashtray. A car slowed down. I could hear the tires squealing against the curb in front of our house.

A car door opened. A man said something in French. Bonnie replied in the same language. It was a joke of some sort. My Louisiana upbringing had given me a casual understanding of French, but I couldn't keep up with Bonnie's Parisian patter.

The car drove off. I took a deep drag on the Pall Mall I was nursing. She made it to the front step and paused. She was probably smelling the mottled yellow-and-red roses that I'd cultivated on either side of the door. When I'd asked her to come live with us she said, "As long as you promise to keep those rosebushes out front."

The key turned in the lock and the door swung open. I expected her to lag behind because of the suitcase. She always threw the door open first and then lifted the suitcase to come in.

My chair was to the left of the door, off to the side, so the first thing Bonnie saw was the crystal bowl filled with dried stalks of lavender. She was wearing dark blue slacks and a rust-colored sweater. All those weeks in the Air France stewardess uniform made her want to dress down.

She noticed the flowers and smiled but the smile quickly turned into a frown.

"They came day before yesterday."

Bonnie yelped and leapt backward. The little yellow dog jumped out of hiding, looked around, and then darted out through the open door.

"Easy," she cried. "You scared me half to death."

I stood up from the chair.

"Sorry," I said. "I thought you saw me."

"What are you doing home?" Her eyes were wild, fearful.

For the first time I didn't feel the need or desire to hold her in my arms.

"Just curious," I said.

"What are you talking about?"

I took two steps toward her. I must have looked a little off wearing only briefs and an open bathrobe in the middle of a workday.

Bonnie took a half-step backward.

"The flowers," I said. "I was wondering about the flowers."

"I don't understand."

"They been sittin' there since the special-delivery man dropped them off. Me and the kids were curious."

"About what?"

"Who sent 'em." The tone of my voice was high and pleasant but the silence underneath was dead.

"I don't understand," Bonnie said. I almost believed her.

"They're for you."

"Well?" she said. "Then you must have seen the note."

"Envelope is sealed," I said. "You know I always try to teach my children that other people's mail is private. Now what would I look like openin' your letter?"

She heard the *my* in "my children."

Bonnie stared at me for a moment. I gestured with my right hand toward the tiny envelope clipped to an upper stem. She ripped off the top flowers getting the envelope free. She tore it open and read. I think she must have read it through three times before putting it in her pocket.

"Well?"

"From one of the passengers," she said. "Jogaye Cham. He was on quite a few of the flights."

"Oh? He send all the stewardesses flowers?"

"I don't know. Probably. He's from a royal Senegalese family. His father is a chief. He's working to unite the emancipated colonies."

There was a quiet pride in her words.

"He was on at least half of the flights we took and I was nice to him," Bonnie continued. "I made sure that we had the foods he liked and we talked about freedom."

"Freedom," I said. "Must be a good line."

"You don't know what you're talking about," she said, suddenly angry. "Black people in America have been free for a hundred years. Those of us from the Caribbean and Africa still feel the bite of the white man's whips."

It was an odd turn of a phrase——"the white man's whips." I was reminded that when a couple first become lovers they begin to talk alike. I wondered if Jogaye's speeches concerned the white man's whips.

I didn't respond to what she said, just inhaled some more smoke and looked at her.

After a brief hesitation Bonnie picked up her suitcase and carried it into our bedroom. I returned to the big chair, put out the butt and lit up another, my regimen of only ten cigarettes a day forgotten. After a while I heard the shower come on.

I had installed that shower especially for Bonnie.

If someone were to walk in on me right then they might have thought that I was somber but calm. Really I was a maniac trapped by a woman who would neither lie nor tell the truth.

I'd read the note, steamed it open, and then glued it shut. It was written in French but I used a school dictionary to decipher most of the words. He was thanking her for the small holiday that they took on Madagascar in between the grueling sessions with the French, the English, and the Americans. It was only her warm company that kept his mind clear enough to argue for the kind of freedom that all of Africa must one day attain.

If she had told me that it was a gift from the airlines or the pilot or some girlfriend that knew she liked lavender, then I could have raged at her lies. But all she did was leave out the island of Madagascar.

I had looked it up in the encyclopedia. It's five hundred miles off the West African coastline, almost a quarter million square miles in area. The people are not Negro, or at least do not consider themselves so, and are more closely related to the peoples of Indonesia. Almost five million people lived there. A big place to leave out.

I wanted to drag her out of the shower by her hair, naked and wet, into the living room. I wanted to make her tell me everything that I had imagined her and her royal boyfriend doing on a deserted beach eight thousand miles away.

The bouquet had been sent to her care of the Air France office. Her boyfriend expected them to hold it there. But some fool sent it on, special delivery.

I decided to go into the bathroom and ask her if she expected me to lie down like a dog and take her abuse. My hands were fists. My heart was a pounding hammer. I stood up recklessly and knocked the glass ashtray from the arm of the chair. It shattered. It probably made a loud crashing sound but I didn't notice. My anger was louder than anything short of a forty-five.

"Easy," she called from the shower. "What was that?"

I took a step toward the bathroom and the phone rang.

"Can you get that, honey?" she called.

Honey.

"Hello?"

"Easy, is that you?"

I recognized the voice but could not place it for my rage.

"Who is this?"

"It's EttaMae," she said.

I sat down again. Actually, I fell into the chair so hard that it tilted over on its side. The end table toppled taking the lamp with it. More broken glass.

"What?"

"I called Sojourner Truth," she was saying, "and they said you had called in sick."

"Etta, it's really you?"

Bonnie came rushing out of the bathroom.

"What happened?" she cried.

Seeing her naked body, thinking of another man caressing it, holding onto the phone and hearing a woman that I had been searching for for months——I was almost speechless.

"I need a minute, baby," I said to both women at once.

"Hold on a minute," I said to Etta while waving Bonnie back to her shower. "Hold on."

Bonnie stared for a moment. She seemed about to say something and then retreated to the bathroom.

I sat there on the floor with the phone in my lap. If I had a gun in my hand I would have gone outside and killed the yellow dog.

The receiver was making noise so I brought it to my head.

". . . Easy, what's goin' on over there?"

"Etta?"

"Yes?"

"Where have you been?"

"There's no time for that now, Easy. I got to talk to you."

"Where are you?"

She gave me an address on the Pacific Coast Highway, at Malibu Beach.

I hung up and went to the bedroom. Three minutes later I was dressed and ready to go.

"Who was that?" Bonnie called from the bathroom.

I went out of the front door without answering because all I had in my lungs was a scream.

I DON'T REMEMBER THE DRIVE from West L.A., where I lived, to the beach. I don't remember thinking about Bonnie's betrayal or my crime against my best friend. My mind kind of shorted out and all I could do for a while there was drive and smoke.

There wasn't another building within fifty yards of the house, but it looked as if it belonged nestled between cozy neighboring homes. The wire fence had been decorated with clam and mussel shells. The wooden railing around the porch had dozens of different colored wine bottles across the top. The house had been built on ground below street level so that it would have been possible to hop on the roof from the curb. It was a small dwelling, designed for one or maybe one and a half.

I opened the gate and descended the concrete stairs. She met me at the door. Sepia-skinned and big-boned, she had always been my standard for beauty. EttaMae Harris had been my friend and my lover in turns. I hadn't seen her for almost a year because I was the man who had gotten her husband shot.

"You look wild, Easy," was the first thing she said.

"What?"

"Your hair's all lumpy and you ain't shaved. What's wrong?"

"Where's LaMarque?"

"He's with my people up in Ventura."

"What people?" I asked. My heart skipped and for an instant Bonnie Shay was completely out of my mind.

"Just a cousin'a mines. She got a little place out in the country around there."

"Where's Mouse?"

Etta peered at me as if from some great height. She was a witch woman, a Delphic seer, and Walter Cronkite on the seven o'clock news all rolled into one.

"Dead," she said. "You know he is."

"But the doctor," I said, almost pleading. "The doctor hadn't made the pronouncement."

"Doctor don't decide when a man dies."

"Where is he?"

"Dead."

"Where?"

"I buried him out in the country. Put him in the ground with my own two hands."

It was certainly possible. EttaMae was the kind of black woman who made it so hard for the rest. She was powerful of arm and iron willed. She had thrown a full-grown man over her shoulder and carried him from the hospital after knocking out a big white orderly with a metal tray.

"Can I go to the grave?"

"Maybe one day, baby," she said kindly. "Not soon, though."

"Why not?"

"Because the hurt is too fresh. That's why I ain't called you in so long."

"You mad at me?"

"Mad at everything. You, Raymond. I'm even mad at LaMarque."

"He's just a child, Etta. He ain't responsible."

"The child now will become the man," she preached. "And when he do you can bet he will be just as bad if not worse than what went before."

"Raymond's dead?" I asked again.

"The only thing more I could wish would be if he would be gone from our minds." Etta looked up over my head and into the sky as if her sermon of man-hating had become a prayer for deliverance from our stupidity.

And we were stupid, there was no arguing about that. How else could I explain being ambushed in an alley when I should have been at home lamenting the assassination of our president? How could I ever tell Mouse's son that he got killed trying to help me out with a little problem I had with gangsters and thugs?

"Come on in, Easy," she said.

THE LIVING ROOM was decorated like a sea captain's cabin in a Walt Disney film. A hammock in the corner with fish nets full of glass-ball floats beside it. The floor was sealed with clear coating so that it looked rough and finished at the same time. The windows were round portals and the chandelier was made from a ship's wheel.

"Sit down, Easy."

I sat on a bench that could have easily been an oarsman's seat. Etta lowered herself onto a blue couch that had gilded clamshells for feet.

"How have you been?" she asked me.

"No no, baby," I said. "It's you who called me outta my house after more than eleven months of me searchin' high and low. Why am I here?"

"I just wondered if you were sick," she said. "They said at work that—"

"Talk to me, Etta. Talk to me or let me go. 'Cause you know as much as I want to see you and try to make it up to you, I will walk my ass right outta here if you don't tell me why you called after all this time."

Her face got hard and, I imagined, there were some rough words on the tip of her tongue. But Etta held back and took a deep breath.

"This ain't my house," she said.

"I could see that."

"It belongs to the Merchant family."

"Pierre Merchant?" I asked. "The millionaire from up north?"

"Lymon," Etta said, shaking her head, "his cousin run the strawberry business north'a L.A. I work for his wife. She has me take care'a the house and her kids."

"Okay. And so she let you stay here when you come down to town. So what?"

"No. She don't know I'm here. This is a place that Mr. Merchant has for some'a his clients and business partners when they come in town."

"Etta," I said. "What you call me for?"

"Mrs. Merchant have four chirren," she said. "The youngest one is thirteen and the oldest is twenty-two."

I was about to say something else to urge her along. I didn't want there to be too much silence or space in the room. Silence would allow me to think about what I had just learned——that my best friend since I was a teenager was dead, dead because of me. For the past year I had hoped that he was alive, that somehow EttaMae had nursed him where the hospital could not. But now my hopes were crushed. And if I couldn't keep talking I feared that I would fall into despair.

But I didn't push Etta because I heard a catch at the back of her throat. And EttaMae Harris was not a woman to show that kind of weakness. Something was very wrong and she needed me to make it right. I grabbed on to that possibility and took her hand.

A tear rolled down her face.

"It was hard for me to call on you, Easy. You know I blame you for what happened to Raymond."

"I know."

"But I got to get past that," she said. "It's not just your fault. Raymond always lived a hard life an' he did a lotta wrong. He made up his own mind to go with you into that alley. So it's not just that I need your help that I'm here. I been thinkin' for some time that I should talk to you."

I increased the pressure of my grip. EttaMae had a working woman's hands, hard and strong. My clenching fingers might have hurt some office worker, man or woman, but it was merely an embrace for her.

"Mrs. Merchant's second-to-oldest is a girl named Sinestra. She's twenty and wild. She been a pain to her mama and daddy too. Kicked out of school an' messin' around with boys when she was a child. Runnin' from one bad egg to another now that she's a woman."

"She too old for you to look after, Etta," I said.

"I don't care about that little bitch. She one'a them women that ambush men one after the other. Her daddy think that they doin' to her but he don't see that Sinestra the rottenest apple in the barrel."

"What's that got to do with me?"

"Sinestra done run away."

"She's twenty," I said. "That means she can walk away without havin' to run."

"Not if her daddy's one of the richest men in the state," Etta assured me. "Not if she done run off with a black boy don't have the sense to come in out the rain."

"Who's that?"

"Willis Longtree. Hobo child from up around Seattle. He showed up one day with a crew to do some work for the Merchants. You know the foreman of their ranch would go down near the railroad yards in Oxnard whenever he needed to pick up some day labor. They got hobos ride the rails and Mexicans between harvests all around down there. Mr. Woodson—"

"Who?" I asked.

"Mr. Woodson, the foreman," she said. "He brought about

a dozen men down to the lower field around four months ago. They was buildin' a foundation for a greenhouse Mr. Merchant wanted. He grows exotic plants and the like. He's a real expert on plants."

"Yeah," I said. "So was my cousin Smith. He could grow anything given the right amount'a light and rainfall."

"Mr. Merchant don't have to rely on nature."

"That's why they build greenhouses instead'a churches," I said.

"Are you gonna let me talk?"

"Sure, Etta. Go on."

"All that Willis boy owned was a guitar and a mouth harp on a harness. Whenever they took a break he entertained the men playin' old-time tunes. Minstrel, blues, even some Dixieland. I went down there one day after young Lionel Merchant, the thirteen-year-old. The music was so fine that I stayed all through lunch."

"I bet Sinestra loved his barrelhousin'," I said.

"Yes she did. Everybody did. It took the crew four days to dig the foundation. After that Mr. Merchant himself offered Willis a job. He made him the assistant groundskeeper and had him playin' music for his guests when he gave parties."

"Mighty ungrateful of that boy to think he deserved the boss's daughter," I said.

"It's not funny, Easy. Mr. Merchant got a whole security force work for him. They use it to keep the Mexicans in line on the farms. He told the top man, Abel Snow, that he'd pay ten thousand dollars to solve the problem."

"And he sees the problem as what?"

Etta held up her point finger. "One is Sinestra bein' gone from home, and two," Etta held up the next finger, "is Willis Longtree breathing the same air as him."

"Oh."

"Is that all you got to say? Oh?"

"No," I replied. "I could also say, what's it to you? Boys run away with girls every day. Daddies get mad when they do. Sometimes somebody ends up dead. Most of the time she comes home cryin' and it's all over. That's the way it was in Fifth Ward when we were kids. I remember more than one time that Mouse got jealous'a you. Usually we got the poor fool outta sight before Ray's .41 could thunder."

"Grow up, Easy Rawlins. We ain't in Houston no more and this ain't no joke I'm tellin' you." There was that catch in her throat again.

"What's wrong, Etta?"

"Willis ain't no more than nineteen. He thinks he's a man but he barely older than LaMarque. And Abel Snow is death in a blue suit."

"You like the boy, huh?"

"He'd come around the kitchen in the afternoon and play for me, tellin' me all the great things he was gonna do. If you just closed your eyes and listened to him, you might believe it'd all come true."

"Like what?"

"All kindsa things. One minute he was gonna be in a singin' band and then he talked about bein' in the movies. He said that he looked like Sidney Poitier and maybe he could play his son in some film. He wanted to be a star. And then Sinestra got her hooks in him. She couldn't help it. It was just kinda like her nature. Girl like that see a man-child beautiful as Willis and she cain't think straight. She just wanna make him crazy, make him run like a dog with her scent in his nose. I saw it happen, Easy. I tried to talk sense to him."

"Maybe you worried about nuthin', Etta," I said. "L.A.'s a

big town. The police hardly catch anybody unless they com-
mittin' a crime or they just turn themselves in."

"Abel Snow ain't no cop. He's a stone killer. And he got
Merchant's money behind him."

"That don't mean he's gonna find Willis. Where would he
look?"

"Same place I would if I was him. Jukes and nightclubs on
Central. Movie studios and record studios and any place a fool
like Willis would look his dreams. He told everybody his
plans, not just me."

"You know I'm still just a janitor, Etta."

"Easy Rawlins, you owe me this."

"If he's big a fool as you say, it's really only a matter of time.
You know no matter how hard he try a fool cain't outrun his
shadow."

"All I know is that I got to try," she said.

"Yeah. Yeah," I said. "I know."

I was thinking about Bonnie and her African prince. It still
hurt but the pain was dulled in the face of Etta's maternal des-
peration. And she seemed to be offering me absolution over
the death of her husband.

"I don't even know what the boy looks like," I said. "I don't
know the girl. It's a slim chance that I'll even catch a glimpse
of them before this Snow man comes on the scene."

"I know that."

"So this is just some kinda blind hope?"

"No. I can help you."

"How?"

"Drive me up to the Merchant ranch outside of Santa
Barbara."

I grinned then. I don't know why. Maybe it was the idea of
a long drive in the country.

*   *   *

LYMON MERCHANT was known as the Strawberry King, that's what EttaMae told me. But there wasn't a strawberry field within ten miles of his ranch. Lymon lived up in the mountains east of Santa Barbara. The dirt road that snaked up the mountain looked down on the blue Pacific. We strained and bounced and even slid a time or two, but finally made it to the wide lane at the top. The dirt boulevard was flanked by tall eucalyptus trees. I rolled down my window to let in their scent.

"This the place?" I asked when we came to a three-story wood house.

"No," Etta said. "That's the foreman's house."

The foreman's house was larger and finer than many a home in Beverly Hills. The big front door was oak and the windows were huge. The cultivated rosebushes around the lawn reminded me of Bonnie. I felt the pang in my stomach and drove on, hoping I could leave my heartache on the road behind.

THE MERCHANT MANSION was only two floors but it dwarfed the foreman's house just the same. It was constructed from twelve- and eighteen-foot pine logs, hundreds of them. It was a fantastic structure looking like the abode of a fairy tale giant——not for normal mortals at all.

The double front doors were twelve feet high. The bronze handles must have weighed ten pounds apiece.

Before we could knock or ring a bell the front door swung open. I realized that there must have been some kind of private camera system that monitored our approach.

A tall white man in a tuxedo appeared before us.

"Miss Harris," the man said in a soft, condescending voice.

"Lawrence," she said walking past him.

"And who are you?" Larry asked me.

"A guest of Miss Harris."

I followed her through the large foyer and down an extremely wide hall that was festooned with the heads and bodies of dead animals, birds, and fish. There were boar and swordfish, mountain lion and moose. Toward the center hall was a rhino head across from a hippopotamus. I kept looking around wondering if maybe Lymon Merchant had the audacity to put a human trophy up on his wall.

We then came into the family art gallery. The room was twenty feet square, floored with three-foot-wide planks of golden pine. Along the walls were paintings of gods and mortals, landscapes, and of course, dead animals. In one corner there stood a white grand piano.

"Easy, come on," Etta said when I wandered away from her lead.

There was something off about the color of the piano. The creamy white seemed natural and I wondered what wood would give off that particular hue. Close up it was obvious that it was constructed completely from ivory. The broad lid and body were made from fitted planks while the legs were formed from single tusks.

"Easy," Etta said again. She had come up behind me.

"They must'a killed a dozen or more elephants to build this thing, Etta."

"So what? That's not why I brought you here."

"Does anybody ever even play it?" I asked.

"Willis did now and then when they had cocktail parties in here."

"He played piano too?"

"Willis was as talented as he thought he was," Etta said

with motherly pride. "That's why it broke my heart when he talked about his dreams."

"If he got the talent maybe he'll get the dream."

"What drug you takin'?" Etta said. "He's a poor black child in a white man's world."

"Louis Armstrong was a poor black boy."

"And for every one Armstrong you got a string of black boys' graves goin' around the block. You know how the streets eat up our men, especially if they got dreams."

She turned away from me then and made her way toward yet another door. I lagged back for a moment, thinking about a black woman's love being so strong that she tried to protect her men from their own dreams. It was a powerful moment for me, bringing Bonnie once more to mind. She loved me and urged me to climb higher. And now that I was way up there the only way to go was down.

The next room was a stupendous kitchen. Three gas stoves, and a huge pit built into the wall like a fireplace. Cutting-board tables and sinks of porcelain and a dozen cooks, cooks' helpers, and service personnel. The various workers stared at me, wondering, I supposed, if I was a new member of the hive. A man in a chef's hat actually stopped me and asked, "Are you the new helper?"

"Yes," I said. "But I only work with one food."

"What's that?"

"The jam."

THE NEXT ROOM was small and crowded with hampers over-flowing with cloth. Even the walls were covered in fabric. The only furniture was a pedal-powered sewing machine built into its own table and two stools, all near a window that was flooded with sunlight.

On one of the stools sat a white woman with long, thick brown hair. She was working her foot on the pedal, pulling a swath of royal-blue cloth under the driving needle.

"Mrs. Merchant," Etta said.

The woman turned from her sewing to face us.

She was in her forties, but young-looking. Etta was in her forties then too, though I always thought of her as being older. Etta's skin was clear and wrinkle-free but the years she'd lived had still left their mark. Etta was a matron, while the white woman was more like a child. Mrs. Merchant's face was round and her eyes were gray. She'd been crying, was going to cry again.

"Etta," she said.

She rose from her stool. Etta walked toward her and they embraced like sisters. EttaMae was much the larger woman. Mrs. Merchant was small-boned and frail.

"This is the man I told you about, Brian Phillips," Etta said, using a name I had suggested on the drive up.

The white woman put on a smile and held out her hand to me. I took it.

"Thank you for coming, Mr. Phillips," she said.

"I'm here for Etta, Mrs. Merchant."

"Sheila. Call me Sheila."

"What is it you need?" I asked.

"Hasn't Etta told you?"

"Your daughter has run away with one of your employees. That's really about all I know."

"Sin is a full-grown woman," Sheila Merchant said. "She didn't run away, she just left. But she also left a note behind for her father, informing him that she was leaving with Willis. That poor boy has no idea what game she's playing with him."

"Now let me get this straight, Mrs. Merchant," I said. "You're worried about the black man? His well-being?"

"Sin is like a cat, Mr. Phillips. She'll always land on her feet, and on a pile of money too. This is just a game she's playing with her father. She doesn't believe he loves her unless she can make him mad."

"I guess shackin' up with a poor black hobo is about as mad as he's gonna get."

"He loves Sin more than any of the other children," she said. "It's really unhealthy."

I waited for her to say something else; maybe she wanted to but at the last moment she held back. I noticed then the errant strands of gray in her hair.

"When Etta told me about your daughter and Willis," I said, "I told her that there wasn't much I could do. I mean, L.A.'s a big town. People around there move from house to house like you might go from one room to another."

"I know something," she said. "Something that neither Lymon or Abel are aware of."

"What's that?"

Sheila Merchant looked from side to side as if there might be spies in her sewing room.

"There's a big bush next to the left-hand post that marks the beginning of the eucalyptus drive. It bears red berries."

"I saw it."

"Under that bush is a basket. It's in there."

"What is?"

"A little journal that Willis carried with him. He could barely read or write, but there are some notes and lots of clippings."

"Excuse me, Sheila, but what are you doin' with Willis's diary?"

"He asked me to hold it for him," Sheila Merchant said. "He didn't want somebody to steal it out of the bunkhouse.

And we were always talking about music. In my house, when I was a child, we all played an instrument. All except for Father, who had a beautiful tenor voice. None of my children are musical, Mr. Phillips."

"What about that ivory piano I saw?"

"That is an abomination. It cost thirty thousand dollars to build and the only one who ever played it was Willis Longtree."

"I see," I said. "So you said he was talkin' to you one day . . ."

"Yes. He was telling me about how much he loved music and performing. He showed me his journal, really it was just a ledger book like the accountants use. He had articles clipped about movie stars and L.A. nightclubs."

"If he couldn't read then how would he know what to clip?" I asked.

"You not here to give nobody the third degree," Etta warned.

"No I'm not. I'm here to help you. Now if you want me to do that, just button up and let me ask the questions I see fit."

EttaMae glared at me. I'd seen her strike men for less.

"It's alright, Etta," Sheila said. And then to me, "Willis had people read to him. He'd go through the newspaper until he saw words he knew, like Hollywood, or pictures of performers, and then he'd have someone read the article to him."

I got the feeling that she had read to the young man once or twice.

"What do you want from me, Mrs. Merchant?"

"Find Willis before Abel does," she said. "Tell him what Sin did. Try and get him somewhere safe."

Sheila Merchant reached into her apron and came out with a white envelope.

"There's a thousand dollars in here," she said. "Take it and find Willis, make sure that he's safe."

"What about your daughter?"

"She'll come home when she runs out of money."

Sheila Merchant looked away, out the window. I looked too. There was a beautiful pine forest under a pale blue and coral sky. It seemed impossible that someone with all that wealth, surrounded by such natural beauty, could be even slightly unhappy.

"I'll see what I can do," I said.

ON THE FRONT PORCH Etta and I were confronted by a sandy-haired man with dead blue eyes.

"Hello, Mr. Snow," Etta said quickly. She seemed nervous, almost scared.

"EttaMae," he replied.

He was wearing gray slacks and a square-cut aqua-colored shirt that was open at the collar. Folded over his left arm was a dark blue blazer. He wore a short-brimmed straw hat, tilted back on his head.

His smile was malicious, but that's not what scared me about him.

EttaMae Harris had lived with Mouse most of her adult life; and Mouse was by far the deadliest man I ever knew. Not once had I seen fear in Etta's face while dealing with Mouse's irrational rages. I had never seen her afraid of anybody. Abel Snow therefore had a unique standing in my experience.

"And who is this?" Abel asked.

"Brian Phillips," I said.

"What are you doing here?"

"Seein' how the other half lives."

I smiled and so did Abel.

"You lookin' for trouble, son?"

"Now why I wanna be lookin' for somethin' when it's stand-in' right there in front'a me, pale as death?"

Etta cleared her throat.

"You here about Willis Longtree?" Abel Snow asked me.

"Who?"

Snow's smile widened into a grin.

"You got something I should know about in your pocket, Brian?"

"Whatever it is, it's mine."

Snow was having a good time. I wondered if his heart was beating as fast as mine was. We stared at each other for a moment. That instant might have stretched into an hour if Etta hadn't said, "Excuse me, Mr. Snow, but Mr. Phillips is giv-in' me a ride to L.A."

He nodded and stepped aside, grinning the whole time.

THE BASKET was where Sheila Merchant said it was. I flipped through the ledger for a minute or two and then put it in the trunk.

ETTA FELL ASLEEP on the long ride back to L.A. I asked her a few more questions about Mouse, but her story never wavered. Raymond was dead and buried by her own hand.

I dropped her off at the mariner's house in Malibu and then drove back home. That was about nine o'clock.

BONNIE WAS WAITING for me at the front door wearing the same jeans and sweater.

"Hi, baby," she said.

"Can I get in?" I asked and she stepped aside.

The house was quiet and clean. I had straightened up now

and then but this was the first time it had been clean since she was gone.

"Where the kids?"

"They're staying with Mrs. Riley. I sent them because I thought we might want to be alone." Bonnie's eyes followed me around the room.

"No," I said. "They could be here. I don't have anything to say they can't hear."

"Easy, what's wrong?"

"EttaMae called."

"After all this time?"

"Mouse is definitely dead and she knows a young boy who's in trouble." I sat in my recliner.

"What? You found out all that?" Bonnie went to sit on the couch. "How do you feel?"

"Like shit."

"We have to talk," she said in that tone women have when they're treating their men like children.

I stood up.

"Maybe later on," I said. "But right now I got to go out."

"Easy."

I strode into the bathroom, closed the door, and locked it. I showered and shaved, cut my nails, and brushed my teeth. When I went to the closet to get dressed Bonnie was already in the bed.

"Where are you going?" she asked me.

"Out."

"Out where?"

"Like I told you, to look for that boy Etta wants me to help."

"You haven't even kissed me since I've been home."

I pulled out my black slacks and yellow jacket. Then I went

to the drawer for a black silk T-shirt. It wasn't going to be Easy Rawlins the janitor out on the town tonight. A janitor could never find Willis Longtree or Sinestra Merchant.

I had put on dark socks that had diamonds at the ankles. I was tying my laces when Bonnie spoke to me again.

"Easy," Bonnie said softly. "Talk to me."

I went to the bed, leaned over, and kissed her on the forehead.

"Don't wait up, honey. This kinda business could take all night."

I walked to the door and then halted.

Bonnie sat up, thinking I wanted to say more.

But I went to the closet, reached back on the top shelf, and took down my pistol. I checked that it was working and loaded, and then walked out the door.

THE GROTTO was the first black entrepreneurial enterprise I knew of that cast its net beyond Watts. It was a jazz club on Hoover. Actually, the entrance was down an alley between two buildings that were on Hoover. The Grotto had no real address. And even though the owners were black it was clear that the mob was their banker.

Pearl Sondman was the manager and nominal owner of the club. I remembered her from an earlier time in Los Angeles; a time when I was between the street and jail and she was with Mona El, the most popular prostitute of her day.

Mona seduced everybody. She loved men and women alike. If you ever once spent the night with her you were happy to scrape together the three hundred dollars it cost to do it again——that's what they said. Mona was like heaven on Earth and she never left a John, or Jane, unsatisfied.

The problem was that after one night with Mona a certain

type of unstable personality fell in love with her. Men were always fighting and threatening, claiming that they wanted to save her. It wasn't until Mona met Pearl that that kind of ruckus subsided.

Pearl had a man named Harry Riley, but after one kiss from Mona, or maybe two, Pearl threw Riley out the door. For some reason most men didn't want to be implicated in trying to free Mona from a woman's arms.

A TRUMPET, a trombone, and a sax were dueling just inside the Grotto's doors. It brought a smile to my face if not to my heart.

"Hi, Easy," Pearl said.

She was wearing a scaly red dress and maybe an extra twenty pounds from the last time we met. Her face was flat and sensual, the color of a chocolate malted.

"I thought you was dead," she told me.

"That was the other guy," I replied.

Pearl's laugh was deep and infectious—like pneumonia.

"How's Mona?" I asked.

"She okay, baby. Thanks for askin'. Had another stroke last Christmas. Just now gettin' around again."

"That's a shame."

"Oh, I don't know," Pearl said. "Mona says that she's lived more than most'a your everyday people by three or four times. You know she once had a prince over in Europe pay her way, first class, every other month for two years."

"What ever happened to him?"

"He wanted her to be his mistress. Offered her all kindsa money and grand apartments but she said no."

"Why?"

"'Cause she liked the life she was livin'. With me and our two crazy dogs."

I wanted to ask her how she could share a love with some stranger, but I held it back.

"I'm lookin' for a boy named Longtree," I said.

"Pretty boy with a wild white bitch?"

"That's him."

"He come in here Sunday night. Said he could play. When I asked him what, he said, 'guitar, piano, or whatever.'"

"Not too shy, huh?"

"Not a bit. An' he wasn't wrong neither. He played the afternoon shift for twenty bucks. I think he might'a got twice that in tips. He didn't play nuthin' like bebop but he was good."

"I need to find him."

"Just look on the sidewalk and follow the trail'a blood."

"It's that bad?"

"That girl's eyes made contact with every dangerous man in the room. She flirted with one of 'em so much that he told Willis that he wanted to borrow her for the night."

"Did they fight?" I asked.

"No. I told that big nigga to sit'own 'fore I shot him. They know around here that I don't play. I told Willis to take his woman outta here and damn if she didn't give that big man a come-on look while they were goin' out the door."

"You think she might'a told him where they were stayin'?"

"I wouldn't put it past her."

"What was this guy's name?"

"Let's see, um, Art. Yeah, Art, Big Art. Big Art Farman. Yeah, that's him. He lives down Watts somewhere. Construction worker."

I found an address in the phone booth of the Grotto. Listening to jazz and worrying about how big Big Art was made Bonnie fade to a small ache in my heart.

✦   ✦   ✦

THE MAN WHO CAME to the apartment door was not big at all. As a matter of fact he was rather tiny.

"Art?" I asked.

"No," he said.

"Does Art Farman live here?"

"Do you know what time it is, man?"

I pulled a wad of cash from my pocket.

"It's never too late for a hundred bucks," I said.

The small man had big eyes.

"Wha, what, what do you want?"

"I come to buy somethin' off'a Art. He know what it is." I could be vague as long as the money was real.

"I could give it to him when he comes in," the little man offered.

"You tell him that Lenny Charles got somethin' for him if he come in in the next two hours."

"Why just two hours? What if he don't come in before then?"

"If he don't then somebody else gonna have to sell me what I need."

"What's that?" the little man asked. His coloring was uneven, running from a dark tan to light brown. He had freckles that looked like a rash and had hardly any eyebrow hair at all.

"I need to find a white girl called Sinestra."

"What for?" The greedy eyes turned suspicious.

"Her daddy asked his maid, my cousin, to ask me to ask her to come back home. He's willin' to pay Art a century if he can help me out."

"What's your name again?"

"Len," I lied. "Yours?"

"Norbert." He was staring at my wad. "What you pay me to find Art?"

"Where is he?"

"No. Uh-uh. I get paid first."

"How much you want?"

"Fifty?" he squeaked.

"Shit," I said.

I turned away.

"Hold up. Hold up. What you wanna pay?"

"Thirty."

"Thirty? That's all? Thirty for me and a hundred for Art?"

"Art can give me the girl, can you?"

"I can give you Art. And she's with him. That's for sure."

I considered taking out my gun but then thought better of it. Sometimes the threat of death makes small men into heros.

"Forty," I said.

"You got to bring it higher than that, man. Forty ain't worth my time."

"I'll go find Willis myself then," I said.

"You mean that skinny little kid?" Norbert laughed. "Art kicked his ass and took his girlfriend from him."

"He did?"

"Yeah," Norbert bragged. "Kicked his ass and dragged that white girl away. 'Course she wanted to go."

"She did?"

"'Course she did. Why she want that skinny guitar man when she could have Big Art in her bed?"

I handed Norbert a twenty dollar bill.

"Where was it that Art did this?"

"Next to that big 'partment buildin' down on Avalon. Near the Chevron station with the big truck for a sign."

I handed him another twenty.

"It was the only blue house on the block."

"How do you know all that?" I asked.

"I drove him over there."

"Did Sinestra mind Art beating up her boyfriend?"

"Didn't seem to," Norbert shrugged.

I handed him another twenty dollar bill.

"Where's Art now?"

"At Havelock's Motel on Santa Barbara. That's where we go when we got a woman, you know, to let the other man get some sleep. I mean we ain't got but two rooms up in here."

I handed over another leaf of Sheila Merchant's money and went away.

ONCE IN MY CAR I had a small dilemma. Should I go after the girl or Willis? It seemed to me that no one really cared about her, except maybe her father. Willis was the one that Etta was worried about. I knew that if I asked her she would have told me to make Willis my priority.

But I was raised better than that. No matter what she had done I couldn't leave Sinestra Merchant at the mercy of a kidnapper and possible rapist. I couldn't take Norbert's word that she maybe wanted some rough action from some big black man in Watts.

HAVELOCK'S WAS A LONG BUNGALOW in the shape of a horseshoe. When I got there it was closing on midnight. A night clerk was in the office, sitting at the front desk with his back to the switchboard. I parked across the street and considered.

The motel sign said that there was a TV and a phone in each room.

I went to a phone booth and dialed a number that hadn't changed in sixteen years.

"Hola," a sleepy Spanish voice said.

"Primo."

"Oh, hello, Easy. Man, what you doin' callin' me at this time'a night?"

"You got a pencil and a clock?"

I gave Primo a number and asked him to call in seven minutes exactly. I told him who to ask for and what to say if he got through. He didn't ask me any questions, just said "okay" and hung up the phone.

"HI," I SAID TO THE NIGHT CLERK five minutes later. "Can you help me with a reservation?"

It was a carefully constructed sentence designed to keep him from getting too nervous about a six foot black man coming into his office in the middle of the night. Thieves don't ask for reservations. They rarely say hello.

"Um," the white clerk said. He first looked at my hands and then over my shoulder to see if somebody else was coming in behind. "I can't make reservations. I just rent out rooms for people when they come."

"Yeah," I said. "That's what I thought. But you know I work at a nightclub down the street here and the only time I can really make it in is after work. Do the daytime people take reservations?"

"I don't know," the clerk said, relaxing a bit. "People usually just look at the sign. If there's vacancy they drive in and if not they drive on."

He smiled at me and the phone rang. He turned his back and lifted the receiver.

"Havelock's Motel," he said in a stronger tone than he'd used with me. "Who? Oh yes. Let me put you through."

He pushed the plug into a slot labeled "Number Six." I was smiling honestly when he turned back to me.

"That's really all I can say," he said. "Just look for the sign."

"All right."

I COUNTED THE DOORS on the north side of the building and then I went around the back, counting windows as I went. Number six's curtains were open wide. The only light on in the room was coming from a partially closed door, the bathroom I was sure. There were two double beds. One was neat, either stripped or made. The other one had something on it, a pair of shoes tilted at an uncomfortable angle.

The window was unlocked.

Big Art—his driver's license said Arthur—Farman had been dead for some hours. The cause of death probably being a bullet through the eye. Before he'd been killed he was bound, gagged, and beaten. A pillow on the floor next to him had been used to stifle the shot.

There was no trace of the girl named Sinestra. But that didn't mean she hadn't been there at the time of Art's death.

I climbed out of the window and made it back to my car. The dead man, who I'd never met in life, was the strongest presence in my mind.

IT'S HARD LOOKING FOR a blue house at three in the morning. There's white, black, and gray, and that's it. But I saw the big apartment building. It was on a corner with only one house nearby. It helped that the lights were on.

I knocked on the door. Why not? They were just crazy kids. There was no answer so I turned the knob. The house was a mess. Pizza cartons and dirty dishes all over the living room and the kitchen. Half-gone sodas, a nearly full bottle of whiskey, it was the kind of filth that many youths lived in while waiting to grow up.

I couldn't tell if the rooms had been searched. But there wasn't any blood around.

I GOT HOME a few minutes before four.

Etta picked up the receiver after the first ring.

"Hello."

I told her about Big Art and Sinestra's games.

"Old Willis don't have to worry about Abel Snow with that girl in his bed," I said.

"She called her daddy," Etta said. "She told him where she was and asked him to come and get her."

"Then she lit out?"

"I don't know. All I know is what Mrs. Merchant said. She told me that Mr. Merchant sent Abel down to get her."

"Did he bring her back?"

"No."

"Damn."

"Do you think he's found 'em, Easy?"

"I'm not sure, but I don't think so. Mr. Snow don't mind leavin' blood and guts behind him."

"Maybe you better leave it alone, Easy."

"Can't do that, Etta. I got to see it through now."

"I don't want you to get killed, baby," she said.

"That's the nicest thing I been told all day."

I SLEPT ON THE COUCH for the few hours left of the night.

When I opened my eyes she was sitting right in front of me.

"We have to talk," Bonnie said.

"I got to go."

"No."

"Bonnie."

"His name is Jogaye Cham," she said. "We, we talked on the plane when everybody else was asleep. He talked about Africa, our home, Easy. Where we came from."

"I was born in southern Louisiana and I still call myself a Texan 'cause Texas is where I grew into a man."

"Africa," she said again. "He was working for democracy. He worked all day and all night. He wanted a country where everyone would be free. A land our people here would be glad to migrate to. A land with black presidents and black professionals of all kinds."

"Yeah."

"He worked all the time. Day and night. But one time there was a break in the schedule. We took a flight to a beach town he knew in Madagascar."

"You could'a come home," I said even though I didn't want to say anything.

"No," she said, and the pain in my chest grew worse. "I needed to be with him, with his dreams."

"Would you be tellin' me this if them flowers didn't come?"

"No. No." She was crying. I held back from slapping her face. "There was nothing to tell."

"Five days on a beach with another man and there wasn't somethin' to say?"

"We, we had separate rooms."

"But did you fuck him?"

"Don't use that kind of language with me."

"Okay," I said. "All right. Excuse me for upsetting you with my street-nigger talk. Let me put it another way. Did you make love to him?"

The words cut much deeper than any profanity I could have used. I saw in her face the pain that I felt. Deep, grinding pain that only gets worse with time. And though it didn't make me feel good, it at least seemed to create some kind of balance. At least she wouldn't leave unscathed.

"No," she whispered. "No. We didn't make love. I couldn't with you back here waiting for me."

A thousand questions went through my mind. Did you kiss him? Did you hold hands in the sunset? Did you say that you loved him? But I knew I couldn't ask. Did he touch your breast? Did he breathe in your breath on a blanket near the water? I knew that if I asked one question that they would never stop coming.

I stood up. I was dizzy, light-headed, but didn't let it show.

"Where are you going?" she asked.

"I got a job to do for Etta. A woman already paid me so I got to move it on."

"What kind of job?"

"Nuthin' you need to know about. It's my business." And with that I showered and shaved, powdered and dressed. I left her in the house with her confessions and her lies.

WITH NO OTHER INFORMATION available to me I went to see Etta at the Merchants' seaside retreat. She only pulled the door open enough to see me.

"Go away, Easy," she said.

"Open the door, Etta."

"Go away."

"No."

Maybe I had gained some strength of will working for the city schools. Or maybe Etta was getting worn down between losing her husband and working for the rich. All I knew was that at another time she could have stared me down. Instead the door swung open.

Inside, sitting on the blue couch with golden clamshell

feet, was a young black man and young white woman, both of them beautiful. They were holding hands and huddling like frightened children. They *were* frightened children. If it wasn't for the broken heart driving me I would have been scared too.

"They came after you called me, Easy," Etta said.

"Why didn't you call back?"

"You did what I asked you to already. You found them. That's all I could ask.".

"I'm Easy," I said to the couple.

"Willis," the boy said. He made a waving gesture and I noticed that his hands were bloody and bandaged.

"Sin," the girl said. There was something crooked about her face but that just stoked the fires of her dangerous beauty.

"What happened to Big Art, Sin?"

Her mouth dropped open while she groped for a lie.

"I already know you called your father," I said.

"I was just mad at Art," she said. "He didn't have to beat up Willis and hurt his hands. I thought my father would come and maybe do something." Her eyes grew glassy.

"What happened?"

"I told Art that I was going down to the liquor store and then I called Daddy. I told him that I was with a guy but I was scared to leave and he said to wait somewhere near at hand. Then I waited in the coffee shop across the street. When I saw Abel I got scared and went to get Willy. When we came back to get my clothes he was . . . ." She trailed off in the memory of the slaughter.

I turned to Willis and said, "You'd be better off holding a gun to your head."

"I didn't mean for him to get killed," Sinestra said angrily.

"What now?" I asked Etta.

"I'm tryin' to talk some sense to 'em. I'm tryin' to tell Sin to go home and Willis to get away before he ends up like that Art fella."

"I'm not going back," Sinestra proclaimed.

"And I'm not leavin' her or L.A."

"She just had a big man break your fingers and then she went and fucked him."

"She didn't know. She was just flirtin' and it got outta hand. She's just innocent, that's all."

My mouth fell open and I put my hand to cover it.

Etta started laughing. Laughing hard and loud.

"What are you laughing at?" Sinestra asked.

I started laughing too.

"Shut up, shut up," Sinestra said.

"Yes. Please be quiet," Abel Snow said from a door in the back.

He had a pistol in his hand.

"There's a man in a car parked out front, Sinestra," Snow said. "Go out to him. He'll take you home."

Without a word the young white woman went for the door.

Etta looked into my eyes. Her stare was hard and certain.

"Sin," Willis said.

She hesitated and then went out the door without looking back.

"Well, well, well," Abel Snow said. "Here we are. Just us four."

Willis was sitting on the couch. Etta and I were standing on either side of the boy. He turned on the blue sofa to see Snow.

"You gonna kill us?" I asked, my voice soaked with manufactured fear.

"You're gonna go away," he said, and smiled.

I took a step to the side, away from Etta.

"You gonna let us go?" Willis asked, playing his part well though I'm sure he didn't know it.

Snow was amused. He was listening for something.

Etta put her hands down at her side. She raised her face to look at the ceiling and prayed, "Lord, forgive us for what we do."

At a picnic table Snow's grin would have been friendly.

I took another step and bumped into the wall.

"Nowhere to run," Snow apologized. "Take it like a man and it won't hurt."

"Please God," Etta said beseechingly. She bent over slightly.

A car horn honked. That was what Snow was waiting for. He raised his pistol. I closed my eyes, the left one a little harder than the right.

Then I forced my eyes open. Abel Snow brought his left heel off the floor, preparing to pivot after killing me. EttaMae pulled a pistol out of the fold of her dress, aimed it at his head, and sucked in a breath. It was that breath that made Snow turn his head instead of pulling the trigger. Etta's bullet caught him in the temple. He crumpled to the floor, a sack of stones that had recently been a man.

"Oh no," Willis cried. He pulled his legs up underneath himself. "Oh no."

Etta looked at me. Her face was hard, her jaws were clenched in victory.

"I knew you had to be armed, baby," I said. "If he was smart he would'a shot you first."

"This ain't no joke, Easy. What we gonna do with him?"

"What caliber you use?" I asked.

"Twenty-five caliber," she said. "You know what I carry."

"Didn't even sound that loud. Nobody live close enough to have heard it."

"They gonna come in here sooner or later. And even before that he ain't gonna report in to Mr. Merchant."

"Tell me somethin', Etta."

"What?"

"You plannin' to go back to work for them?"

"Hell no."

"Then call your boss. Tell him that Abel's not comin' home and that there's a mess down here."

"Put myself on the line like that?"

"It's him on the line. I bet the gun in Abel's hand was the one he used on Art. And if that girl of his finds out about any killing in this house she'd have somethin' on her old man till all the money runs out."

"What about Willis?"

"I'll take care of him. But we better get outta here now."

I DROVE ETTA to a bus station in Santa Monica. She kissed me good-bye through the car window.

"Don't feel guilty about Raymond," she said. "Much as was wrong with him he took responsibility for everything he did."

"What you gonna do with me?" Willis Longtree asked as we drove toward L.A.

"Take you to a doctor. Make sure your hand bones set right."

"I'm still gonna stay here an' try an' make it in music," he told me.

"Oh? What they call you when you were a boy?" I asked.

"Little Jimmy," he said. "Little Jimmy because my father was James and everybody said I looked just like him."

"Little Jimmy Long," I said, testing out the name. "Try that on for a while. I can get you a job as a custodian at my school.

Do that for a while and try to meet your dreams. Who knows? Maybe you will be some kinda star one day."

"Little Jimmy Jones," Willis said. "I like that even better."

I GOT HOME in the early afternoon. Bonnie wasn't there but her clothes were still in the closet. I went to the garage and got my gardener's tool box. I clipped off all the roses, put them in a big bowl on the bedroom chest of drawers. Then I took the saw and hacked down both rose bushes. I left them lying there on either side of the door.

The little yellow dog must have known what I was doing. He yelped and barked at me until I finished the job.

I went off to work then. I got there at the three o'clock bell and worked until eleven.

When I got home the bushes had been removed. Bonnie, Jesus, and Feather were all sleeping in their beds. There were no packed suitcases in the closet, no angry notes on the kitchen table.

I laid down on the couch and thought about Mouse, that he was really dead. Sleep came quickly after that and I knew that my time of mourning was near an end.

GATOR GREEN

"**E**ASY?" Bonnie's voice came from the kitchen window.
"Yeah," I said.

I was sitting in a maple chair on the concrete apron that spread out around our back door. I'd just started Jesus's advanced sailboat-building book. It was going to be his reading assignment for the next three weeks and I wanted to make sure I understood it before he and I started our lessons.

"There's a man at the front door."

"He want you or me?" I said in an unfriendly tone.

"Easy."

She was outside now. All I had to do was turn around and I could see her. But I didn't turn. I pretended to go on reading even though the words had turned into squirming worms across the page.

"He wants to talk to you," she said.

I put Juice's book down on the chair and stood. I stared straight ahead, childishly avoiding her gaze. She touched my arm as I passed her. She always touched me when I was close enough. Especially lately, when I was so upset that I couldn't even sleep in my own bed.

"**WHY YOU SLEEP** in the livin' room, Daddy?" my adopted daughter, Feather, asked when she came upon me one morning and realized that she couldn't watch cartoons on the living room TV set.

"I been restless," I said.

"Why don't you go to a doctor?"

"There's nuthin' the doctor got for this."

I must have sounded sad because Feather put her little golden hand on my neck and sat over me until I fell back to sleep.

"MORNIN', MR. RAWLINS," the small white man hailed. He was standing in the doorway between the kitchen and the living room.

"Saul," I replied. "What are you doing here?"

"Got a little problem I thought you might help me with."

"Would you like some coffee, Mister . . . ?" Bonnie asked.

"Lynx," the man told her, "Saul Lynx. And yeah, I'd love a little java in a cup with some milk."

Saul Lynx was a private detective. He and I worked a case that he started and I took over some years before. When I first met him I didn't trust him. I didn't trust many white people. But as it turned out he was okay. It wasn't until some time later that I found out he had a black wife and three children as light as Feather.

"What's up?" I asked, herding him into the living room.

"That your wife? She's beautiful."

"Bonnie Shay. She lives here with us. Now what is it you want, Saul?" It was Saturday and I was tired from a hard couple of months of work—both on and off the job.

My son, Jesus, had dropped out of school but I was still teaching him every evening; making him read to me and then having him explain what he read. My lover, Bonnie, had admitted that she'd gone away to Madagascar with an African prince who was trying to liberate the continent. She said that they slept in separate rooms but still I couldn't bring myself to kiss her good night.

I had been slipping back into the street in spite of my respectable job as supervising senior head custodian at Sojourner Truth Junior High School. In less than three months I had investigated arson, murder, and a missing person. I had also been party to a killing that the police might have called murder.

But worst of all, I had found out that my best friend in life was definitely dead. Raymond Alexander, Mouse, had died trying to help me. There wasn't a place in my mind that I could turn to for hope or a laugh.

THE COFFEE WAS ALREADY BREWED. Bonnie brought Saul his cup and I led the way into the backyard carrying a maple chair for him. We sat side by side looking up at the enormous shade tree that dominated half the yard.

"Good coffee."

"Yeah," I said. "She can burn."

Saul gave me a questioning glance and then he smiled. He was a small man who always wore brown. That day it was cotton brown trousers with a brown, blue, and green sweater that had an argyle pattern on the chest. He was also wearing tennis shoes, so I supposed he was on a job.

Saul had a big shapeless nose and a face you would forget two minutes after you saw it. But he had emerald-colored eyes that Hollywood starlets would have paid a hundred thousand dollars to possess.

"I have a cousin-in-law named Ross Henry," he said.

"Don't we all." I was responding to his tone more than his words.

Saul laughed.

"I've missed you, Easy."

"Ross Henry," I said.

"Yeah." Saul put his cup and saucer down on the deck and leaned forward, clasping his hands. "Ross is a good kid, man really, he's thirty-seven. But . . . he never learned how to make it in the white man's world."

I grunted and Saul grinned again. He lived among black people and understood the humor in his words.

"But it's worse with Ross," he said. "He had an argument at work with his boss which led to a scuffle. He broke the boss-man's nose."

"Then it's lucky he lives up here," I said. " 'Cause down in Mississippi they just might have strung him to a tree."

"Not so much Mississippi as it is Louisiana." Saul shook his head.

"Say what?"

"Eggersly Oliphant," Saul said. "Known to the world as 'Gator.' He owns and operates a six-lift garage down on Lincoln, near the beach."

"Six lifts." I was impressed.

"Not only that. He owns a small used-car lot across the street and a motel two blocks down. Oliphant is president of the Santa Monica Board of Commerce and a power broker in local politics. A northern Dixiecrat."

"Ross broke Gator's nose?" I asked.

"No. Gator's tough. Very much so. It's his cousin, a runty little man named Tilly. Tilly called Ross a name that white men shouldn't use on black people and then he picked up a ten-pound monkey wrench. Ross figured that he had a reason and that the difference in size was made up for by the steel."

"I'd have to agree with the brother on that," I said.

"Maybe I would too," Saul agreed. "But Ross went overboard. He kicked Tilly when he was down and made him lie there while he bad-talked him."

"So now Ross is in trouble with Tilly or with Gator?"

"Gator. Well, really it's with the SMPD."

"For assault?"

Saul shook his head. "Robbery."

"He robbed him?"

"No. They fired Ross on the spot. That night the garage safe, where they kept the proceeds from all of Oliphant's businesses, was robbed."

"And Ross did it?" I asked.

"Gator says so but Ross denies it."

"But Eggersly is an important man and so the police arrested your wife's cousin for the job." It wasn't hard to figure out.

Saul nodded. "It was definitely an inside job. That's why Ross could even be arrested. Whoever it was knew exactly where the safe was and what tools they needed to crack it open."

"What did they use?"

"An acetylene torch from the car lot."

"And Ross worked there?" I asked.

"He worked all over," Saul explained. "Ross is a natural mechanic. They used him wherever they had a need. He could fix the ventilation system at the motel and crack open an automatic transmission for the garage."

"So the cops have it that he broke into the car lot, stole the torch, toted it over to the garage, and then burned the lock off the safe?"

"Actually," Saul corrected, "it was an old safe. All the guy had to do was burn off the hinges."

"How much?"

"Between cash receipts, checks, and past due bills, they reported forty-nine thousand and some change."

"And all the cops got on Ross is that he broke a man's nose and then they fired him?" I said. "I doubt if they could convict a man on that kinda evidence."

"Well . . ." Saul looked down at his coffee cup, hesitating, "it's not that simple."

"Oh no?"

"No. You see, when Ross was younger he was arrested for assault and robbery. They even convicted him but all he did was six months."

"Why?"

"It was a dispute he had with a bartender on Central. He had fixed up a TV on a platform so they could play the baseball games at the bar. Ross told the bartender, a man named Grey, that he'd do it for thirty-five dollars, which was his rent at that time. Grey said okay, but when it came time to pay up he said that he had agreed on twenty-five . . ."

There was real feeling in Lynx's words. I could see that he and Mr. Henry were close.

"Ross fought with Grey, knocked him out and took his thirty-five from the till."

"And they arraigned him for felony assault and robbery but then argued it down because of extenuating circumstances," I said, finishing the all-too-common tale.

"There was a woman in the bar, the waitress. She heard the deal and the judge was feeling merciful that day," Saul said, wrapping up the story.

"So? What he needs is a lawyer. What do you want with me?"

"We got him representation," Saul said. "But she's gonna

need some help if we want to prove he's innocent. The problem is if Ross didn't do it, then somebody else had to."

"What else they have on him?"

"He was the only one to use the torch. And he was the only
one who had access to all the keys except for Gator and his
cousin."

"Why didn't they take his keys when they fired him?"

"He'd left them at home that morning because it wasn't his
day to lock up."

"It sure is a mess," I said. "But what could I do about it that
you can't?"

"That's just it, Easy. I made the mistake of going over there
when Ross got in trouble. I went up against Oliphant and he
called me a kike. I didn't do anything, but let's just say that
there's no love lost between us."

"And so you want me to what?"

"He likes people from down around where he comes
from," Saul explained. "Southerners, especially from
Louisiana. They got a machinist opening now that Ross is
gone . . ."

"I got a job, man," I complained.

"Yeah, I know. For a favor, Easy."

It never hurt to have a white man owe you a favor, that's
what I believed. And Saul was a good guy. Even the fact that
he was there giving a bad-tempered black man the benefit of
the doubt made me want to help him.

And then there was Bonnie and Mouse. Him dead and her
—a dead place in my heart.

"Where is this Ross Henry now?"

"We got him out on bail. His mother put up every cent she
has for the bond. He's down in Watts, at his mother's place."

*   *   *

SOMEBODY IN ROSS HENRY'S apartment building had a very bad cough. We heard it from the bottom of the stairs. It was one of those deep, wet, rolling coughs that, in my childhood days, almost always preceded a funeral.

They lived on the third floor of the building, which had been constructed from wood some time before the First World War. The stairs sighed with each step. The colorless paint had separated with the grain of the drying wood planks. The screen door we stopped at was divided into two equal panes. The top screen was as old as the house, rusted and crumbling. The bottom one was brand new, gray, and supple.

The cough was coming from inside the apartment.

Saul knocked but I didn't think anyone could hear it over that rheumy hacking, so I tried pulling the door open. It was latched from the inside.

I was glancing over to the right, looking for a button or something harder than knuckles to knock with, when Saul said, "Um, Easy."

Behind the ancient haze of the upper screen I saw a sour-faced black woman with staring yellow eyes.

She coughed.

"I thought you might not have heard us knocking," I said lamely. "I mean—"

"I'm sick, not deaf," the woman said and then she suppressed a cough.

"Hello, Clara," Saul said. "This is Easy Rawlins. He's a specialist that I'm using to help Ross. Is your son in?"

Clara Henry was tall and dark. She had manly shoulders and hands that had seen so much work that they seemed too large for her body. She looked me up and down and curled her lip.

"I guess," she said, and unlatched the door for us to enter.

Then she called, "Ross, it's that white man and somebody for ya."

The entryway of the apartment was bisected by a wall that separated two parallel halls. Clara Henry went coughing down the hall to the right. I was about to follow her when a man's voice called out from the other way.

"Send 'em on down."

After about twelve feet the hallway veered off to the left depositing us into a room that had no one particular purpose. There was a green couch that doubled as a bed, and a card table used for dining. In one corner there was a sink set upon a small patch of tiles. The rest of the floor was wood so deeply rutted and splintered that a mop would have been torn to shreds in any attempt to wash it.

The big man stood up and extended his hand when we entered.

"Hey, Saul," he said.

"Ross."

Ross had orange-brown skin and a thick mustache that didn't stop at the corners of his mouth but went straight back and up until it blended with the hair just above his ears. He had a receding hairline and shoulders inherited from his mother.

Behind him there was a youngish white woman still seated on the couch. Her short hair was brown and styled into a flip. Her nose slanted toward the right which made her seem as if she was standing in profile even when she was looking straight at you.

She had obviously just put on her sweater. I imagined that her bra was under the couch somewhere.

She noticed me noticing her nipples under the thin pink cotton and turned away, smiling slightly.

"And this is Ross Henry," Saul was saying to me.

My heart was doing a kind of double-knocking throb in my chest.

"Mr. Henry," I said.

"Mr. Rawlins. This is Amiee," he said. "She come by to visit."

"Hello," she said. Even her words were sexy. She added, "I better be going, baby."

"No." Ross put out a hand. "No, don't go. I just got to tell these men somethin' and then we can, we can . . . you know, visit."

"Um," Saul said delicately.

"Naw, man," I said. "This business is only between us three. Maybe your friend would wanna wait with your mother."

"Oh no," Amiee said holding up her hands in a defensive pose. She stood up from the couch with a sinuous, snakelike motion. "Some other time, baby."

Getting up on tiptoes she kissed Ross's cheek. At the same time however, she managed to meet my eye with a smile.

She was slight and in her thirties but young-looking, dressed better than a secretary or waitress. She wore no ring.

I had been looking at women lately. Ever since I found out about Bonnie's royal holiday. I'd been looking but I didn't have the spirit to follow up. When I lost the desire to kiss Bonnie it seemed to extend to all other women too.

That's what bothered me about Amiee. Her crooked glances managed to get under my skin. It was hard for me to think about anything more than her sidelong smiles. For that reason I was happy to see her pass out of the door.

"Man, why you wanna go an' threaten her with my mama?"

On cue the hacking cough sounded through the walls.

"Wasn't no threat," I said. "I just needed her out of here so we could talk about keepin' your ass outta prison."

"I'm not goin' to jail, man," he said. "Shit. I'll have my ass down on some Alabama farm 'fore I go to no jail."

Saul met my gaze. He shrugged slightly.

"Your mother put up her life savings against a fifteen-thousand-dollar nut," I said. "What you gonna do, make her work the rest of her life 'cause you a coward?"

"Motherfucker!" Ross yelled.

He threw a long looping right hand but it was useless because I hit him on the side of the jaw with a left that also blocked his punch.

Ross went down hard on the desiccated floor.

Someone cackled behind me.

Mrs. Clara Henry was standing in the doorway gleefully clasping her hands.

"That's right, mister," she said encouragingly. "Hit him again, hit him again. Maybe you hit him hard enough you might knock some sense into his thick skull."

She even did a little jig. But all that laughing and capering was too much for her condition. She fell into a bout of coughing that brought her elbows down to her knees.

Saul was crouched down next to Ross, who seemed stunned by the mere fact he'd been hit. He was rubbing his jaw and watching his mother's show.

"Mama, what you doin' back here?" the full grown man said. "This my room."

Mrs. Henry recovered enough to laugh once more.

"You show him, mister," she said to me. "Knock some sense inta him."

With that Ross's mother went off down the hall.

"I'm gone, Saul," I said.

"Hold up, man." That was Ross. "Hold up."

He stood and held out a hand.

"No hard feelings, brother," he said. "It's just that you caught me right in the middle'a the pussy, man. I was gettin' it but when she heard you comin' she jumped up off me and put on her clothes. Then when you made her leave—shit, I lost it."

"Are you crazy, Ross?" Saul asked. "Why do you want to have a woman in here when you're in so much trouble?"

I think I was the first one to laugh. But Ross and Saul followed soon after. We all knew the answer to that question.

"All right now," I said. "It's time to talk turkey." The smiling stopped.

Ross rubbed his mustache and leaned against the sink. Saul sat in the sill of a small window.

"You didn't rob your boss?" I asked.

"What kinda shit question is that?" Ross said, half rising from his perch.

"You swing on me again and I'll break that jawbone."

"No, man. No. I did not rob Gator."

"Then who did?"

"How should I know?"

"I don't know, but if the cops don't have nobody else they gonna give you to the judge. And you and I both know what he's gonna do."

"Over twenty-five guys work for him," Ross said. "They come and go all the time. Must be a hundred different people know about the safe and that torch."

"How many of them have access to a key?" I asked.

Ross winced and turned his head away.

"How'd you come up with the money for Amiee?" I asked.

"What you mean?"

"She's a prostitute, right?"

"Man," Ross said. "You just wanna get your ass kicked, don't you?"

"She's your girlfriend?"

"Today," Ross replied. "Maybe not tomorrow."

"Lemme see your wallet."

Ross turned to Saul but only got the shrug.

You could see around Ross's eyes that he was in his thirties. But in his heart he was still a young man, barely out of his teens. That's why I treated him like a child.

He took out a black wallet that was maybe ten percent leather and the rest paper. He had a driver's license, a library card, and three dollars. Under the secret flap he had a two-dollar bill that had the upper right corner torn away to avoid the bad luck associated with that denomination. If he had robbed a safe of thousands of dollars his wallet would have been stuffed with cash—I was sure of that.

"You do much reading?" I asked him.

"So what?" he replied.

I handed him the wallet and asked, "What kind of job could I get if I go down there?"

OLIPHANT'S GARAGE was an ultramodern auto repair and body shop. Everything was chrome and concrete, glass and white paint. The gleaming cylinders for the hydraulic lifts were well oiled and flawless. There was no trash or built-up grease in the corners. The mechanics wore dark-blue coveralls.

There were white men and blacks working together. If I was unemployed this would be the first place I'd look for a job.

"Can I help you?" a red-headed kid asked. He was no more than fifteen, with a big friendly smile on his face. I felt that I'd met him before but put that down to his engaging manner.

"Lookin' for a job's all," I said.

"What kind of job?"

"Mechanic."

For a frown the young man smiled just a bit less brightly.

"You been a mechanic before?" he asked.

"Sure have."

"I wanna be a mechanic on racing cars," he said. "Those guys travel all over the world and make real money."

"I guess they do," I said.

"You ever work on race cars?"

"I was in a few drag races when I was a hothead down south. I worked on those cars but I've never been a professional."

The kid was looking right at me but I had no idea what he saw.

"I'm learning everything I can here," he said. "By the time I get out of high school I'll know everything I need."

"I wish you luck," I said, wondering how to get to applying for the job.

"I'm gonna buy a dirt bike tomorrow," he said. "That'll be great. I can start to learn about bikes and bike racing. We don't fix motorcycles here."

"Do you know if there's a job opening?"

"I don't know," he said. "But it's not up to me. You see the main office over there?"

He pointed toward a room encased by glass walls. Three men in blue coveralls were sitting around smoking and laughing with a big white guy in a green suit.

"Yeah," I said.

"That's Gator's office," the boy said. "He's the one in green."

"Gator?"

"Mr. Oliphant if you want the job."

* * *

I KNOCKED ON THE GLASS DOOR. Gator turned his head in my direction. He took me in for a moment and then gestured with his head and lips for me to enter.

It was a good-sized room with two tables and a desk. The mechanics sat at one table. The other one supported a partly deconstructed car engine.

"Mr. Oliphant," I said as I stuck out my hand. "I'm Larry Burdon."

It was one of many names that I typed in as dead or missing during my stint as a statistics sergeant during WWII.

"How can I help ya?" he replied.

The other men took this as their notice to leave. They filed out into the unnaturally clean garage and took up various posts.

"Lookin' for a job," I said as they were leaving.

Gator was perched at the edge of his desk. He was as tall as Ross, but whereas Saul's cousin-in-law was burly Oliphant was long and lean. I didn't think I could get inside his offense and I wouldn't have wanted to try.

"For what?" he asked.

"My specialty is heating and cooling but I can do anything mechanical."

"Oh really? Where you from, Larry?"

"Lake Charles."

"You don't say? Some good old boys down in Lake Charles. And they can eat."

"Blue crab gumbo and crawdad pie to die for," I said. "Put all that on a plate with some dirty rice and red beans and you will be in heaven."

Oliphant smiled and a rough laugh escaped his lips.

He would have been handsome except for the pits on his

cheeks and throat. In one way he was the exact opposite of Saul Lynx. The tall Cajun had brown eyes and green clothes.

"You know your food but do you know engines?"

"Oh yeah," I said like they did down home. "Poor man got to know how to fix his car 'cause a place like this cost you a week's wages."

Again Oliphant laughed. "If you lucky."

He picked up a slender stick and tapped the bottom of the engine.

"What's that?" he asked me.

"Oil pan."

"And that?" he asked tapping the upper region.

"Injector over the intake manifold."

"What about down here?"

"Flywheel."

We went on like that for a while. After I'd named twenty parts of the engine he began asking me how I'd fix various problems. I guess he was happy with my answers. I did know about cars.

"You say you're a hot-and-cold man but you know your cars."

"I know boiler rooms and air conditioners too," I said. Working as the building supervisor I had to know how every machine at a school worked.

Oliphant rubbed his ravaged jaw and regarded me.

"I do have a position open," he said. "But how'd you know about it?"

"Sam Houston," I said.

"And here I thought the great man had died." Oliphant's smile was somewhat sinister.

"Not the original," I said. "This one's from Texas too, but

he's black and owns a restaurant in L.A. called Hambones. He found out about it somewhere."

I doubted that Oliphant would go so far as to check my story but I'd already asked Sam to cover for me.

"Last boy to work here didn't work out," Gator said. "Broke my supervisor's nose and broke into the safe too."

"Was he from Louisiana?"

That got Gator laughing again. He liked to laugh.

"Okay, Larry," he said. "We'll try you out. If you can work as good as you talk you'll do just fine."

We smiled into each other's eyes. He had the kind of eyes that made you feel that he knew what was going on in your mind.

TILLY MONROE was the first man I had to deal with. I knew his name from the moment I saw him—that wasn't hard. First off he had a bandage over his black-and-blue swollen nose. Then he was short, five-five tops. He also wore red coveralls with the name TILLY stitched over his heart. All he needed was good sense and six inches and he could have been a matinee idol.

"So you the new buck?" he said, and I wondered why Ross had waited so long to bust his face.

"Just a mechanic," I said.

"This ain't no penny-ante backyard garage here, son," he said. "This here's a first-class operation. You get a job and a time estimate and you better believe that you will finish on time and keep your station clean."

I inhaled through my nose and held it, trying to keep from saying something angry.

"No personal phone calls," Tilly added, "except in emergency, and no sick pay. You get paid for hours worked and you work every hour you here. Understand?"

"Yes sir." I hated myself for saying it.

I was given three engines and told that I had a week to overhaul them for the used-car lot across the street. That way, Tilly said, he could make sure that it was me and not some other man doing the job.

I signed up for the evening shift and worked into the night. It didn't bother me not being home. Bonnie and I barely spoke but still it hurt my heart to have her near.

I SPENT SIX HOURS there and didn't find out one thing that would help clear Ross Henry.

Gator was well named. He cruised around the garage like a huge green predator. He had the same kind of evil grin as the alligator and seemed to come up out of nowhere. I met eight men other than Oliphant, Tilly, and Ed. Ed was the kid I met coming in. I don't remember anyone else's name. They all worked hard and laughed well. Maybe one of them robbed the safe. It was beyond my ability to tell.

The garage closed at eight that Sunday night. I dawdled around until nearly nine, cleaning up my station.

"See ya, Larry," Ed said to me.

"Later, kid."

His bright smile shone in answer and Ed turned toward the door.

"You about finished, Burdon?" Tilly asked me.

When I looked up to see the small man, I saw Gator beyond him, looking at us both through the glass wall of his office. His brow was dark and dangerous.

"Just about," I said.

"'Cause we don't want any of the brothers around when we're not here to watch 'em, if you know what I mean." Tilly was standing nearly on top of me, which was unsettling because

I was down on my knees putting my tools into an iron chest.

I stood to my full height and Tilly fell back, one step and then another.

"Didn't that man who stole your money break your nose for you?" I asked him.

"What of it?"

"Nuthin'," I said. "It's just that you should go home and study your eyes and that nose in the mirror. See if you can find a correlation between the two."

"Corra-what?"

I never expected to return to Oliphant's garage. Why not give them a glimpse of the man who hid from them in plain sight?

"See you tomorrow," I said.

I stripped the blue coveralls off of my street clothes and marched out of the mechanic's glare into the briny night.

ED WAS STANDING on the corner, waiting for a ride I supposed. He was a good kid. Talked a little too much. But whenever he did Gator came out and set him straight without embarrassment. If anybody was going to let something drop, it would be Eddie.

I wanted to go home, to sleep on my sofa. But Saul was a friend and I had made a promise. So I went to the corner thinking this would be my last stab at getting information on the robbery.

"Hey, Ed."

"Mr. Burdon."

"Goin' home?"

"Yeah. My mom's coming to get me. I won't get my license for three more months. Then I can drive myself. You need a ride?"

"Yeah, which way you goin'?"

"Up to Sea Breeze, but my mom can give you a ride anywhere around here."

I had no idea where Sea Breeze was and I had my own car. I just wanted to hang around Ed until he answered a question or two.

"They say the guy I'm replacing broke old Tilly's nose," I ventured.

"Sure did," Ed said. "Ross is a good guy and that Tilly's just mean. He don't like black people too much, you know. He's from the South."

"So's Gator," I said. "You got a little twang there yourself."

"Ah yeah, but Gator's great. He's my dad."

No one had mentioned this during the day. But it made sense once Ed said it. I thought Gator was looking out for him because he was the only kid at the place. But thinking about it, Gator wasn't just being a boss, he was being paternal in a cold sort of way; like the lizard he emulated.

A white Cadillac pulled up to the curb.

"That's my mom," Ed said.

The car door opened and a woman said, "Come on now, Eddie. I got to—"

She didn't finish her sentence because I turned and she saw my face. She was looking straight at me but her face still seemed to be in profile. That grin still thrilled my heart.

"Hey, mom," Ed said. "This is Larry Burdon, the new mechanic. He needs a ride."

"Easy?"

"No, it's Larry," Ed corrected.

"Oh."

Amiee came around the side of the car to shake my hand. She grabbed onto two fingers, squeezed, and pulled.

"Pleased to meet you, Mr. Burdon. You look familiar."

"That's funny," I said. "So did your son when I met him."

"Mr. Burdon did the best of anybody on dad's test," Ed was saying.

We were looking into each other's eyes. I was ready dive to in, right there.

"You don't have a car, Larry?" Amiee asked.

"I took the bus, Mrs. Oliphant," I said. "I live a ways up, near Sepulveda."

"I'd be happy to give you a ride."

As I climbed into the car I looked over at the garage. The lights went out just as I turned and so I couldn't be sure that I glimpsed Gator standing in the glass door, staring in our direction.

We dropped Ed off at the Oliphant's front door on Sea Breeze Lane. Then Amiee drove off in the opposite direction from my fictitious home.

"I was surprised to see you," we both said at the same time.

"Twice," she added.

"You mean when I came up on you in the clenches with Ross?"

"No," she said. "When I saw your handsome face come in that room."

I was a full-grown man, forty-four at that moment. I had been on three different continents and seen everything from birth to death many times over. With all that experience one would think that a slip of a girl with an uneven face would hardly even make an impression. But Amiee had my heart fluttering and my mouth watering to the point where I had to swallow.

She smiled at my discomfort.

"What's goin' on, Amiee?"

My question had extra meaning as we were pulling into a

parking lot that bordered the Pacific Ocean. The low-slung three-quarter moon sent a corridor of light rippling from the horizon to the shore, not twenty feet from our car door. The moonlight and that woman filled my chest with awe.

"You working for Ross?" she asked me.

"After a fashion. You workin' on him, or with him?"

"I was just giving him a little justice," she said.

"Justice?"

"I told him that I knew he didn't rob Gator but all I could do was to give him the secret knowledge that he had the boss-man's woman before he ran."

"No wonder he was so mad when we interrupted you."

Amiee smiled and gestured at me with her jaw.

Only that morning I thought that I'd never kiss another woman.

We wrestled around for a minute or two. Her hands were quick and clever. I felt every hormone and instinct in my body surging but still, I took Amiee by the shoulders and pressed her back against the door—at arm's length. Not daunted by the distance she pressed a bare foot against my erection and smiled.

"No," I said.

"Not yet," she replied. "But it's comin'."

"No," I said again. "It's not."

Amiee composed herself then accepted my refusal without anger.

I felt a powerful urge to jump out of the car and run back to Bonnie. I wanted to tell her something, but I had no idea what.

"I'll never forget you, Easy Larry," Amiee said.

"Why's that?" I asked in a voice much deeper than usual.

"I never had a man frustrate me twice in the same day."

We both laughed.

"You still need a ride home?" Amiee asked. She leaned over to give me a half-friendly kiss.

"Naw," I said. "My ride is a couple'a blocks away from the garage."

"You gonna tell me why you workin' there?"

"To see if there's some other explanation for the robbery."

"You find anything?"

"Nope."

"But you're there to help Ross?" she asked.

"Yeah."

"Why?"

"For a favor to Saul. That's the guy I was with."

"What if I told you something?" she said. "I mean, could I trust you to keep secret where you heard it from?"

"Yeah," I said. "But I don't know how to prove it."

"Oh I'll take your word, honey. I can feel how much you wanted me and still you held back. Some woman has made an honest man outta you."

Her words seemed to be full of meaning.

"Any man that true," she continued, "will keep his word if he can."

"All right," I said. "You got my word. So what can you tell me?"

"Gator and Tilly are movin' stolen sports cars."

"From the used car lot?"

"Uh-uh. They work on 'em late at night and then sell 'em from off the street."

"How so?"

"They get the car in and paint it, then they leave it on some corner and send the buyer the key."

"How long they been doin' that?"

"Couple'a years."

"And was Ross in on it?"

"I don't think so."

"And how do you know about it?"

"Eggersly don't give two shits about me. He got at least two girlfriends at any one time an' he ain't hardly ever home. When he is he treats me like a piece'a property. He brags about what he's doin' like I wasn't in the room. Talk about women he had, men he beat, and the cars too. Gator always says that he was born poor white trash but he was smart and tough and made somethin' outta himself. But my mama always said that you could put trash in a silver ashcan but it's still just trash."

I'd known men like Oliphant. Men so proud of their strength and their accomplishments that they forget even the greatest fighter can be stabbed in the back.

"So you think Gator or Tilly knows who stole the money?" I asked.

"Not himself. He wasn't in there that night, 'cause it was Tuesday. On Tuesdays he drops Eddie off at Little League practice and then goes off. Nobody sees him again till Wednesday."

"So what does that mean for Ross?"

"Ross don't know none of it. He don't know that most nights Tilly and Gator up in there with stolen cars. How's he gonna be so smart to pick the one night you can be sure nobody's there?"

It was a good question.

"YOU DIDN'T GET IT? What the fuck is wrong wit' you, Easy?" Mouse asked.

It wasn't really Mouse but just a specter in my mind. Lately, whenever I was disturbed or distressed, I'd start telling the story to the air and from somewhere in my mind I'd imagine my dead friend's opinions.

"No," I said in the empty car. "No. I haven't set things straight with Bonnie yet."

"Lemme get this straight, Ease. She had her hand down in your pants, had a hold'a yo' dick, and you still pushed her off?"

"Yeah," I said on a heavy sigh.

And there was no reply. It was new ground for Mouse and me. What could he say? There was no experience he'd ever had with a friend who would have said such a thing.

I PULLED UP INTO THE DRIVEWAY at about eleven. The lights were on. Bonnie was sitting in the reclining chair reading and waiting for me. Her recreational reading was mostly in French. I'd always felt that it was a barrier between us, like her French-speaking African prince.

She put the book down when I came in.

For a while after I found out about her holiday she tried to act normal. She'd smile at me when I came through the door and kiss me the way she always had. But after a few weeks of me being cold and turning away she stopped pretending.

"Easy."

That's all she said, just one word, and I wanted to put my fist through the wall.

"Hey, baby," I said instead. "What you readin'?"

That threw her off guard. She was about to say something else but those words never came out.

"A book," she said. "Nothing. It's about a young girl in love with a man who doesn't even know that she's alive."

I pulled a wooden chair up next to the recliner and sat down.

"Just because somebody loves someone else that don't mean she got to love him back," I said. I was hoping for better words to come out; words like she'd been reading in that novel.

Bonnie wanted to say something but all she could do was reach out and touch my cheek.

"I was mad at you," I said. "I wanted to take my love away from you 'cause I thought that's what you did to me. And maybe it is. Maybe you love somebody who don't know it. But all I know is that you're here with me, inside me. And so I wanna say that you can go off now or tomorrow or next month. You can go have that life you read about and I will let you go. And . . ." I was talking from a place inside me that I didn't even know was there; saying words that had been worked out in a part of my mind that I was unaware of. ". . . and you can leave knowin' that I love you. It doesn't matter that you love him or don't love me. It doesn't matter what you did or wanted to do. I'm not mad at you anymore. And the good feeling from my lovin' you is stronger than the pain of seein' you do what you got to do."

As soon as those words were out I felt like a fool. My ears got hot and I expected Bonnie to laugh in my face. But she didn't laugh. Her hand fell down against my chest and pressed. Whether it was a caress or pushing me away, I didn't know.

"You wanna come to bed, baby?" she whispered.

"Not tonight," I said. "I got things to think about."

"What Mr. Lynx wanted you to help him with?"

"Yeah. Tryin' to help his cousin stay outta jail."

"Okay. But will you come back to bed when this is over?"

"If you still want me."

Bonnie's eyebrows furrowed and her hand moved away.

She kissed me on the cheek and left without saying another word.

I laid back on the sofa and for the first time since before Mouse had been shot I fell instantly to sleep. It was a place beyond images, way past normal, everyday rest. It was the kind of sleep that you fall into after surviving a high fever or grave illness. It was the healing sleep of infants and wild animals. My dreams, if there were any, were shapeless and feral notions far beyond any small problems of humankind.

When I awoke early the next morning it took a few minutes for me to remember who I was and where. It was a new world and a new life opening up for me. And I was ready to challenge the world.

BUT FIRST I had to go to work.

I was there early prowling the school, looking hard for unlocked doors or broken windows. I found an overturned trash bin on the upper campus. Instead of making a report for one of my custodians, I opened a hopper room and got myself a broom and dustpan. I had almost finished when the principal came upon me.

"Good morning, Mr. Rawlins," she said.

"Principal Masters," I said.

It took Hiram Newgate shooting himself in the head to make me call him principal.

"Is sweeping in your job description?" Ada Masters asked.

"When I used to go to school down in Louisiana," I said, "the last thing we did every night was to sweep, dust, and pick up the classroom. Wasn't any slot in the budget for a janitor. If you see a mess, you take care of it if you can. How else a child or an employee gonna learn unless somebody sets the example?"

Mrs. Masters's smile beamed. That's how my luck ran. Under the previous principal I couldn't do a thing right. But since Masters had come she only saw me in my best light, even though I had lost my way and spent many days away from work on made-up illnesses.

"How are you, Mr. Rawlins?" she asked.

"As near to bliss as a poor man can hope for."

Again she smiled.

I SPENT THE DAY checking between the cracks, making sure that my school was in tip-top shape.

Mrs. Plates called in and said that her husband had died that morning. It was no surprise, he'd been bedridden for years, but she was still broken up.

The students had put up an art show down the main hall of the arts building. Some of those black children had real talent. Portraits and landscapes, abstractions and stories about the good life of being young. Most of them would end up trading in their paintbrushes and watercolors for janitors' brooms and mail sacks.

There was one painting of me. It was a full body portrait. I was wearing my herringbone jacket and pointing the way to a small boy, probably First Wentworth. I was pointing on ahead and looking in that direction. There was a smile on my face, my teeth were showing.

"You like it, Mr. Rawlins?" Nora Dewhurst, the art teacher, asked.

"That's somethin' else. Who did it?"

"Starla Jacobs. It's her first attempt with oils. You know, she's a natural painter. See how she made the paint thicker in your face and hands. I think she knew intuitively that that application would make the portrait come to life."

It wasn't the person I saw every morning in the mirror; not the hard-knocks black man from the Deep South. Not my jaw-line exactly. But it had my spirit and my style. She caught the pride in my eye from being able to help a young boy make it on his way. It was the Easy Rawlins they knew at Sojourner Truth.

"You think she'd take seventy-five dollars for it?" I asked.

Nora Dewhurst had blue-gray hair. Her eyes were nearly clear with just a touch of blue to them. She was close to retire-ment, had taught in Los Angeles public schools since 1926. But her eyes bulged with such surprise that you'd think no one had ever purchased one of her students' paintings.

"Mr. Rawlins, I don't know what to say. You would make a painter out of Starla if you were to do such a thing."

"She's already a painter."

"You know what I mean."

And there we were, a black man from the Deep South and a white woman from New York City, both aware of how little chance those kids had. We didn't quite say it because neither of us wanted to know what would happen if we let the truth out of the bag.

"Tell her to put a matte board around it and I'll pick it up on Friday after the last class."

Nora kissed me on the cheek. Two little girls standing nearby gasped and ran away.

THAT EVENING I was in my car, down the street from Oliphant's garage. I'd parked next to a vast concrete wall, far away from any streetlamp. And I sat low so that any passing cruiser wouldn't see me watching.

Redheaded Ed came out at eight-fifteen. He wheeled a small motorbike to the corner. Five minutes later Amiee drove up. She opened the trunk and Ed put the bike in.

Everybody but Tilly and Eggersly had gone by nine. At ten they were still in there. They were playing cards, throwing down money and pulling from the deck.

Just past eleven a yellow Porsche drove up to the garage door and was admitted. Fifteen minutes later a red sports car pulled up. It must have been European because I didn't recognize the make.

After that Tilly Monroe put up ten-foot opaque screens in front of the glass doors. That didn't bother me though. I had already scoped out a building behind the garage that had a fire escape. I made my way back there and climbed up halfway between the second and third floors. From there I had a night bird's eye view through the skylight.

There had been two men in each car. By the time I reached my perch they'd donned blue coveralls and covered the floor with a heavy tarp. Then they put up clear plastic tents around the cars. Tilly was already taping the chrome.

I decided at that moment I should take a class in photography.

The yellow car turned a dark green while I watched.

They were just turning their attention to the red car when a police cruiser pulled up to the door. I smiled. The job was being done for me. Any lawyer could punch holes in Oliphant's story about Ross if he had been arrested for painting stolen cars.

But it was just a friendly visit. The police came in and conversed with Oliphant while the red car turned white. They received an envelope and a handshake and went on along their way.

Two of the thieves were rolling up the tarp and washing off the spray-paint nozzles by the time the cops left. The other two were shining powerful lamps on the newly painted cars. I watched them clean and dry while Tilly and Gator went into the glassed-in office and smoked.

The thieves were through with their work by three. Three of them drove off in the stolen automobiles but one walked away.

He went over to Pico and turned east. I followed him for two blocks, taking one-and-a-half steps for every one of his. When I was right behind him he turned his head to the side.

"Don't turn around," I said. "Unless you want I should shoot you."

I pressed the muzzle of my .38 in between his shoulder blades and took out his wallet.

"You robbin' me?"

The short, white car thief sounded surprised. I guess he figured that a man committing a crime was immune from being held up. Like a first-class passenger thinking that his plane can't crash.

"Oliphant sent me," I said.

"What for?"

We had stopped walking by then. We were standing there at the corner, two men on a short line to nowhere.

"He wants his money or your blood," I said, reading the name on his license, "Mr. Tremont."

"Then what you take my wallet for?"

"To see if you had one of his thousand dollar bills."

"He had thousand dollar bills in there?"

"Don't try and play me, man," I said. "Just gimme the money and I bust your leg. That'll make us all even."

"I swear I didn't do it," the thief cried.

"Step over here, out of the light," I said.

Alan Tremont did as he was told. We walked into the entry-way of a bank building. He tried to turn around but I cuffed him on the ear, saying, "Eyes front."

He started trembling then.

"Please, man. I didn't do it. I swear I didn't do it."

"Then why Oliphant put me on you?"

"I don't know. I don't know."

"Gimme somethin' then," I said. "Gimme somethin' or I blow out the back'a your head."

"I wasn't even there, man," Alan Tremont said. "I wasn't even in town. We had a line on a car down in San Diego. Me and Pete did."

"I'm goin' to see Pete right after I kill you." I wanted to put my intentions in plain language. Simple terms are often the most frightening.

"I can't prove it, man. If you think it was me and Pete what, I mean . . . Listen, I got thirty-six hundred dollars I been savin' up . . . I could give it to you."

I paused for a moment, letting him think I was considering the offer.

"I could get it for you tonight," Alan said.

"Who do I hang it on then?" I asked.

"You could just say that I got away from you."

"Better to have the man who did it. You say it wasn't you, right?"

"No. But I don't know who did it. All I know is that it wasn't me and it wasn't Pete neither. We weren't in town."

"Then who?"

"It could'a been anybody. No one was workin' that night and we all knew it. That was Tuesday and Tuesdays Oliphant spends with Thana Jamieson. Nobody works if Oliphant ain't there."

"Who do you think though, Alan? 'Cause you see, boy, I got to kill somebody. I'd like your money but I got to kill somebody or else I got to take Eggersly out. 'Cause if I don't get you he bound to come after me."

"Maybe it was the one they said. Maybe it was the, the colored guy." He almost said "nigger" but held back due to the cast of my own words.

"He's out."

"Then Tilly's your man," Alan said. "Tilly hates Oliphant. He's always talkin' behind his back. He's been fuckin' Ollie's wife for over a year. He does it on Tuesdays, when Ollie's with Thana. Tilly stoled it if anybody did."

"Okay. Okay. You know the Farmer's Market up on Fairfax and Third Street?"

"Yeah."

"You know the Du-Parr's restaurant up there?"

"Sure."

"Meet me there at six tomorrow with the money in a paper bag."

"You bet."

He tried to turn around but I cuffed him again.

"You'll see my face tomorrow," I said. "When the job's over."

"But how will I know it's you?"

"I'll be reading a book," I said. "*War and Peace* by Tolstoy. You can read, can't you?"

"Sure I can," he said, but I wasn't convinced.

"Then get your ass outta here. Go on, run!"

I pushed Alan Tremont out onto the curb and he ran. He was good at running. Most thieves are.

WHEN I GOT BACK to the gas station Tilly Monroe's big blue Buick was the only car left. I stood across the street for a good ten minutes weighing my luck in life up to that moment. I had been shot before, and stabbed and sapped and kicked. I'd been on a few hit lists. There were still a few people around who would have liked to see me dead.

But Tilly had no reason to want to hurt me. He didn't even know my real name.

I DIDN'T NEED TO WORRY. Tilly Monroe was slumped down dead over a scattering of playing cards and cash. His hands were up at the sides of his head as if he were trying to surrender before he was slaughtered.

Five twenty-dollar bills had been dropped on the side of his face. They were old, 1934 issue, silver certificates from a time when the government backed up its currency.

My watch said four A.M.

I took the twenties and left for work.

IT WAS ALL IN THE AFTERNOON *Examiner.* Tilly Monroe shot dead, Eggersly Oliphant mysteriously missing, an argument over a poker game was the suspected cause of the falling out between cousins. But there was also evidence that there had been illegal activities surrounding the garage. Police detective Benjamin Suffolk told the press that Eggersly had been suspected of moving stolen cars for the past eleven months.

"Yeah," I muttered. "And they'd'a gone on suspecting him for eleven years if not for those twenty dollar bills."

"What's that, Mr. Rawlins?" Willis Long, my newest janitor and pet project, asked.

"Nuthin', Willie," I said. "It's just that some people in this world bigger fools than even young men like you."

"The fool fool himself that he's happy is better off than the smart man foolin' that happy don't mean a thing."

"That gonna be your new song?"

"Maybe it is. Maybe."

❖   ❖   ❖

AT TEN-THIRTY I decided to ring the doorbell. The last visitor left the Sea Breeze Lane home at about nine-fifteen. I'd spent the time yawning and napping in the front seat of my car. I hadn't gotten a good sleep for two nights. An old white woman opened the door.

"Yes?" she asked.

"Is Amiee in?"

"She's not seeing anyone."

"I'm not anyone, ma'am. I'm Easy Larry."

"That's all right, Myra," Amiee said from about twenty feet away. She was wearing a long-sleeved blousy white dress that went all the way to the floor. Her hair was brushed out but not styled. Her nose was still wayward and sexy.

"But, Amiee," Myra complained. "How would this look?"

"Go into some other room and close your eyes, dear," Amiee said as she approached.

Myra huffed off through a doorway and I never saw her again.

"There you are again," Amiee said.

There was fire in her eyes and my gut. But I wasn't there for kisses.

"And there you are, the grieving wife abandoned by a faithless husband, cheated of her domestic bliss."

"Why, Easy Larry, I do believe that you have read a book or two."

"Where's Ed?" I asked.

Amiee's brash smile disappeared then. She looked down and shook her head.

"He's upstairs cryin' his heart out. The doctor came with a sedative for me but he ended up givin' it to Eddie. He's up there right now cryin' in his sleep."

I took the thirty-year-old twenty-dollar bills from my pocket and handed them to the siren.

"Where'd you get these?" she asked.

"Somebody had used this instead of pennies to cover Tilly's eyes."

"Oliphant," she said uttering her own last name as if it was already alien to her.

"What does it mean?"

"That either Tilly or Eggersly robbed the safe. My husband got these from his first gas station back at the end of the war. It was the first money he made fixing a fancy car."

"And he kept it in the safe?"

"Yes."

"Do you think that Tilly was such a fool that he'd throw down this money in a poker game?"

"Maybe he would. I don't know that Eggersly ever told Tilly about that hundred dollars."

"Was Tilly up in here with you the night the safe was robbed?"

Amiee hesitated for a moment before saying, "Yeah. He knew I was open to him when I knew Gator was with his whore."

"Then that rules him out," I said. "Who else knew about the bills?"

The truth dawned in Amiee's eyes. I could see it clearly.

"Where was Ed when you were playing with Tilly?"

"Tilly come over after Ed was asleep."

"You think he might have ever got up and went to the toilet?"

ED WAS MOANING and shifting around in his bed. When we came in he cried and called out, "Mama?"

"Sh, baby, go back to sleep."

It was definitely a boy's room. It smelled of sour socks.

There was a little box record player on a table and three baseball bats leaning into a corner. He had comic books and stacks of blue-lined paper jumbled on his desk. There was an accordion paper file folder in the closet that contained Oliphant's receipts and maybe forty-two hundred dollars in cash.

"You stay here," Amiee said. "I'll go downstairs and get rid of Myra."

When she was gone a few minutes I pulled an orange stool up to the side of the bed.

"Ed?"

"Uh."

"Eddie."

"Mmmm. What?" he whined.

"Are you awake?"

"No."

"Why did you rob your father's safe, son?"

"Tilly wanted to sell me the dirt bike. He said he wanted a hundred dollars."

"What are you doing?" Amiee was standing at the door.

"Where's Myra?" I asked.

"Already gone. What were you doing to Ed?"

"He was getting upset. I was just trying to calm him down."

Amiee needed love in her life, not for herself but for the boy. She smiled and touched my sleeve, then motioned for me to follow downstairs.

We spent almost two hours at the kitchen table wiping down every surface of the accordion file. Not the money; I took that.

"I guess he was just doin' what boys do," Amiee said at one point.

"Don't believe it," I said. "He stole that money and then paid

Tilly for a motorbike with those twenty-dollar bills the day of the poker game. He was workin' some serious mojo there."

"What do you mean?" Amiee asked. But she knew.

"Tilly's been up in here with you." I said. "Up in Ed's father's bed on Tuesday nights. He knew it."

"I've seen you looking at my nose," she said. "You know it used to be straight. I had what they call an aristocratic nose."

I adjusted my dishwashing gloves. They were small on me and made my hands sweat.

"Oliphant broke it," she sneered, "that was back when he still loved me. But I didn't care about that. What made me mad was how he ignored Eddie. Wouldn't stay around for a baseball game or ask about school. That's why Eddie worked down at the garage. It was the only way he could see his father."

"Sons love their fathers," I said. "He set up Tilly. Did a good job of it too. Even if his cousin would have said that he got the money from Ed, Oliphant would have never believed it."

"But he didn't think his father would have killed him," Amiee said.

"He wasn't thinkin' about what would happen at all," I said. "Only how he could make his father as mad as he was."

Soon after that we'd finished the wipe-down.

"Put this somewhere down in the basement and leave it there for a day," I told her. "Then bring it back up here. Get a few prints on it. Call the cops and tell 'em you found it looking for your husband's legal papers."

"Okay." She was looking into my eyes. "Stay with me tonight."

"I can't."

"It's because I been with so many men," she said. "You think I'm some kind'a whore."

"No." I put my hand on her side. "I think you saved my heart from turnin' back to stone."

"What?"

"That's why I'm helpin' you. Because you gave me somethin' and you didn't even know it."

I kissed her for a moment longer than I should have but then I leaned back.

"Thank you," I said.

"HI, DADDY," Feather said, as I came out of the bedroom the next morning.

She was all dressed for school in a green outfit and brown shoes. She looked taller.

"Baby."

"You better?"

"Better than what?"

"You not nervous no more?"

I remembered our talk and sat next to her at the breakfast table.

"Yeah, baby," I said. "I'm better. It was just that I was jealous that Bonnie goes all over the world and meets such wonderful people."

"And you wisht that you could go?" Feather asked.

"No. I was wanting her to stay home and not have anybody but us as friends."

"But she can't do that because, because that's her job."

"Yeah," I said. "I know."

"Everybody got to do their job," Feather added.

"Yes, ma'am," I said, and Feather giggled and kissed me.

GRAY-EYED DEATH

A CAR DOOR SLAMMED on the street somewhere but it didn't mean anything to me. I was at home drinking lemonade from the fruit of my own trees on a Saturday in L.A. Nobody was after me. My slate was clean. Bonnie had gone out with her friend Shirley, Jesus was taking sailing lessons near Redondo Beach, and Feather had gone down the street to her little boyfriend's house, a shy red-headed child named Henry Hopkins.

Just four weeks before I would have spent my solitary time wondering if I should ask Bonnie to be my bride. But she had spent a weekend on the island of Madagascar with a man named Jogaye Cham. He was the son of an African prince born in Senegal while I was raised a poor black orphan.

Bonnie swore that the time they spent together was platonic but that didn't mean much to me. A man who expected to be a king, who was working to liberate and empower a whole continent, wanted Bonnie by his side.

How could I compete with that?

How could she wake up next to me year after year, getting older while I made sure the toilets at Sojourner Truth Junior High School were disinfected? How could she be satisfied with a janitor when a man who wanted to change the world was calling her name?

Sharp footsteps on concrete followed the slamming door.

Bonnie had made my life work perfectly for a while. She never worried about my late-night meetings or when I went out for clues to the final fate of my old friend Mouse. I knew he was dead but I needed to hear it from the woman who saw him die. EttaMae admitted that she buried him in a nameless grave.

The footsteps ended at my door. They were the footsteps of a small man. I expected Jackson Blue to appear. Maybe he wanted my advice about his crazy love affair with Jewelle now that Mofass was dead. Or maybe he had some scheme he wanted to run past me. Either way it would be better than moping around, wishing that my woman wasn't born to be a queen.

The knocking was soft and unhurried. Whoever it was, he, or she, was in no rush.

When I pulled the door open I was looking too high, above the man's head. And then I saw him.

He pushed me aside and went past saying, "If it wasn't for ugly, Easy, I woulda never even seen you again."

"Raymond?" I could feel the tears wanting to come from my eyes. I was dizzy too. Torn between the two sensations I couldn't go either way.

"You know I been drivin' up an' down Pico for the last hour and a half tryin' to figure out if I should come here or not," Mouse was saying.

He wore dark gray slacks and an ochre-colored jacket. His shirt was charcoal and there was gold edging on three of his teeth. On his baby finger he wore a thick gold ring sporting an onyx face studded with eight or nine diamond chips. His shoes were leather, honed to a high shine.

He wore no hat. Kennedy killed hats by going bareheaded to his inauguration, any haberdasher will tell you that. And if Mouse was a slave to anything it was fashion.

"Where the hell you been, Ray?"

He grinned. He laughed.

That was one of the few times I ever hugged a man. I actually lifted him off the floor.

"All right now, Easy. Okay. It's okay, brother. I missed you too, baby. Yeah."

Mouse was still laughing. It wasn't a guffaw or even a roll. It was a calculated chuckle that only debutantes and killers had mastered.

"Where the hell you been?" I asked again.

"You got somethin' to drink around here, Ease?" he replied. "I know you don't drink but I thought maybe your woman did."

Bonnie kept a bottle of brandy on the top shelf in the kitchen, behind the mixing bowls. I poured Mouse three fingers and refreshed my lemonade. Then he got comfortable on my recliner and I sat on the loveseat Bonnie brought from her home when she moved into mine.

"Well?" I asked after his first sip.

"Well what?"

"What happened?"

"You saw me get hit, didn't you? You saw me sprawled out there at Death's door. Shit. I was almost dead, Easy. Almost. Everything looked different. Slow and like black-and-white TV through red sunglasses. I heard Etta cryin'. I heard the nurse tellin' her I was dyin'. I believed her. As far as I was concerned I was already dead."

Mouse stared at the kitchen window through the door, his gray eyes amazed with the memory of his own demise.

"Where did Etta take you?"

"Mama Jo's," he said. "That's why I'm here, partly."

"You were too hurt to be taken all the way down to Texas," I said. "Your heart wasn't even beating."

"Jo moved up around Santa Barbara six years ago," Mouse said. "Etta knew about it but she never told no one. Domaque had got himself in trouble down Harrisville and she helped 'em move here."

"She called me."

"Etta?" Mouse asked.

"No. Jo. Couple'a months ago. She called and asked if I knew where you were. It was that same deep voice. Yeah. I couldn't place it at the time. She healed you?"

"Yeah, baby. You know Jo's a witch." I remembered Mouse saying the same words when we were only nineteen. He'd taken me to her cabin in the woods outside of Pariah, Texas. Jo was twenty years older than we were. She was tall and jet black, crazy and full of need.

She seduced me and then saved my life when I came down with a fever.

"She used powders and ointments," Mouse continued. "Stayed up all night by my side, every night for six weeks. She sat next to me almost the whole time. Etta and LaMarque was in the corner worryin' and Domaque did all the work. You know, Easy, I believe that her standin' sentry was why Death couldn't pull me off. When my heart got weak she held foul-smellin' shit up under my nose. And then one mornin' I was awake. Everything looked normal. My chest hurt but that was fine. I was walkin' in seven days' time. I woulda been fuckin' but Etta was mad at me for gettin' myself shot."

He sipped while he talked. After each swallow he hissed in satisfaction. As the moments ticked by I got used to seeing him. That was easy because Mouse had never really been dead for me. I took him with me everywhere I went. He was my barometer for evil, my advisor when no good man would have known what to say. Raymond was proof that a black man could live by his own rules in America when everybody else denied it. Why couldn't he crawl up out of the grave and return to life whenever he felt like it?

"Damn," I said. "Damn."

Mouse grinned again. I refilled his glass.

"Good to see you, Easy."

"I looked everywhere for you, Ray. I asked just about everybody here and down in Texas. I asked EttaMae but she said you were dead."

"She told me about that. You know I was mad at her for not gettin' me to help that musician boy." Mouse held up his glass in a toast to his wife. "But she's a good woman. She didn't want me hangin' 'round you 'cause she said that she thought that you'd get me in trouble."

"Me?" I said. "Me get *you* in trouble?"

Mouse chuckled again. "I know what you mean, Ease, but Etta got a point too. You know you always on the edge'a sump'n'. Always at the wrong door. I did get shot followin' you down that alley."

Mouse winked at me then. We were both in our mid-forties but he didn't look thirty. His smile was as innocent as Eve's come-on in the Garden of Eden.

"I'm sorry," I said. A tear did escape my eye. "I really am."

Mouse ignored the emotion I showed. "Anyway," he said. "She don't know that a man cain't be worried 'bout every Tom, Dick, and Harry wanna do him some harm. There's always somebody out to get ya. Always. You cain't hide from it. Shit. At least we friends, right?"

"Yeah," I said. "We sure are."

Mouse focused those cloud-colored eyes on me. "Domaque's in trouble again."

"What about?"

"Ugly," the dapper killer said. "Ugly brought him into this world and ugly gonna take him out."

"What's wrong with him?"

"Wrong with him? Don't you remember?"

Domaque was Mama Jo's son. He had the soul of an artist, the strength of a mule, and the looks of a fairy-tale ogre. His nasal passages didn't work right and so his drooling mouth was always open. One eye was larger than the other and between his arms and legs no two of them were the same length. He had a curve in his spine that made him hunchbacked and, though he was very intelligent, he had the emotional makeup of a twelve-year-old.

"I mean, what trouble is he in?"

"They say he robbed a armored car on its way to the Bank of America in Santa Barbara."

"Did he?" I asked.

"No."

"Did you?"

That made Mouse laugh. But it wasn't his debutante titter. It was a snort that was meant to be a warning. I had seen dogs run away from him when he'd made that sound.

He'd only been alive for ten minutes and I was already under threat.

"So what did happen?" I asked.

"Some white girl been hangin' 'round, that's what Jo says. She met Dom down at this cove where he went fishin' and started sweet-talkin' him. One day she disappears and the next thing they know the cops come up to Jo and Dom's house."

"They get him?"

"Naw. Jo got a false floor with a hole for Dom to hide under. She told them cops that Dom was down in Texas, that he'd been there for two weeks. They didn't believe her. But they couldn't find Dom neither."

"Where is he now?"

"Compton. With Etta."

"Etta's here?"

"Yeah. After you two killed that white man she decided to come back. You gonna help me with Domaque, Easy? You know you owe me after all the shit I gone through."

There it was, the offer of redemption. I could pay Mouse back for the guilt I'd taken on. I just nodded. What else could I do?

"YEAH, EASE," Mouse opined as we drove south toward Compton. "You ain't got no reason to feel guilty. The way I see it it helped me gettin' shot and all."

"Helped you how?"

"Well, you know I was so upset back then, wonderin' if all the violence I lived through was wrong. But when Jo patched me up she said that I'm just a part of a big ole puzzle, a piece. I fit in where I go and I do what I do. She said that and it stuck with me. Now I'm just fine with who I am."

Etta's new house wasn't as nice as the servants' quarters of the mansion she lived in, in the mountains above Santa Barbara. It was a small wooden cottage on a street of wooden cottages—all of them painted white. The only protection her little home had from harm was a wire fence that was twelve feet long and three-and-a-half feet high.

Mouse opened the gate and we scaled the three granite steps to the door. Before he could get his key into the lock it came open.

"Hey, Ray!" Domaque shouted. "Easy Rawlins!"

He was almost exactly the same as the last time I'd seen him, in the summer of 1939. Barrel-chested and lopsided, drooling and full of glee.

"I saw you comin'!"

"You don't have to shout and spray like that, Dom," Mouse said. "Damn."

I offered my hand to Dom and he almost crushed it.

"Good to see you, Dom," I said through clenched teeth.

"Wanna go fishin' like we did back in Pariah?" he asked.

The outing came back to me with all the pain of those miserable days. I was coming down with a virus that nearly finished me. Mouse took Dom and me fishing with a pistol instead of a pole. He stunned the fish by shooting the water with a flat-nosed soft-lead bullet, shoveling them into a bag before they could regain their senses and escape. Raymond also killed three dogs and their master, his own stepfather. After that he married Etta and I joined the army for the comparative safety of World War Two.

"No time for relaxation, Dom," Mouse said. "Easy got to get you outta trouble before Jo loses her mind."

A pitiful emotion spread over Dom's already damaged face.

The front door led into a makeshift dining room. There was a dark wood table just inside the door, surrounded by six chairs.

I grabbed a seat and turned it backward.

"Who was this girl you'd been seeing, Domaque?" I asked. I wanted to get down to business quickly.

"You ever learn how to read books, Easy?" he asked.

"Yeah. Yeah."

When I'd met Dom and his mother I knew how to make out what words I needed to pick through instructions or read a love letter from a girl. But when I saw him read hard books out loud I got jealous because I realized that he could go further than I could in the world of his mind. It struck me that it was because of Dom that I learned to read.

"Her name is Merry," Dom said. "E-R-R-Y Merry not A-R-Y the way it is usually. She was just on the beach one day while I was fishin'. You know you cain't shoot the water in the sea for fish, Raymond. It's too big."

"Dynamite prob'ly work though," Mouse replied.

"Tell me about Merry," I said.

"She was real pretty, Easy. Real pretty and nice. She didn't care I was ugly and humpbacked. She liked to laugh. For a few days she'd come around and talk to me. She even kissed me on the cheek and let me hold her hand." A sigh shuddered through Domaque's diaphragm. He was more upset about the girl than the police intent on sending him to prison. "But then she had me go to a supermarket-like place on the coast highway one day. She said that the guy who ran the place always tried to make her kiss him and she hated him. But she owed him some money and said for me to take it there."

"Did the armored car come while you were there?" I asked.

"Uh-huh. It did. You know how much I like trucks and other big cars. I looked at it and they told me to get away."

"Did Merry tell you that you could see the money car if you went down to pay her debt?"

"Sure did. But they didn't have no record of her owin' money and they told me to get away from there."

"And the next thing you know the car is robbed?"

"Not till the next week," Dom said, shaking his head. "It was a week later that we found that bag in the bushes."

I glanced at Raymond. He just hunched his shoulders and looked away.

"What bag?"

"Jo fount a bag in the bushes outside our house," Dom said.

"Was that after the cops came?"

"Uh-uh. She got the sight, you know. She felt somethin' and started nosin' around. That's when she made me hide in the space. She knew the cops would be there."

Before I could ask what was in the bag Raymond pulled it out from a closet next to the table.

It was a Wells-Fargo bag that had three stacks of a hundred twenty-dollar bills and a short .38 with a rough black handle the shape of a lightbulb. I didn't touch the money or the gun.

It was a beautiful frame: the girl with the fake name that nobody ever saw; the witnesses at the country market and evidence poorly hidden in the bushes.

"But what about the guards?" I asked out loud. "I mean there's no mask in the world that could hide Dom."

"Dead," Mouse said. "Both of 'em shot in the head. And I bet you ten to two that it was this here .38 done it."

"Damn."

"She prob'ly had partners," Mouse said. "I mean Dom says she wasn't big or tough or nuthin'."

"Yeah," Dom put in. "She was prob'ly tricked by some guy wanted to fool me too. I don't wanna get her in trouble for that."

"You see why I called on you, Easy," Mouse said. "If I knew who they were it would be a piece'a cake. But I got to find 'em before I could convince 'em to let up on my cousin here."

I had to laugh then. It was really funny. Maybe I wasn't an

African prince but I had my own domain. I wasn't a sovereign maybe and I didn't wear a crown or signet ring. But I too spent my time working for my people.

"What the hell you laughin' about, Easy?" Mouse complained.

"It's good to see you, Ray. It really is."

THE FRONT DOOR OPENED and a tall and lanky youth came in tripping over his own big feet.

"LaMarque!" Dom shouted.

The boy, who was at least six foot three, winced.

"Is that you, LaMarque?" I asked.

"Hi, Mr. Rawlins."

"Boy, you've grown a foot."

"Yes sir."

His skin had grown darker in just the few months since I'd last seen him, and he had brooding eyes. His shoulders slumped and his head hung down. He was Jesus's age, seventeen, and prey to all of the sour emotions of an adolescent.

"Say a proper hello to Easy and your uncle," Mouse ordered his son.

"He's not my uncle," LaMarque replied.

"What you say?" Mouse asked.

I stood up and stuck my hand out. "It's great seeing you, son."

After a moment's hesitation LaMarque took my hand.

"Ray," I said. "Let's go somewhere where we can talk. This is some serious business and it should just be us three involved."

"You gonna say hello to your uncle?" Mouse asked his son.

"Hello, Uncle Dom."

Dom grinned and waved with his long arm.

The level of drama around Mouse was always higher than it was anywhere else in the world. A week in Raymond's company would age a normal man a year or more.

He smiled at LaMarque and said, "Okay, Easy. I got a place we could go."

"What you want me to tell mama?" LaMarque asked his father.

"That I went out. That you don't know where I went or who I was wit'."

The brooding boy nodded and turned away toward the kitchen.

WE CAME TO A SMALL HOUSE with a brick façade off of Denker. Mouse had the key and so we went in the front door. The door opened onto a good-sized living room. There was a picture of a shapely black woman and a bespectacled black man on the coffee table. The table was flanked by two sofas. Dom and I sat on one couch and Raymond took the other.

"Whose house is this?" I asked.

"Pamela Hendricks and her husband Bobby."

"They friends of yours?"

"She is. I don't think he likes me too well."

"Where are they?" I was wondering what Mouse thought I meant when I asked for privacy.

"He took her up to Frisco for a vacation. They gonna be gone another ten days."

"And they gave you keys to their house?"

"She did. He prob'ly don't know about it. But even if he did—what's he gonna do?"

"So nobody's gonna come around?"

"No sir." Mouse grinned.

I shook my head. Mouse still lived in the fever of our

youth. At that degree he should have died long before he was shot down in that alley.

"Did Merry have a last name, Dom?"

"Not that I know."

"Did she tell you anything about herself, anything? About her parents, her school, where she's from—"

"She said she was from Pasadena," Domaque blurted out. "She said that when she moved out from her parents she moved to, to . . ." the damaged man pressed his powerful fingers against his dark brow. ". . . Culver City. Uh-huh, Culver City."

"Think hard, Dom," I said. "Did she ever say anything about her last name or her parents' last name?"

"I think," he said. "I think that it had the sound 'Bick' in it somewhere."

"Bickman? Becker? Buck somethin'?"

"Uh-uh. No. Not like that. I don't know, Easy."

"She have any scars or marks? What color was her hair?"

"Light, light blond. Almost white. But brown eyes though. Most'a your blond-haired peoples got blue eyes but not Merry. And she had a little nose and her canine teef was sharp. She bit me one time and laughed."

Mouse sighed and stood up. "I'ma go in the other room," he said. "Stretch out a minute."

He walked out. I knew he was bored by all of my questions. The only questions Mouse had patience for could be answered by "yes" or "no," either that or with a number.

"How tall?" I asked Domaque when Raymond was gone.

"Five-five," he said, and then he ducked his head and grinned. "She showed me her butt," he whispered.

"What?"

"She showed me her butt. One day we was playin' around

down by the sand at Horth's Cove. She'd pushed me and then run before I could push her back. I got kinda hard an' she point at my pants and laughed. Then she pulled down her jeans and said was that what I wanted. I told her yeah and she said to go down to the market and wait for her in two days. And I did but then the people who owned the place made me go away."

"That was the day of the robbery?"

"Yeah," Dom said. There was a glimmer of suspicion in his eye but it faded quickly.

Raymond had left the Wells-Fargo bag on the sofa. I opened it and took out the gun. It was a peculiar design. The barrel was silver or at least silver-plated. It had ornate designs etched all over—wandering vines with small dog heads instead of flowers. The butt was made from ebony wood capped with hammered gold. The cylinder was extra-large with eight chambers. Four bullets had been discharged.

I used my shirttail to wipe my fingerprints off and then put the gun back and checked out the bag. It was double-ply canvas, tough and coarse. On the very bottom it was lined with a leather strip. Along the seam of the strip was a dark stain: blood of the corpses whose dead fingers pointed at one of the only people that Raymond loved.

Dom and Ray were raised together in the now defunct town of Pariah, Texas. They ran together because they were both outcast from the other poor children. Dom because of his birth defects and Raymond because he had always been crazy.

"Did Merry ever say that she had a boyfriend?" I asked Domaque.

He pouted and turned to the side, away from me.

"Did she?" I asked.

"That was all over. She said it was."

"I'm sure it was," I said, and he turned a quarter of the way back. "But maybe if I could locate him he might know something about her that could help me find out what happened."

"Like what?"

"Like her last name."

This didn't seem so bad to Dom. A name wasn't like looking at the comely girl's butt.

"His name was Dean," he said. "That's what she told me. But he wasn't nice to her and I was and that's why she liked to come see me at Horth's Cove."

"Was there anything else about him?" I asked. "A last name or maybe what he looked like."

"He was strong but not as strong as I was. And he had stringy black hair that got in her eyes when he made her have sex with him."

I asked a hundred questions but didn't learn much else.

Finally I asked, "How did Merry come across you in the first place?"

"I go down to the cove all the time to fish. You know I love fishin', Easy."

"Anybody else know that you went down there?"

"Jo."

"Other than Jo."

"There's Axel."

"Who's that?"

"Axel Myermann. He's a guy live up in the hill over Santa Maria. Axel come down and fish wit' me now and then."

"Jo ever meet Axel?"

"Yeah. Onceit."

"Did she like him?"

"Not too much. She said that he had twisted eyes."

*   *   *

RAYMOND WAS ASLEEP. I reached for his shoulder but before I could touch him he grabbed my wrist. For a small man Raymond was very strong.

"You finished, Easy?"

"If your friends won't be back for a few days I think you should leave Dom here," I said. "You wouldn't want the police showin' up at Etta's place and findin' a suspected murderer."

"Where we goin' next?" Mouse asked with a smile.

"I'm gonna strike out solo for a while. You know, quiet like."

"Okay, Ease. Do what you got to. But remember—I will do anything and kill anyone to keep Jo from comin' to grief."

Those words rattled around my mind for weeks after it was all over.

I SPENT THAT NIGHT with Bonnie and my brood. Feather had been reading her first book with no pictures while Jesus put the finishing touches on the hull of his single-sail schooner. Bonnie was reading a French-African journal published in Mali. I made pigtails and black-eyed peas with white rice. There was pumpkin pie in the refrigerator for dessert.

We ate and talked loudly, laughing and making fun. At least the ladies and I did. Jesus was almost always silent. But he had a good time. He loved the family I had cobbled together around him. He'd have done anything for Feather and the way he looked at Bonnie sometimes made me feel like putting my arm around her waist.

They spoke together in Spanish sometimes. Bonnie knew five languages.

She would reach out and touch my arm now and again, somehow sensing that I was giving her up in my heart, that I felt unequal to her black prince. We made love passionately every night. I think she was trying to hold on to me. For my part every moment was precious because I knew that one day soon she would leave me for her throne.

"Ray came by today."

"What?" all three of them said.

"He's alive. Etta lied. Our old friend Mama Jo nursed him back to health."

"No," Bonnie said. "You're joking."

"No ma'am. He walked right up to the front door and knocked."

"What did he want?" Jesus asked.

There was feeling behind my adopted son's question. He knew Ray almost as well as I did.

"Nuthin' much," I said, but I doubted if either Jesus or Bonnie believed me.

"ARE YOU IN TROUBLE, EASY?" Bonnie asked after we had made love.

"No. Why?"

"It was the way you mentioned Raymond. It was as if you were hiding something by being so simple."

I turned toward her under the covers. The clock over her shoulder said 11:30.

"He's got a friend in trouble and I'm the best one to figure it out."

"Is it dangerous?"

"Not anymore. I'm just a snoop like. Just askin' a few questions here and there."

"Just don't stick your neck out," she said. "I wouldn't know what to do without you."

"Without me you'd be a queen."

She kissed my lips and said, "Why would I want to settle for second best?"

I DROVE UP TO SANTA MARIA and looked Axel Myermann up in a phone booth at an Esso gas station. He lived at number five Elmonte Crook.

"What's a crook?" I asked the station attendant.

"Say what?" He was over sixty but his thick hair was still mostly blond.

"I mean like a street," I said. "It says here Elmonte Crook."

"Oh," the man said. He had the name DELL stitched on his breast pocket. "You mean Elmontey. Some rich old family bought up the land around there and started usin' different names for streets. Lane and Circle and Way weren't good enough for 'em so they started with that stuff like Crook and 'Y' and 'U.' If you got money you could do what you want. Now me, I can't even get the town to come over and fill in a pothole. I been callin' every Monday for three years almost. Every Monday and that hole gets bigger every time it rains."

"Down where I used to live," I said, "the city once left a dead dog in the street for over two weeks. It was one of those big dogs. Some guys and me tried to put it out for the trash collectors but they just left it moldering in the can."

"Damn Democrats," Dell said. "Damn Republicans."

I didn't have anything to add so we stood there a moment. I pulled out my wallet to pay for the three dollars' worth of gas that he'd pumped. I handed him a five.

When he was giving me my change I asked, "How do I get up to this crook?"

"Follah Stockton all the way up the mountain till you get to Reynard. Turn there and stay on it till you get to a dirt road with no sign. Take that for a little less than a mile and you'll see Elmontey. All the mailboxes are there together at the foot of the road."

THE LOOSE DIRECTIONS worked perfectly. Twenty-three minutes after leaving the Esso station I was at the foot of Elmonte Crook. Number five did indeed belong to Axel Myermann. It was country out around there, dusty shrub country. There were no farms or even big trees. Just dirty green leaves, rocky terrain and blue sky.

Elmonte Crook was a hilly path that was well named. I passed two unlikely driveways before coming to a dark lane that had a small sign that read MYERMANN'S. The path was too steep for my car so I pulled off the road as far as I could and hiked my way down. I got as far as a small brook when I saw the house. Really it was just a cabin. Painted dull red and roofed in green, it had only one window that I could see and one step, even though the doorway was a good two feet above the ground.

The door was unlocked and Axel was not quite dead.

"Help me," the elder man said.

He was sitting in a chair and holding his chest where blood was still escaping. He was small with a wiry build. Through his sparse beard you could see that he had a weak jaw. He wore a jeans jacket and denim pants too. His T-shirt had been white before the bleeding started. His shoes were brown with eyes but no laces.

"They shot me," the man said.

"Dean and Merry?" I asked.

He nodded and winced.

"You Axel?" I asked him.

"Yeah. Who're you?"

"Friend of Domaque."

"I'm sorry 'bout him. It was just the money was all. The money they said we could get. I shouldn'ta done it. Shouldn'ta."

Axel coughed and dribbled blood down into his beard.

"You better save your breath," I said.

"Help me."

"You got a phone?"

"They pult it outta the wall."

"Why'd they shoot you?" I asked.

"So to keep the money and be sure I didn't tell."

"You told them about Domaque?"

"I'm sorry about that. I really am."

I looked around for something to use to stop Axel's bleeding. His home was just one big room, messy, unadorned, and pretty bare. There was a white-enameled wood stove in one corner and a bed in another. Next to the bed was a pile of clothing that he probably chose from now and then when he needed to change. I took out two long-sleeved shirts and shredded them to make a bandage that I could tie around his chest.

"What are you doin' here, Mister?" Axel asked while I worked on his wound.

It wasn't bleeding much. The hole, below his right nipple, was even and pretty small.

"Tryin' to find Merry and Dean. They framed Dom and Dom's my friend."

"They're in L.A.," the old man said. "Spendin' my money and laughin' at us fools."

"Where exactly?"

"He's a surfer. Likes the water. So they're down near the ocean somewhere, that's for sure."

"Did they live around here?"

"In a trailer on Bibi Wyler Road. Bibi Wyler Road," he said again. Then he coughed up a great deal of blood and died.

I WENT BACK DOWN to the Esso station and called the cops, then I got a map and made my way to Bibi Wyler Road.

There was only one trailer on the three-block street. It was abandoned. There were clothes strewn around but no mail or written material of any kind. In one pants pocket I found an empty billfold with a photograph folded into the "secret compartment." It was of a blond girl with a sharp smile standing arm in arm with a brutish-looking man whose black hair went down to the collar of his shirt.

I considered asking the neighbors about the occupants of the trailer but then I decided that the fewer people who saw me the better. After all, there had already been three murders in Santa Maria and the only suspect was a black man.

I GOT HOME in the late afternoon and played with my children. Bonnie watched me from the back door. I think she was worried but she didn't say anything.

That night I dreamed about fishing in the ocean with Domaque and Raymond. We were in Jesus's boat far out on the ocean. Mouse was catching one fish after the other, reeling them in to Domaque's squeals of delight. I had my line in the water with bait on the hook but no fish nibbled or bit.

"Don't worry, Easy," Mouse said to me. "As long as you got friends you can eat."

Those words soothed me and I clambered down into the bottom of the boat and slept on a rocking sea of deep silence.

✽   ✽   ✽

"GOOD MORNING, MR. RAWLINS," Ada Masters greeted. It was the next day and we were in the main hall of Sojourner Truth junior high school.

It was 5:30 A.M.

"Good morning to you too but you know you shouldn't come to the school so early, Mrs. Masters," I said. "It's not safe for a woman alone."

I was one of the few people who could tell it like it was to our new principal. She liked me. I liked her too.

"I'm not worried, Mr. Rawlins. And this is my school. I like to walk around and see what it looks like before children come in. How are you?"

Somehow Mrs. Masters knew that I had been in a funk. Her pale blue eyes saw past my façades. The suit she was wearing cost more than most other women's wardrobes but you had to know something about clothes to tell that. We were perfect partners for the maintenance and care of the body and spirit of Truth.

"Doin' pretty good," I said. "Pretty good. If I don't fall off, the horse I'm on might make me a winner."

AFTER THE CUSTODIANS had left the maintenance office for their daily rounds, I pulled out the telephone and phone book. I made calls from eight o'clock until almost eleven. It was the thirty-second call that paid off.

"Why yes, Mr. Auburn," Herschel Godfried said. "There was an eight-chambered thirty-eight caliber pistol and it did have a bulblike handle. It was a Lux-Tiger design from about 1895, an English design. The only one I know of in southern California is owned by Grant West in Pomona."

Mr. West had sold the pistol in question to Harold Stout, a businessman who lived in Beverly Hills.

I left work at 1:45 and made it to Stout's address by nine to two.

It was a large house on Doheny, only about two-and-a-half miles from my home.

He might have lived within walking distance from me but Stout was rich. I could tell by the pink marble that made up his walls and the manicured lawn surrounded by dozens of different varieties of rosebushes. I could tell by the imported stained-glass windows and the ugly Rolls-Royce parked in the driveway. The front door was heavy oak, at least ten feet high and five wide.

The small woman who answered the door wore cotton pants the color of a rotten lemon and a pink-and-white polka-dot shirt. Her hair was strawlike in both color and texture. She looked like she belonged in a trailer park drinking lemonade laced with straight alcohol.

"Yes?" she asked.

"Jay Auburn looking for Harold Stout." If she had heard me over the phone she would have thought it was a white man speaking.

"Harry's very sick," she said. "He can't talk."

"I'm sorry," I said. "What's wrong with him?"

"Same thing's wrong with all men," the white woman said in a husky voice. "Thinkin' about a woman's butt and then wonderin' why they got shit for brains."

I laughed hard, not so much at her joke but at the shock of hearing such language from a white woman in those sedate surroundings.

"My name's Alice," the woman said. "You wanna come in, Jay?"

"Can't think of anything better," I said.

❖   ❖   ❖

THE ENTRANCE HALL had yellow stone floors lit by slender three-story windows, which also threw light on the curving, cream-colored staircase leading to the higher floors. To the left was a dining room with a table set for fifteen, and a maroon carpet. To the right was a sunken living room with yellow sofas, chairs, and carpeting.

Alice led me into the living room.

She offered me scotch but I demurred. She poured herself a shot. It wasn't the first one she'd had that afternoon. She asked if I had a cigarette. I gave her a Chesterfield and lit it. She steadied my hand with her fingers. Her hands were large and powerful, callused and misshapen by a life of hard work or hard time.

"I knew a girl got lynched just for touchin' a nigger," she said after her first lungful of smoke. "Selena was her name. The boy was Richard Kylie. You know, they had known each other since they were babies. They wanted each other all the more since it was a crime. She told me about their first kiss. Said it was so sweet it was like drinkin' water from Jesus' own hand. Said that all he had to do was kiss her neck and she'd shout out for the Lord."

"I wish you would keep from saying the word 'nigger,'" I said. "It hampers conversation."

"It bothers you?" She sounded surprised. "It's just a word back where I come from. I'm a cracker, you're a nigger, Pablo's a beaner, and Chin's a chink. But okay. I don't have to use the word, though."

I nodded, thanking her for the restraint.

"Richard fucked Selena every day for six weeks," Alice said, continuing with her story. "Every time she told me about it she was more upset. At first she was just playin'. It was taboo and sweet to her evil side. But sometimes her and Richard would steal away for a whole day. She'd say she was in school and he pretended to be lookin' for a job down Minorville. You know, Jay, when a man make a woman feel like she turn inside-out, she cain't help but be in love with him—nigger or not. Oh, excuse me."

I took a breath. Alice was missing an upper front tooth but other than that she started looking good. Forty maybe. She had a tight body in her button-up cotton blouse and her yellow pants. I was almost glad for the insults; they meant that I would never let my guard down for the sex-crazed southern woman.

"I need to know something about Mr. Stout's gun collection," I said.

"Shoot," she said, and then she laughed, realizing the pun.

"Did he have a Lux-Tiger?"

"A what?"

"It's an English pistol," I said. "A thirty-eight. Holds eight cartridges and has a handle looks like a rubber squeeze pump."

"Oh yeah," Alice said. "You know, Jay, you could fuck me right here on this couch and Harry wouldn't even hear it."

"What if he came downstairs to go to the toilet?"

"He don't go nowhere without me helpin' him."

"I see. Well, maybe in a little while. You see, I need to know about that pistol first."

"What for?"

"It showed up at a friend's house and I was wondering if it was stolen."

"It sure was," Alice declared. She had a wide mouth and healthy teeth except for the missing one. That made me think that someone had socked her, at least once.

"What happened to it?"

"That girl took it. That whore." She winked at me even though her words were angry.

"Who was that?"

"Doreen Fitz. Little whore drove Harry out of his mind. She had a boyfriend come up here and beat the shit outta Harry. That's partly why he's laid up now. They took all kinds of stuff from him. Rings and money and that old pistol. Harry loved that gun. He liked that it was so fat but hardly had no kick."

"Are you Harry's wife?" I asked.

"No. Just his cousin from Arkansas. Just his cousin come to make her fortune by pickin' his bones. You could share some of it with me if you want."

"You're stealing from him?"

"Have you ever seen a sharecropper's farm, Jay?"

"Yes, ma'am," I said.

I thought about all of the poor black and white people I'd seen straining over hard dirt, going deeper into debt with each passing season. I saw all that pain in her callused hands.

"You wanna go up and see Harry?" she asked.

IT WAS A BRIGHT BEDROOM with a picture window that allowed strong sun to beat down upon the occupant. He was a tall man but slender as a child. Even though he was under the sheet you could see the outline of his skeleton. His eyes were intelligent and the only part of him that moved. When he saw me a worried look crossed those eyes.

"Hey, Harry," Alice said. "I brought a nigger up to look at ya. I fucked him on your couch. He nearly broke me in two."

"Mr. Stout, my name is Jay Auburn. I'm looking for the people who stole your Lux-Tiger. Alice is just joking with you. She has some sense of humor."

Stout was looking deeply into my eyes, pleading with me.

"Did Doreen Fitz take your pistol?"

With a supreme effort Harry Stout nodded.

"She had a boyfriend named Dean?"

Again he made his head move.

"Do you think that they might still be around?"

He didn't nod that time but it might have been because he was exhausted.

Alice took a drag on her cigarette and coughed.

I went to the window and pulled the drapes closed.

"Hey," Alice complained. "He needs a little color."

"Keep the drapes closed and take care of him like you're supposed to," I said. "Do that or your free ride'll be over."

"What the hell do you mean?"

"I'm a cop," I said. "Looking into a murder right now but I'm calling social services the minute I get back to the precinct."

"You can't come in here without telling me you're a cop. That's against the law."

"Sue me," I said. "Tomorrow morning a social services agent, Saul Lynx, will be here. You better either be taking care of this man or be on your way."

THERE WAS ONLY ONE D. Fitz in the phone book. The number had been disconnected. But I went over to the house anyway. The address was on South Robertson, the left half of a two-family home composed of salmon stucco.

There was a concave entranceway with the doors to both apartments facing each other. I knocked on the D. Fitz number I got from the phone book.

An old woman came to the door.

"Oh," she said instead of a greeting.

"Miss Fitz?"

"Who?" she asked instead of replying.

"I'm looking for a Doreen Fitz."

"No," she said. "Not me."

"She moved out," a man's voice said from behind me.

I turned to see a tall and elderly white man. He had kind eyes and stooped a bit but still he had the posture of a soldier. His smile was mild. It wasn't joyous or even happy. The expression was more relief than anything else. Remembering him in the narrow doorway he seemed like he was in a coffin, made up for death.

The door behind me slammed.

"You know Doreen?" I asked.

"Why, yes I do. I tried to help her out when I could."

"World War One?" I asked him.

"Yes sir," he replied.

MR. PALMER—that was the veteran's name—invited me in for coffee. He led me through a living room that was twice the size of a dressing room at the May Company department store, through a transitional space that was so small that it could have no name or purpose, and into a small kitchen that was connected to a screened-in porch.

The porch had two redwood chairs and looked into the boughs of a tall magnolia. It was cool out there and I relaxed.

". . . wasn't a bad girl really," he was saying about Doreen.

We had been out there for an hour or more. Every once in a while the little white woman from the other apartment would come out onto her little porch to see if I was still there.

Palmer told me about the war and the trenches, about the mustard gas and wild dogs that fed on soldiers who had fallen alone. He had three children, two dead wives, and had come out to California after the war because the war had taken too many friends from his small Iowa town.

I told him about my leaving the South for pretty much the same reasons, except that most of my friends had died in Houston rather than on the battlefield.

It was a nice talk. He was the perfect host; a lonely old man who didn't worry about race or wildness in girls. I guided him into a discussion about Doreen, telling him that I had a friend who knew her in Santa Maria and who worried that she might have been in trouble because of a guy named Dean.

"It was that Dean who got to her," Palmer agreed. "He was handsome and drove a motorcycle. Girls like that. They think they want a wild man until they drop their first kid. Then it's fuddy-duddies like you'n me they want, Mr. Auburn."

I liked being called a fuddy-duddy.

"My friend wanted me to drop by and see if Doreen had moved back here," I said.

"No," Mr. Palmer said. "She never came back. But I send her mail on to an address down in Venice. I think it's Dean's brother. Here, I'll get it for you."

The veteran weighed no more than a hundred and ten pounds but he had to use all of his strength and a lot of leverage to get up and out of his chair. While he was gone the old lady next door spied on me from her kitchen window.

I felt that I deserved her distrust. There I was lying to the friendly old man. If it wasn't for Domaque and my blood debt to Mouse I would have left then.

"It's a place down in Venice," Palmer said when he returned. "I drove her down there once before the state took my license. They say I can't see well enough. Anyway, it's a small place not far from the water. But his brother isn't a friendly fellow. I wouldn't go there alone if I were you, Mr. Auburn. If you know what I mean."

It was his only reference to race. Even then he might have meant I'd have trouble because of my fuddy-duddy status.

I had an extra cup of coffee and swapped a few war stories. He walked me to the door as evening came on.

"Come back and see me again sometime, Jay," Mr. Palmer said as I left. "It's nice to talk to somebody smart now and then."

I DROVE DOWN TO THE ADDRESS Mr. Palmer gave me. It was on a small street a mile or so south of Pico. The house was smaller than the gaping garage, and the lawn was covered with rusting cars and motorcycle parts. I saw three men and one white-blond girl sitting on a bench, drinking whiskey from a quart bottle. One of the men and the girl had been in the photograph I took from the Santa Maria trailer.

The men were a rough-looking lot. They had long greasy hair that came down past where their collars would have been if they wore proper shirts. But they wore T-shirts and leather jackets, dirty jeans and heavy boots.

I drove by quickly and then headed back toward Compton.

I MULLED OVER THE PROBLEM of Dean's brother's place all the way. Mr. Palmer was probably right about me walking up there alone. Even in a gesture of friendship those men would have probably shown me the door—with a tire iron. And I didn't want Doreen or Dean to know I was looking into them, not until I had a plan.

I needed backup but there was only one man I knew who could take that ride. And it scared me to death even to consider his help.

ETTA ANSWERED THE DOOR when I got there. Her eyes turned to stone when she saw me through the screen.

"How did you find us?" she asked in a whisper.

"Why'd you lie to me, Etta?" I replied.

"Who is it?" Mouse called from somewhere in the house.

"Nobody," Etta said.

"It's me," I said, raising my voice.

"Come on in, Easy," Mouse said.

Etta stared death at me a moment more and then stepped aside.

Raymond was sitting at the dining table playing solitaire, dressed in a soft gray shirt and dark gray pants. These colors made his gray eyes spark like fire.

Etta moved to a corner and stared at me like Feather's little yellow dog does sometimes.

"Don't be gettin' all mad, Etta," Mouse said. "I told Easy I was here. You know we gonna need him if we want Dom to get out from under that police investigation."

Etta turned on her heel and strode from the room. We could hear her slamming pots and pans around in the kitchen.

"What you know, Easy?" Mouse asked.

"Too much," I said.

"It's them books, brother. Readin' ain't all that good, you know. It softens up your brain."

"We can't kill 'em, Ray."

His teeth were smiling but he was staring gray-eyed death.

"Really, man," I said. "If you kill 'em then Dom will go down for the murder."

"Okay, baby. I got ya. No killin' 'cause it's for Dom. Okay."

"I need an out-of-town car," I said. "That and the money bag."

"We could keep the money, though," Mouse said. "Right?"

"Most of it. Hopefully they got more money at the house."

"What house?"

"Down in Venice."

Mouse grinned again. "You're good, Easy. Damn good."

WE PICKED UP A CAR from a friend of Raymond's. It was a purple Chrysler, from San Diego we were told. We headed out for Venice at about nine-fifteen. On the way we decided that Mouse should approach the family, to make sure that Dean and Doreen were there. I tried to think of something better. Putting Mouse in the face of the enemy more often than not ended up in a war. But I made him promise that he'd keep his gun in his belt loop and his knife in his pocket. That didn't mean much, though. Mouse had killed people with his hands, feet, and once with his teeth.

I waited down the block while he approached them with the promise of good weed that he could procure. He was gone over an hour and a half.

I sat in the car worried that the men got suspicious and overpowered my friend. If he died this time there'd be no solace for me. I was just about ready to take the eight-chambered .38 and rush the houseful of long-haired white men.

But then Mouse strolled up.

He was singing a song. "Feelin' Good."

Once next to me again I could see that he was pretty high.

"Damn, Easy. If them boys wasn't all up against Dom I'd like 'em pretty good. You know I offered 'em my weed but they had golden hash. Damn. Wow. That shit twist up your mind."

"Dean and Doreen there?" I asked.

"Sure is. Both of 'em. But they headed out to Canada tomorrow morning. Leavin' the country—'just in case,' they said."

"Tomorrow?"

"Bright and early."

"Shit."

"What we gonna do, brother?" Mouse asked.

He was grinning, looking at his face in the rearview mirror.

"Wait here." I took out the Wells-Fargo bag and made it down the street.

I went into a driveway two houses down from the house of the motorcyclists and jumped over three fences. This brought me to a stand of fruitless banana trees that separated Dean's brother's house from his neighbors. There was loud rock and roll music playing from the open back door.

I took a deep breath and made my way across the cement patio and to an open window. Inside the window a balding man with a beard was kissing Doreen. It was a long, slow kiss. They were lying on a mattress on the floor, pressed up into a corner. The bald man put a hand up under her dress and she made a grunting sound that surprised me.

Then Dean came in.

"What the fuck," he said.

Doreen jumped up immediately. She was a little slow on her feet, though.

The balding man was laughing.

"Just a little kiss, Dean. That's all, man. You don't mind if your brother gets a little kiss from his future sister-in-law."

"Get the fuck in our room, Dorrie," Dean said.

"Oh come on, baby," she said. "It wasn't nuthin'."

I felt something brush against my ankle. When I looked down I expected to see a cat but instead it was a rat standing on its back legs, baring uneven yellow fangs.

I know I made some kind of sound but luckily Dean and his brother's cursing drowned it out.

They argued for a minute or more and then took it out of the room with Doreen trailing after.

I tossed the money bag into a corner and then ran for all I was worth.

Mouse was listening to the radio when I got there. He was lost in the soul of Otis Redding and I couldn't stop from breathing like a spent dog.

"WE COULD JUST CALL THE POLICE," I was saying. We were still parked down the block.

"Ain't LAPD's case," Mouse argued. "They ain't gonna come runnin' on a phone call. And even if they do come they'll stop at the front door and that'll be that. No, Easy. My way is the only way and you know it."

I finally agreed. Mouse was crazy and unread but he was smart in spite of that.

I DROVE DOWN THE STREET going about thirty. Mouse, who was sitting in the backseat, lowered his window. When we got in front of the bikers' house, he opened fire with his cannon-like .41. He shot all six chambers and reloaded with amazing precision while I made a U-turn at the end of the block. He opened fire again on our return route. On our third pass a man was standing out in front of the house holding a rifle or maybe a shotgun.

"Don't kill him, Raymond!" I shouted as my friend opened fire.

The rifleman fired too, blowing out the rear window.

"I hit him!" Mouse declared. "In the leg, Easy. In the leg."

The next time we went down the block the man was crawling toward the house. Gunfire flared from the windows and our stolen Chrysler was hit with a few slugs.

I threw a bundle of money onto the lawn.

Mouse was laughing.

"One more time," he said.

"No," I told him. "If that don't do it then nuthin' will."

I DROVE SEVENTEEN blocks north to the nearly vacant parking lot of a Safeway supermarket. We left the wounded Chrysler there and went on foot to my car, which was four blocks farther on.

Then we came to the hard part.

I drove back down to Venice, to the street where we had played cowboys and Indians. The police were there arresting the occupants of the house. I saw them put Doreen into the back of a squad car.

". . . THERE WAS A VIOLENT shootout in Venice last night," the radio announcer was saying at 5:15 the next morning. I was on my way to work. "When the police arrived at the scene they discovered a bundle of cash in a Wells-Fargo wrapper. Inside the house police found a number of unregistered handguns and more evidence from the armored car robbery that occurred in Santa Maria last week. Arrested were Anthony Gleason, who was wounded in the shootout, Mickey Lannerman, Doreen Fitz, and Arnold Wilson. A fifth suspect, Dean Lannerman, is believed to have fled the scene on foot. Police sources have informed us that the escaped Lannerman and Miss Fitz are now prime suspects in the armored car robbery. Lannerman is considered armed and dangerous . . ."

The announcer went on to explain that the weapon that might have been used in the robbery-murder was also found at the scene. There was also some speculation that Lannerman and Fitz might have had something to do with the murder of an associate of theirs, a man named Myermann.

I made a U-turn in the middle of Central Avenue headed for Santa Barbara.

I stopped to call EttaMae's number. Luckily she answered.

"What you want, Easy?"

"I need Mama Jo's number."

"She ain't got no phone."

"Then I need her address."

"Why?"

"I think somethin' me and Raymond did might come back on her. I need to get there fast, Etta."

"You want me to get Raymond up? He knows the way."

"I got a map. I'll find my own way."

She hesitated and then gave me what I needed.

I drove along the Pacific Coast Highway part of the way, then followed the map to a dirt road that led up into a forest of pine.

Walking down toward the house I was brought back to an earlier time, a time in the swamplands of eastern Texas. The trees, the smell of soil, insects buzzing around my head, even the fever I'd felt in the primeval wood returned.

The two-story house was rustic. Made from wood and stone, brick and plaster. There were large patches of chicken wire and tarpaper where the more costly materials had crumbled and failed.

The front door was ajar.

I picked up a stone and pushed the door open.

The room I entered was just like the one I had seen twenty-five years before. Shelves along the walls were filled with bottles and jars containing powders, leaves, twigs, and crystals. There was the same rough-hewn table and chairs.

There was even a fireplace with the same skulls—five or six armadillos and one human, Domaque Sr.

"Easy," she whispered from behind a drawn curtain.

I jumped nearly across the room.

"What's wrong?" the curtains opened and Jo walked out.

She didn't look a day older, except maybe around the eyes. Black skin and dark hair with some silver showing here and there. She stood erect, an inch taller than I. She was wearing a coral-colored robe drawn tight around her shoulders.

"We gotta get outta here, Jo," I said.

"Sit down, honey," she said. "Let me make you some tea calm your nerves."

"We got to go," I said again.

"Why?" She smiled. Her teeth were the color of aged ivory. They were big and somehow frightening.

"The man who robbed that armored car and blamed it on Dom was found by the police," I said. "But he got away. We framed him with the same bag he tried to frame Dom with. He might be comin' here."

"Oh?" she said. "Then go on and sit, baby. I done thrown the bones on that one and the girl. They ain't gonna mess around me. Go on—sit."

I did as she said.

She made a pot of tea from her leaves and twigs. She served mine in a wooden mug.

The table was clear except for a worn black velvet bag.

"That's my chicken bones," she said. "That's how I divine the future."

From the first sip I was a little light-headed.

"Really?" I said.

"Uh-huh. You want me to read your future?"

"No thanks." I took a second sip and settled back into the chair. I was still thinking about Dean Lannerman but for some reason I wasn't concerned.

"I know what you mean, honey," Jo said. "Men like you is better off not knowin'. Otherwise you might second-guess what you doin' and get all worried when they ain't nuthin' you could do."

"Yeah," I said. I grinned too.

"Old Domaque was like that," she said waving her hand at the skull covered in dried skin on the mantel. "He died for love of me and my father. He refused to fight and died thinkin' that if he killed my father he would have broke my heart."

"He must have been a great man," someone speculated. That someone was probably me.

"Drink up, baby," Jo said.

I did so. The world around me got sparkly and soft. Jo's deep voice droned on. Some kind of music was playing. It was music that I had listened to years before on scratchy phonographs down in Texas when I was a child. I don't know if the music came out of my memories or if Jo was playing something on an old player.

"You never did nuthin' wrong to Raymond, baby," she was saying. "And you saved Dom for me. Don't you ever worry about what you do, Easy. You are the kinda man who stands up for who he is. You come here because you know what's right. You might not always make it in time but you always on the way. That's all we can ask for, darling child."

I fell asleep to the deep crooning tones of Mama Jo's speech. I felt as if I were being lifted up by a hundred black hands, that I was being carried up the side of a mountain while a thousand women sang. There were drums and trumpets playing. And I was walking down the center of Central Avenue with ten thousand people behind me. We were all walking together toward some unknown destiny.

I came to a door that had my name on it. Then I took a deep breath and trundled off into a deep sleep.

WHEN I WOKE UP I knew it was night. I was in bed and dressed only in my pants. There were voices coming from beyond the curtains. I came out feeling deeply refreshed. Dom and Mouse were sitting with Jo at the country table, eating from tin plates.

"You sleep good, baby?" Jo asked me.

Just that little bit of concern made me want to cry.

"What happened to Dean?" I asked.

"Dead," Mouse said.

"Dead," echoed Dom.

"How?"

"They had a roadblock waitin' for him down on the highway. They knew him around here and spotted him on the road."

"He was comin' for Jo," I said.

"But he was ordained to die on the asphalt," Jo said.

I wondered if her chicken bones had been so specific but I didn't ask.

"Wanna go fishin', Easy?" Dom asked.

"In the mornin'?"

"Now," he cried. "The grunion's runnin'."

I STOPPED AT a phone booth and called Bonnie. She seemed to understand, which surprised me because I was still in the haze of Jo's potion.

"I dreamed I had a door," I said into the receiver.

"It was telling you something," Bonnie said. "Something that you need to know."

*   *   *

AFTER THAT RAYMOND AND DOM and I ran up and down
the beach with our aluminum pails scooping up the spawning
fish and laughing out loud. We were like children in the dark
of the ocean. No one knew we were there. No one cared about
us and that was just fine by me.

AMBER GATE

THERE WAS A SMALL shoe repair shop at 86th Place and Central Avenue back in those days. But Mr. Steinman, the owner and only employee, also made shoes. And if Steinman made you a pair of shoes you'd have to work in a junkyard in order to wear them down. It took him three months to finish just one pair. He charged two hundred dollars but that was cheap for the craftsmanship and style. And he didn't make shoes for just anyone. No. He had to know his customer before agreeing to spend a quarter of a year on a pair of shoes for him. He had to work on your footwear and see how you cared for what you bought in the stores. You had to prove that you would maintain the shine and use a frame to keep up the shape. You couldn't have scuff marks or uneven heel wear from poor posture if you wanted to wear a pair of handcrafted Steinman's.

He was an odd little white man but I liked him quite a bit. And he must have liked me because he had left a message that he'd just finished my third pair of handmade shoes.

When I opened the front door, a small bell tinkled and there was a rustling behind the wall of hanging shoes that stood between Steinman's workroom and the front. The front room was less than three feet deep and just about eight feet across.

There was no chair for waiting because, as Steinman once told me, "I never hurry at my work, Mr. Rawlins. If they want speed, let them buy cardboard soles from Drixor's department store."

We probably didn't have one drop of blood in common but we were cut from the same cloth still and all.

"Mr. Rawlins," Steinman said. He stood in the small opening that led to his workshop.

"Good morning, Mr. Steinman."

We had given each other permission to use first names years before but courtesy kept us proper except at odd, more intimate moments.

"Come on in, in back."

I followed the little cobbler into his workshop, knowing that I was one of only four or five people who were ever given that privilege.

The back room was composed of endless shelves cluttered with pairs of shoes tied together by their laces and marked with yellow tailor's chalk. Women's shoes were held together by string.

"Sit, sit," Steinman said. "I wanted to talk to you. Can I get you something to drink? I have schnapps."

This was unusual even for our cordial relations. Often I sat for a half hour or more and talked to Theodore. I had been part of an invading army that subdued his homeland—Germany. But Steinman had come to America as a child in 1910 and had no patriotism for the Third Reich or its war on the rest of the world. We talked about cities and streets that I'd seen.

"My mother always told me that Germany is one of the most beautiful countries in the world," he often said.

I didn't really agree with her but I always nodded and said, "It sure is."

But he'd never offered me a drink before. If he had, he would have known that I'd stopped drinking soon after my first wife left me.

"No thanks, Mr. Steinman. It's a little early for me."

"Yes. Yes. It is early."

"How are you, Theodore?" I asked, sensing that we weren't conducting simple shoe business.

"Yes," he said, nodding his large bald head. "For me things are fine. I have a good business. My children are doing very well. I have three grandchildren now."

"That's great," I said. I was in no hurry to get to the point. If I had an office, I thought, I wouldn't have had a waiting room either.

"But some people are not so lucky."

"Who for instance?" I asked.

"Mr. Tanous."

I'd never heard that name before and my expression said so.

"He's the man who owns this building," Theodore Steinman said. "The whole block really. He's a nice man. A good man."

"But he's got trouble?"

"Yes. Yes. The police found her in the alley behind this building and they took him right off to jail. Right off. They had no proof but still they took him just like Nazis."

"Who did they find?"

"Jackie Jay, that's what they called her. She was a . . . a loose woman I think you say. She made her living being with men. But then somebody killed her."

"And the police think it was Mr. Tanous?"

The little shoemaker nodded. He had broad shoulders and

thick hands. For all that he was a small man, Theodore Steinman was a powerhouse. It was sad to see him so defeated over his friend's arrest.

"You don't think he did it?"

"No. Definitely not. Musa would never commit such a crime. He is a peaceful man no matter how angry he gets. How else could he run a building this size with all the trouble some people can be?"

"So why do the cops think he did it?"

"Because he is not a white man."

"He's Negro?" I asked, surprised. I thought I knew every black property owner in the neighborhood.

"I don't know where he's from. Somewhere from the Mediterranean, maybe from North Africa. Maybe even Iran, he never really said."

Steinman clasped his hands and stared at the floor. I rubbed my fingers together and considered. A pair of shoes was not worth me getting involved with a murder, but Theodore had given me much more than that. He had always offered me friendship without prejudice.

My weakness had always been the offer of equality.

"This Mr. Tanous in jail?"

"No. He put up five thousand dollars for bail and is waiting for a trial."

"Did he know this Jackie Jay?"

"Most people around here knew her. When she was a little girl she used to come into my store with her father and brother. He father, Robert, would bring me his shoes to fix."

"So why are you telling me all this?"

"They say that you know what goes on in this neighborhood. Maybe you could ask around. Maybe somebody would tell you something that might help Musa."

"You know I probably can't do anything," I said.

"But you will try?"

I hesitated a moment.

"I can't pay you, Ezekiel," he said. "But I can promise you that whenever you need a pair of shoes I will make them. And these," he picked up a package of brown wrapping paper and held it out to me, "these are free."

The time to turn down the job was then, before I laid hands on the package. I should have taken out my wallet and insisted on paying. But that would have insulted my friend and I was raised better than that.

"Your friend might have to pay a little something too," I said.

"He is a rich man," Theodore said.

THEODORE LOCKED HIS FRONT DOOR and put up his CLOSED sign. Then he guided me through the back of his workshop into a long, lime-colored-plaster hallway. The dim corridor led to a stairway lit by small windows at the elbow of each half-flight up. The stairs were well maintained and the window panes were clean. There was no dust in the corners or crevices. I was beginning to like Musa Tanous even before we met.

On the fourth floor we entered another mild-green passageway. This hall was filled with light because there were windows at either end. It was a wide corridor lined with maple doors that were sealed with bright tawny varnish. Theodore led me to the last door on the left side. My heart skipped when we came to that amber gate. I don't know why. There was no sign on it. It was just a door but somehow it seemed perfect. The hinges were brass and the bottom panel was flush to the floor. I imagined that it was hung just right and would open with hardly a squeak.

From inside the room a man's voice rose. There was worry, maybe even fear in his tone.

"Musa," Theodore whispered.

I reached for the brass knob and turned.

The door was noiseless and that's probably what saved me from a slash wound or worse.

It was a good size for an office, rectangular in shape with the long wall leading toward the windows to the street. There was no furniture except for one pine chair. The two men facing each other did not notice the well-oiled door opening. One man was tall and black and powerful, holding a nine-inch butcher's knife. I would have thought the other one was Mexican if I wasn't ready to meet a man named Musa.

The black man felt the draft maybe two seconds after I opened the door. While he turned toward me I threw the shoes, hitting him in the temple. Then I grabbed the chair and tossed it lightly, just enough to block any stabbing he might have been contemplating. I kicked him in the knee and hit him on the jaw with four blows before picking the knife up off the floor. It wasn't a move from any rule book but real fights never are.

The black man, who had a boy's face, fell against the wall but no further. When he saw me with the knife he rolled away and lurched through the door. He pushed Theodore down. I could hear his heavy steps all the way down the stairs we'd taken.

I helped the cobbler up and then turned to the other man in the office.

"Mr. Tanous?"

"Who are you?" he asked in an accent that I couldn't place.

He was looking at the knife in my hand. Maybe he thought I stopped his attacker so that I could kill him myself.

"He is my friend, Musa," Theodore said. "The one I told you about."

"Easy Rawlins," I put in.

I walked past Tanous and went to one of the three large windows that looked out on the street. Central was bustling by then. There was a hardware store, a stationery shop, a grocery store, and a liquor store all squashed together across the street. I put the knife down on the window sill and smiled at the waxed pine floor.

If it wasn't for the obvious threat to Theodore's friend I would have spent a good deal of time appreciating the simple room. The dark wood trim and the antique white walls seemed almost regal.

Instead I turned and asked, "Who was that man I just beat on?"

"He thinks I killed his sister," Musa said. His voice was hollow, removed.

"Mr. Rawlins knows many people around here," Theodore was saying. "People talk to him. Maybe he can find out what happened to Jackie."

"Are you a detective?" Musa Tanous asked me.

"No. I'm just a guy who trades in favors, that's all. And I know folks all over the neighborhood, like Theodore says. The kind of people who would know the habits of a girl like he told me about."

"But you don't have some kind of certification, a license?"

Musa Tanous was slender and very well dressed. His silver-hued suit might have been made from silk. I could tell that it wasn't an American cut because there was only one button. It was a European design probably made in some eastern country. Tanous had a trim mustache and manicured fingers. He was as neat as his office building. There was a heavy and sweet odor mixed in with the sweat of fear coming off him.

"Did that guy with the knife have a license?" I asked.

"What does that mean?"

"It means that the government doesn't regulate the action down here. I would expect that you'd know that, bein' in business and all."

"I don't understand," he said. "I didn't do anything. Why are people mad at me?"

"The kid with the knife have a name?" I asked.

"Trevor McKenzie. I told you he's Jackie's brother."

"Jackie Jay?"

Musa looked over at Theodore. The smaller man nodded.

"Yes," Musa said. "She did not use her last name."

"And what was he doing here?"

"He said that he was going to kill me for what I did to his sister."

"Did you kill her?"

A passionate anger rose in Musa's eyes.

"Listen, man," I said, heading off his tirade. "The cops think you did it. Her brother thinks you did it. That's not proof but it means something."

Emotions passed across the man's face like colors in a kaleidoscope.

He was struggling to get something out. I let this go on a

moment and then I said, "We need to sit down if we want to have a conversation. You got a room with two chairs?"

"My office," Musa said, literally choking on the words.

"Does Trevor know where that is?"

"Yes, but . . ."

"Where do you live, Mr. Tanous?"

"Pacific Palisades."

For some reason that made me smile.

"Hey," I said. "Why don't we go there?"

"We could go to my apartment," Theodore suggested. "I live closer—on Grand."

THEODORE GAVE US the address and we each made our own way. That was L.A. Every man had the right of life, liberty, and the freedom to drive alone.

The building Theodore Steinman lived in was ugly, eight stories high, and constructed from brown brick. His apartment was on the top floor. We got there in an elevator made for three.

The front door opened into a sitting room that was quite spacious. All the windows were open. There were four extra-wide chairs surrounding a glass-top coffee table and a potted fern in the corner.

"Sit," Theodore said, and then he called, "Sylvie."

On cue a woman entered through a small doorway. She was taller than the cobbler but by no means tall. She had white skin, white hair, blue eyes, and wore a dress that was four shades of gray. She was thin, happy to see us, and wordless.

"Mr. Rawlins," Theodore said, introducing me.

Her mouth moved and she smiled but no words were spoken or necessary. She touched my hand and nodded.

"Pleased to meet you," I whispered in return.

"You know Musa," Theodore continued.

Sylvie smiled for the landlord but it was a bit chillier than my greeting.

"Can I get you anything?" Theodore asked us. "Tea, schnapps?"

"Just let us talk for a few minutes," I said. "Then we can get outta your hair."

When Sylvie turned to leave I felt that she was dancing to some music I couldn't hear.

"I'll be right through that door if you need me," Theodore said. "Just call."

He went with his wife: the hard-working dwarf following his elfin dream.

"THANK YOU FOR HELPING ME back at the office, Mr. Rawlins," Musa said. "I don't think he would have really hurt me but you didn't know that."

"Imagine how many people come up to the Pearly Gates," I replied, "shaking there heads and sayin', 'I never thought he'd really do it.'"

Musa smiled and we moved to the coffee table.

I sat first and the maybe–Middle Eastern man sat directly across from me. He leaned back in his chair and concentrated on his left hand.

This tactic amused me. Usually when a man's in trouble his defenses break down. He sits next to you and then leans forward, he looks you in the eye. But Musa Tanous leaned back, downplaying the deadly game he was involved in.

"Why did you drive over here, Mr. Tanous?" I asked at last.

"Because Theodore seems to think that you could do something for me."

"You don't?"

"You aren't a licensed detective. You don't know the people involved. How can you help me?"

"I can't if you don't want me to," I said.

"And if I said I wanted you to help then something would be different?"

"No."

"I don't understand."

"I'm here because of Theodore too," I said. "He asked me to see what I could do and I intend to try. But if you don't open up and admit you got trouble, I have no way in."

Musa Tanous sat up and then leaned toward me, maybe an inch.

"What do you charge?"

"Did you kill Jackie Jay?"

The elegant man stood up. He didn't step away or even turn his head. It was a threat of dismissal but nothing more.

"Sit down, Mr. Tanous."

"I don't intend to stay here and take insults from you."

"I'm not insulting you. People out there seem to think you did kill her, and I have to hear from your own lips that you didn't before I can tell you what it will cost to get you off the hook."

He hung his head and sat down again.

"No," he said.

"No what?"

"I did not kill her."

"Do you know who did?"

"No."

"How did the cops convince the prosecutor to charge you?"

For the first time sadness showed in his eyes. He looked at the Steinmans' sheer curtains undulating on the breezes.

"Jackie and I went to the Dinah Motel the night before the morning she was found. We stayed there together and in the morning I went off to work," he said. "She stayed in bed. Jackie liked to sleep late. The last time I saw her she was, she was sleeping."

"What time was that?"

"Close to five."

"Early."

"I like to have the whole building checked over before people come in. That way I know what needs to be done."

I liked that answer. It was how I worked.

"How'd you meet Jackie?"

"Trevor worked for me. He did cleaning and some fixing but then he stole from one of my tenants. He took a turntable and a pair of speakers from room C-fifteen and tried to sell it to Mr. Dodson, who owns the hardware store across the street. I went over to his house, to speak to his mother. I told her that I would call the police if I did not get the things he stole or the money they were worth."

"And did she pay you?"

"A week later Jackie came to my office with the money." Musa's lips began to quaver, his hands were unsteady. "When I opened the door she came right in and looked me in the eyes. She said that she had my money. She was so beautiful. I asked her to come in. I have a little couch in my office, Mr. Rawlins. A chaise lounge. Instead of going to a chair she went right to the chaise lounge and patted a place next to her." Musa patted the arm of his chair to show me. "We were kissing before three more words. I loved her."

"Did she give you the money?"

"I bought her a new dress and shoes with it. Then we drove to San Diego and went to the zoo." Tears welled in his eyes. "She taught me how to dance."

He certainly loved her enough to kill her.

"How long this go on?"

"Months," he said. "Three . . . no, four months."

"Love at first sight."

He smiled at me and shook his head.

"My wife left me. She took the children but I didn't care. Even now that Jackie's dead I don't regret. Have you ever loved like that, Mr. Rawlins?"

It sounded more like a contest than a profession of love.

"No," I said. "Cain't say that I have."

We were both silent there for a while. It was a pleasant day. I thought about my good friend Raymond Alexander. When I believed he was dead I was as distraught as the man before me.

"What happened to her?" I asked.

"Somebody had beat her. . . . They found her in the alley, behind my building."

"What was she doing there?"

"I don't know. She had the key. Maybe she was coming to surprise me."

Tremors shook Tanous's forearms and knees.

"Okay," I said. "I'll do it. I'll try and find out who killed her. But I warn you, man: I *will* find out who did it so it better not be you."

"You haven't told me your price."

"Who rents that office we found you in?"

"No one. It's been vacant for over a month. I was trying to do my work from there without anyone knowing. But Trevor found me somehow."

"If I find out who did it and get you off, you give me that office for twenty dollars a month for as long as that building is in your family," I said. "The rent stays the same, forever."

My demand amused him. He smiled for a moment and then nodded.

For my part I was surprised. I had no need for an office but somehow that room seemed as if it had been waiting for me. I wanted to go back there, sit in a chair, and look out of the window at the street.

"Where does Trevor live?" I asked.

He gave me the address. It wasn't far.

"And I'll need a picture of Jackie. Do you have one in your wallet?"

"No," he said. He seemed rather embarrassed. "I have some at home."

"Then let me have your address and telephone number. I'll call before I come by, probably tonight."

COX BAR WAS A DIVE in a back alley off of Hooper, not far from Steinman's Shoe Repair. I don't think the alley had a name. It had been paved at one time but most of the asphalt had worn away, leaving a rutted dirt path that ruined the alignment of any car that drove on it.

It was a boxlike structure tiled with tar paper flaps that had green-and-red pebbles pressed into them. The sign was a hand-painted flat board leaned up against the front wall.

I parked on the street and walked the hundred yards or so to the screen door. The room smelled of cigarettes, smoked sausage, and stale beer. At noon its only inhabitants were Ginny Wright and Raymond Alexander.

She was the girlfriend of the now-dead Tiny Cox and he was my best friend.

They sat across from each other in the gloom, under a dim light, playing blackjack. Ginny had sixty years, three hundred pounds, and one of the best memories I had ever encountered on her side. Mouse had what he called the "luck of the black man" on his.

"Easy," he had once told me, "you know a black man has to be luckier than any white guy you ever met."

"How you get that?" I asked.

"Well you know white men had it easy. They had jobs and guns and the western plains for them. All we had was chains and nooses and shit like that. For a white man's father's father to survive was nuthin'. But if one of our people lived it was only because of the best luck. Jackson Blue said it to me. He said that this scientist, Derwin I think, said that you got things from your ancestors through the blood. I got luck from mines."

That didn't explain why Mouse thought he was luckier than other black men, but I didn't question his beliefs because he was the luckiest man I had ever known.

"Twenty-one," Mouse shouted, slapping down a red queen. "Pay up Ginny. You owe me thirty-seven cents."

Ginny Cox was slow and deliberate, more than twice the size of Mouse. She looked at his cards and then looked at hers. Then she brought out a change purse and counted out her losses.

"Another game?" she asked then.

Women liked Mouse. It passed through my mind that she might have lost games often enough to keep Mouse around. Who knows? One drunken night she might just drag him off to bed.

"Not right now if you don't mind, Raymond," I said.

"Easy." Mouse turned to me and smiled, his gold-edged teeth glittering.

"I need your company, Ray."

"You gonna get me shot again?"

"I hope not," I said. "But you never know."

"Well if I could beat Ginny here then I must be on a streak. I might even be lucky enough to survive Easy Rawlins."

With those words he stood and walked out into the alley with me.

WE DROVE THE FEW BLOCKS over to Parmelee, Trevor McKenzie's street. On the way I told Mouse about the girl Jackie Jay and the friend of Theodore Steinman.

"Teddy's cool," Mouse said. "You know him and me go out barhoppin' sometimes."

"You do?"

"Oh yeah. Teddy like them bars with the girls got the naked titties hangin' out. He won't touch 'em though, not him. He wouldn't do that to Sylvie—"

"You know his wife too?" I was shocked. For some reason I didn't imagine Raymond with everyday people.

"Yeah, man," Raymond said. "One time I brought him a pair of rattlesnake boots that Poor Howard made."

Poor Howard was a Cajun who lived in the woods of southern Louisiana. I hadn't thought of him in years. He was a cobbler. All of his shoes were made from the things you could gather in the swamplands. From alligator hide to water moccasin skin, from opossum fur to cougar fleece—Poor Howard made it all.

"Where'd you get that?" I asked.

"Howard up around here nowadays, man. He killed a white boy slapped his woman and then made beeline for L.A."

"He's in town?"

"You know Howard," Mouse said. "He's somewhere. In the woods or down by the sea. Settin' traps and whatnot. Anyway when Theodore got a look at those snakeskin boots, he was my best friend from then on. I like the guy. Them Frenchmen are all right."

"He's not French," I said. "He's a German."

"Same thing," Mouse said with a shrug.

I would have argued further but we were at the McKenzie house.

I knocked while Mouse stood off to the side. After a moment or so a woman answered. She was small and blunt-looking, dark-skinned with eyes that never looked straight at anything.

"Yes sir?"

"Mrs. McKenzie?"

"Miss McKenzie."

"Is your son here, ma'am?"

"Who wants to see him?"

"Tell him that it's the man who hit him in the head earlier today. I came by to apologize and ask him a question."

Miss McKenzie's mouth came open showing no teeth and resembling a cornered Gila monster.

"Trevor?" she said, and the big young man appeared.

He had been standing off to the side just as Mouse was.

"What you want?" Trevor barked.

"I'm working on a job," I said. "Tryin' to prove that Jackie was killed by Musa Tanous."

"You lyin', man. You the one saved him from me."

"I'm the one saved you from the electric chair," I corrected, "just where my client wants to put Tanous."

Trevor squinted and moved his head around as if trying to hear some far-off sound.

"Nuh-uh, man," he said at last. "You hit me upside the head and took my knife."

Trevor pushed the door open, confident that round two would go in his favor. I took a pace backward and Ray took a sidle pace into view. Trevor noticed the periphery movement and swiveled his head.

"Hey, brother," Mouse hailed.

"Trevor," Miss McKenzie cried. "Stop it before you get in trouble."

She would have said those words anyway but I don't think Trevor would have stopped his onslaught if he wasn't worried about my friend.

Mouse had the aura of danger around him. The way he walked, talked, and smiled were all harbingers of violence.

When Miss McKenzie looked at him, her frown deepened. She turned to me and asked. "What you want here, mister?"

"My name is Easy Rawlins, ma'am, and I want prove that Musa Tanous killed your daughter." I said this with absolute certainty. And it was true. If I tried my best to prove Tanous's guilt then maybe I'd achieve the opposite.

"Get inside, Trevor," she said.

He obeyed her and she made room for me and Mouse.

✻   ✻   ✻

THE FRONT ROOM was just that—a room. It had no carpeting or decoration. There was a wooden bench and a couple of wood chairs. There was a stool. Mouse took that. We all sat, even Trevor.

"Who you workin' for?" Trevor asked.

"I can't tell you his name," I said. "He's a married man and he's afraid that his wife might find out. But he paid me to make sure that Jackie's killer gets convicted."

"Is it Durgen?" Trevor asked, "that white man own Trellson's?"

"No," I said quickly, as if avoiding the question. "Tell me what happened the day your sister was killed. Did you talk to her? Did Tanous call her?"

"She didn't stay around here much any more," Miss McKenzie said. "She has her own apartment and most of the time she was out cattin' around. You know men loved her and she loved them too. I tried to get her to stay here with me but she went her own way."

"Did she have lots of boyfriends?"

"What's that got to do with anything?" Trevor said belligerently.

Mouse grinned.

"What you grinnin' at, fool?" Trevor asked him.

"Don't listen to him, Mr. Alexander," Miss McKenzie said. "He too young to know respect."

Mouse shrugged generously.

"I need to know what she was doin' and who she knew," I said. "Because that way maybe I can put Jackie and Musa in the same place at the time she was killed."

"You ain't the police," Trevor said.

"And she's no white girl," I replied. "I hope you don't think the cops gonna work up a sweat over her killer. If Tanous got the money for a good lawyer then he's gonna walk."

"And I'll kill his ass."

"And spend the rest of your life behind bars, or maybe the court will be lenient and execute you."

This prospect seemed to confuse Trevor.

"Yes, Mr. Rawlins," Miss McKenzie said. "She knew a lotta men. She wasn't no prostitute now. Sometimes men helped her with her rent and she was out to dinner every night. But money never changed hands for gettin' in the bed."

"Did you know many of them?"

"Not a lot. Mr. Tanous was really the only one she stuck with. He was nice to all of us."

"He killed Jackie, mama. He killed her. How can you call that nice?"

"The Lord will take care of all that, boy. Yes he will."

Trevor jumped up from his wood chair and stormed out the front door.

After he was gone conversation became easier.

"Other than this Durgen, are there any other men that she might have known, Miss McKenzie?"

"She had started to see a man named Bob Henry. He's got a gas station on Alameda. And then there's Matthew Munson. He does taxes down here on Central."

"How old was Jackie?" I asked.

"She told everybody she was nineteen. She looked twenty-one but she was just seventeen, Mr. Rawlins. Just a girl." Miss McKenzie's eyes filled with tears. "When she moved out she took all of her dolls. And you know she was a good girl. She always said that she was going to buy me my own house in the country where I could have a garden and Trevor could have him a horse."

"WHY YOU WANT me wit'you on this, Ease?" Mouse asked as we rode down Hooper.

He had one foot up on my dashboard and the other knee laid flat on the seat. He wore a yellow short-sleeved shirt that was loose fitting with soft gray slacks and maroon-colored shoes with no socks. Those were his "slumming" clothes.

"Somethin' to wear but not to go nowhere in," as he'd told me more than once.

"I don't know," I said. "I guess I missed runnin' around with you when I thought you were dead. And if the guy who hired me is right and he didn't kill that girl, then I thought I might need you to back me up."

"So you was lyin' when you said that you were tryin' to prove Mustard did it."

"Musa," I said. "And, yeah, I was lyin' but either way I'll do what she would want. If Musa did it I'll find out and if he didn't I'll find out who it was instead."

"An' what's he payin'?"

"It's just a country trade, Raymond. No money."

"Then what do I get wastin' my time when I could be win-nin' money off'a Ginny?"

"Theodore asked me to look into this," I said.

"So?"

"That means he will owe me a pair of handmade shoes."

Raymond lit up there next to me. He might have been a child he was so pleased.

"Drive on, my man," he said. "Drive on."

                    *   *   *

OUR FIRST STOP was a small apartment building on Manchester. Doreen McKenzie had given us the key to her daughter's apartment mostly because she seemed to have a deep regard for Mouse.

"How do you know that woman?" I had asked my friend.

"Don't know her far as I can remember, Ease."

"Then why she show you so much respect?"

"I got a rep, man. People know who I am. You know that."

"Yeah."

Her apartment was built on the model of shotgun architecture of the Deep South. Three rooms in a line from front to back. And because she was on the first floor there was a back door too.

We entered into her bedroom. It was furnished with a big mattress held aloft by a cherry frame, and a vanity with lipsticks, powder cases, and bottles of perfume scattered about. The next room was the toilet. There was makeup crowding the sink and nylons hanging from a rack above the tub.

The last room was the kitchen. It was stacked with dirty dishes and fashion magazines. She had been cutting out pictures of women in sexy poses.

The only food she had was milk that had gone bad and cornflakes, both of them kept in the refrigerator.

Other than the magazines there was no reading material in the house. There were no photographs, no calendar, phone book, telephone directory, or television set. There was a radio on the kitchen counter. It was set on the station KGFJ which specialized in soul music. I knew that because Mouse turned it on.

There were condoms in her medicine cabinet—dozens of them.

There was nothing under the bed.

I was looking between the mattress and box springs when Mouse asked, "What you lookin' for, Easy?"

"Something that might give us an idea about who killed Jackie," I said, a little vexed that he wasn't giving me a hand.

"You mean like this here?" He was holding out a thick sheaf of legal documents.

"Where'd you get that?"

"In the vanity drawer."

Sooner or later I would have checked that drawer. But I had got it in my mind that Jackie was a devious child, that she would have kept her secrets in some pretty obvious hiding place.

It was the deed to a house at the southern outskirts of Compton. She'd paid twelve thousand dollars in cash for the place. It was large enough for a garden but I didn't know if it was zoned for stabling a horse.

On a small piece of paper, folded in between the various documents, she had listed a dozen or so names under an underlined title—$500. Bob Henry was on the list. Ted Durgen was too. Musa Tanous was the second to last name, just before Matthew Munson.

WHEN WE WALKED OUT of the front door I noticed a man pushing a wire shopping cart, stolen from some supermarket, down the street. I say stolen because he wasn't coming home from the grocery store. Neither had he been to the laundromat in the past year or so. His cart was filled with junk he'd picked up along the way. Broken umbrellas, a painting of a white woman holding an apple up to her eye, bottles, cans, newspapers, and various types of clothing. There was a green felt derby in there with a yellow hatband that sported three green feathers and a new-looking powder-blue scarf, festooned with large black polka dots, tied to the guide bar.

Close up the man stank. Mouse refused to get within three steps of him.

"Excuse me," I said. "My name's Easy."

"Hello, Easy," he replied holding out a hand. "I'm Harold."

His hand was big and soft, bloated almost. I didn't want to shake it but I needed to gain the man's confidence.

"You got a cigarette, Easy?" Harold asked me.

I handed him a Chesterfield and lit it. His bloated hand was quivering; there was a line of sweat across his upper lip.

Harold's brown chin sported white stubble and his eyes saw everything and nothing all at once.

"Do you hang out around here much, Harold?"

"Oh yeah. I sleep in that empty lot down the street two, three days a week. You know—when John Bull ain't beatin' the bushes. Sometimes they catch on to me and send me to county jail. It's alright except if it's in with the drunks. You know I hate the smell in there. I stay with my mama sometimes—"

"Did you know a young woman live in here, down on the first floor? Her name is Jackie Jay?"

"Jackie Jay," he said, considering the name for a moment or two. "Jackie Jay. No. No. No I cain't say that I do. My mama's name is Jocelyn—"

"You sure?" I asked. "She's a young black woman . . ." I was wishing that I knew what the woman-child looked like. ". . . a young woman hangs out with men more my age."

"No, sir. Uhp. Whop. Maybe. Did one'a her boyfriends drive a red T-Bird? Convertible?"

"I don't know," I said, honestly. "It could be."

"There's a real pretty young thing wear them, what my mama calls scandalous short skirts. She come outta there every once in a while and this Mexican picks her up in a red sports car. Then they drive off."

"Did you see them last Thursday?"

"Thursday I was in the can," Harold said.

He was short and powerful, maybe fifty years old, but his hairline had just begun to recede. And even though his skin was medium brown you could see the streaks of filth on the back of his hands and across his face.

"Yeah, yeah," he said. "I had a stomach bug, couldn't hardly walk but they said I was drunk and took me off. When I was still sick the next day they took me to the nurse's office and she sent me home. There I was sick like some kinda dog. First they arrest me and then they throw me out on the street. It's a wonder that a colored child ever makes it to be a man."

"Did you notice anything else about the pretty girl and the man in the red car?" I asked. "Did they ever fight?"

But Harold was still thinking about the disservice that the nurse and the police had done him.

"Easy," Mouse said from his three-step distance. "Let's get outta here, man."

"YOU STILL WORKING over at that school, Ease?" Mouse asked me.

We were on the road again, heading back for Ginny's so that Mouse could retrieve his car.

"What else I'm gonna do?" I asked him. "I got to pay the bills."

"What about them apartments you got? Don't they make you some money?"

"I put that away, for Jesus and Feather."

"How is Juice?"

"Almost finished with that boat. It looks good too."

"Why'ont you come to work for me, Ease? I get you rich in no time."

"Doin' what?"

"I got this dockworker gig goin'."

"What's that?"

"I gotta couple'a guys movin' anything from Swiss watches to French champagne for me. I get 'em to drop it off different places and then I make some calls. The people I do business wit' pick the shit up and then they pay me." When Mouse smiled his gray eyes flashed. "Everybody gets paid and the police be scratchin' they heads."

"What you need me for?"

"I don't know, Easy," Mouse shrugged. "You my friend, right? You cleanin' up toilets, right?"

"I'm the supervisor, Raymond. I tell people what to do."

"Whatever. It's the same chump change all these workin' fools bring home. You should live better'n that."

"I like my life just the way it is thank you very much."

"No, baby. That ain't true."

"Why not?"

"If you did like it you wouldn't be out here takin' a pair'a shoes to go out and find a murderer. No, man. You need to come around."

"A man raising children has to set an example, Ray," I said. "Our children, especially our sons look at us to tell what it is they should be doing with their own lives. That's human nature."

"I don't know what you call it but Etta done raised LaMarque well enough to know that if he tried to do like me that he'd get killed inside of a week."

"But it's not just what they think they might be doing," I said. "What they do is buried deep in their minds."

"I don't know about all that shit," Mouse said. "But even if it is true you cain't expect a man to give up everything he is 'cause one day one'a his kids might slip up. This is life, Easy. In the end it's every man for himself."

With those words he climbed out of the car and I drove off. On the way I castigated my friend for his mistaken beliefs. But as I drove I wondered about my own actions; about the late-night visitors, men and women, white and black. I wondered about what my own children saw when they looked at me. At least Raymond's son had seen him seemingly lifeless with a hole ripped in his chest. He looked like a criminal so his son had the ability to make a choice. But to my kids I might have seemed like some kind of hero.

Maybe I was angry with myself and not Raymond at all.

IT WAS JUST A STOREFRONT with a hand-painted canvas sign in the window that read TAXES. There was a camel-colored young woman sitting at a desk set off to the right. She had a sensual face with big orange-tinted lips that must have motivated half the men in the neighborhood to ask her opinion on their taxes.

"Yeah?" she said to me before I could ask my question.

"I need to see Matthew," I said.

"Why?"

"I wanted to talk to him about a five-hundred-dollar murder."

If there had been a movie camera on the receptionist it would have stopped at that frame. She neither blinked nor breathed for a good five seconds.

"What did you say?" she asked at last.

"Get him for me will ya, sister?"

"Matt," she said, raising her voice.

"What?" came a man's voice from the room at the back.

"I think you better come out here."

A medium-sized white man came out. He had thinning hair combed across his head to hide the encroaching baldness. His eyes were blue and his skin yellowy. His lips were almost as large as his secretary's. But his were wrinkled like a day-old balloon that's lost half its air.

"Mr. Munson?"

"Yes?" he asked warily.

"You knew Jackie Jay?"

"Yeah?"

"I'm here representing a man named Musa Tanous. Do you know him?"

"No."

"He owns a building a couple'a blocks down. He was arrested a few days ago for murder."

Matthew gulped and touched his throat with all the fingers of his left hand.

"Rita," he said to the secretary. "I'll be spending a few minutes with this gentleman."

"Yes sir," she said in a thick voice.

I turned her way in time to see her wiping tears from her eyes.

"Follow me, Mister—?"

"Rawlins."

＊   ＊   ＊

LIKE THEODORE, MUNSON had a backroom much larger
than his front office. But most of the space back there went
unused. The only furniture was a pine desk shoved into one
corner. This was crowded with papers and files which were in
turn covered in a fine layer of rubber eraser dust.

The accountant led me to the desk but he didn't sit—
neither did I.

"Now what's this about Jackie?" he asked me.

"I was hired by a man, another man who knew Jackie. He
wants me to make sure that Musa Tanous gets the chair for the
crime."

"You said something about her and a murder?"

"Don't you know?"

"Know what?"

"Jackie was murdered three days ago."

Munson's mouth fell open. His eyelashes fluttered. If he
was acting he was the best I had ever met.

"Who, who is this man? The one you're working for?"

"I can't tell you that, Mr. Munson," I said. "He's married
and, well, you know—important. He doesn't want it to get out
that he was involved."

Munson watched my eyes with a steady gaze. I wasn't worried though. A good liar learns to use his eyes in the tales he
spins. And I was a good liar, a very good one.

"Who are you, Mr. Rawlins?" Munson asked.

"I'm unofficial," I said. "I look into things when people want
to be sure that there's no notes or forms to be filed or remembered. Right now I'm the man looking for Jackie Jay's killer."

Munson winced.

"I thought you said that this Muta guy did it?"

"That's what I thought," I said. "But then I found this list."

I handed him the list I took from Jackie's apartment.

He read it over, then over again.

He held it away from me and asked, "Isn't this police evidence?"

"I got the mother's permission to search Jackie's house. There was no police notice telling me not to look around."

"Well," he said with sudden authority in his voice, "I think I'll hold onto this for the cops if they need it."

I have fast hands. I snatched the list out of Munson's grasp before he could move. He tried to muscle and I slapped him. I didn't think I'd hit him hard but he tipped over and fell on his side. He was up quickly though. There were tears in his eyes.

"Who the hell do you think you are hitting me?" he said.

"You try an' take this paper from me again and I'll kick your ass up and down the block."

He reached for the phone on his desk.

"I'm calling the police."

He picked up the receiver.

I watched him.

He watched me.

"Are you going to give me that list?" The threat was thick and ridiculous on his tongue.

"Why'd you give her the money, Matt?"

The tears were still streaming from his eyes. I doubted if any man ever hated me more than he did at that moment.

"When we met she told me that one day she would ask me for five hundred dollars. She said that I didn't have to give it to her, that I should only do it if I wanted to."

"And did you?"

"What's it to you?" Munson said. He was regaining his feeling of superiority so I reminded him:

"It ain't nuthin' to me, man. But the cops'll be more interested in you bein' on this list than me havin' it."

The accountant's lashes fluttered again. He was so upset that I wouldn't have been surprised if he had started foaming at the mouth.

"Yes," he said.

"You gave it to her?"

"Seven-hundred-and-forty-eight dollars," Munson said, nodding. "And she gave me a letter stating that she owed me the money and that she'd pay off the loan at the rate of five dollars a month."

"Long-term loan. Did she ever make a payment?"

"Yes. Two of them."

I should have felt good. I got what I wanted and I was able to show a superior-feeling white man that he couldn't bully me with his arm or his will. But seeing him so defeated only reminded me of all the defeats me and mine had experienced. I actually felt sorry for him.

"Is Rita's last name Wilford?" I asked.

"No. It's Longtree," he said. "Why?"

"I thought she was a Wilford from down Dallas. Guess I was wrong."

LONG AND LEAN BOB HENRY was sitting at a desk behind a glass wall when I drove up to his Atlas gas station. I asked him about the $500 club and he was easy enough.

"Sure," the copper-haired fifty year old said. "I've spent more on girls give me less in a week than she did in one night.

That girl was sex-crazy. When's the last time you had a twenty year old beggin' you for sex?"

"Seventeen," I said.

"What?"

"Seventeen years old."

"I didn't know that." Bob Henry sat up in his swivel chair. "Any judge in the world look at her and he'd know that she looks twenty."

"She looks dead."

"What?" It was the same question but it took on a whole new tone.

"Murdered. Three days ago. In an alley off of Central."

It's a strange thing seeing a white man go white.

"Who is she to you?" he asked.

"I don't know," I said.

"What's that supposed to mean?"

"She's a complex girl. I didn't know about her until after she was dead but even still she's full'a surprises. Did she start paying you five dollars a week?"

"Yeah. How did you know?"

"Jackie was a very organized young lady. It seems that she paid all of her gentleman friends five dollars a week for a long-term loan."

"What did you say your name was?"

"Easy."

"And what do you have to do with this?"

"I'm looking into it—for the family."

"Isn't this a police job?"

"You'd think so, but I haven't seen one cop looking into it and I bet you haven't either. Look, you didn't even know the girl was dead."

The red-headed man took in my claim with a certain amount of bewilderment.

"What are you saying?" he asked.

"Do you know who might have killed her?"

"No."

"No enemies? No jilted lovers?"

"Jackie had a lot of boyfriends," Bob said. "Sure she did. She never hid that. No. Nobody had any reason to kill her."

TED DURGEN'S HARDWARE STORE was closed by the time I got there. I could wait a day to talk to him. I drove down to a Thrifty's Drug Store on 54th Street and made a call from a phone booth near the ice cream counter.

"Hello," Bonnie said in a musical voice.

"Hey, honey," I said.

"Where are you, Easy? You said that you were just going to get a pair of shoes."

There was a time, when we first got together, that neither one of us would have asked that question. But another man had crossed her path, and though she swore that her love for him was that of a friend, we still asked questions where once there would have been only trust.

"Theodore said if I did something for him that he'd let me have the shoes for free."

"What did he want you to do?"

"Ain't nuthin', honey," I said. "Nuthin' at all. How's the kids?"

"Jesus is sewing his sail and Feather is helping him. Really she's just drinking chocolate milk and talking."

"I got to go out to the Palisades to see this friend of Theodore's," I said. "I'll be back before ten."

"Raymond called. He said if you needed him to call at this number."

I wrote down the number and we hung up.

THE PHONE BOOK TOLD ME that Rita Longtree lived on Defiance Avenue. It was an orange stucco building in the middle of the block. Her door was nestled in a third-floor nook that had a small palm growing in a terra cotta pot right outside.

She was surprised to see me standing there. The orange had been wiped from her lips. Her eyes seemed different.

"Yeah?" It was the same word she used when we first met, only this time the edge was gone.

She'd been crying but that's not what was different. I realized that she was wearing false eyelashes before.

"Rita, I need to talk to you about Jackie."

"I don't know her."

"Yes you do, and if you don't want me to say that to the cops you'll let me in and answer my questions."

As a rule I don't threaten black folk with the law. That's because most of the time I'm trying to help someone black. The police are hardly ever in the position to make a Negro's life easier. They're there to keep us from making trouble. But I needed to know what Rita's connection with the dead girl was and the law opened almost any door in the ghetto.

She let me in and showed me to a chair.

The chair was blue and the couch gray; there were lavender walls and a red-and-brown carpet. It was a poor working girl's apartment, clean and ill-fitted.

She was wearing cranberry slacks and a white T-shirt.

She looked good. Even the sorrow made her attractive.

"What you wanna know?"

"You got a picture of Jackie?"

From a table behind the couch she took a small frame that had an oval aperture. The photograph was of a lovely, smiling young woman, a little heavy but worth every pound.

"She was beautiful," Rita said.

"You knew her pretty well?" I asked.

"Uh-huh. We were friends."

"Did you know her before she got to know Mr. Munson?"

"No. She met Matt at a hamburger stand down Hoover. At first he'd bring her over to the office after I went home but after a while they got sloppy and I'd catch 'em. After that she'd call sometimes when he was out with a client and we talked. She was a really good person." Sorrow constricted the last few words.

"Did she love your boss?" I asked.

Rita smiled through the tears.

"Jackie just liked men," she said. "I mean they had to be older and they couldn't be black but after that she wasn't too picky. She didn't mind if they was fat or bald or plain."

"How about rich?" I asked.

"No. I mean she had her investment plan but you didn't have to be rich to belong to that."

"That was to buy her house?"

"Uh-huh. She fount this house for only twelve thousand dollars in Compton. Then she would ask her boyfriends to put up the money, like an interest-free loan. She had started payin' it back. She called it her rent."

"And where'd she get that?"

"She was a good girl," Rita said. "She was only seventeen you know. And her mama could hardly make enough to pay the rent. And Jackie really liked the men she was with. So what if a couple'a them gave her money?"

It was a discussion held between women that I had been overhearing since I was a child. Poor young women with no money, and no hope for a job, taking a handout now and then from a "friend." Maybe he was called "uncle" or a family friend. He was older and lonely and willing to let her go out dancing when she wanted to. The money was always in an envelope and never in the bedroom. Sometimes there wasn't even sex at all, just a series of well-dressed dates and maybe a kiss or two at the end of the evening.

"Why not black men?" I asked.

"She hated her father," Rita said. "He used to beat her mother and brother. She said that most'a the white men she was with were gentle."

"What about Musa Tanous?"

"She loved him for real. She'd call me after they were together and tell me about his stories about castles in Jordan and Lebanon. His family used to own a castle that was a thousand years old."

"When's the last time she called you?"

"The morning she was killed." Her throat tightened again.

"What time?"

"About eight. We planned to meet at Brenda's Sunshine Diner on Eighty-second at eight-thirty but she never got there."

"Where'd she call from?"

"The motel."

"You sure?"

Rita nodded.

"Can I use your phone?"

"Is it long distance?"

"Station to station but I'll give you two dollars for it."

"You better. It's 'cause of you I lost my job."

"What do you mean?"

"Matt really didn't know that Jackie was dead. When he asked me if I knew and I said yeah he fired me."

"Oh."

"YES?" Musa Tanous said into my ear.

"It's Easy Rawlins," I said.

"I've been waiting for you, Mr. Rawlins."

"Where were you from eight to nine on the day Jackie was killed, Mr. Tanous?"

"Picking up floor wax from a distributor on Alameda. S&J Distributions."

"You were in the place at eight?"

"Yes. Mr. Hind and I were having coffee. He's an old friend."

"What time did you leave Mr. Hind?"

"Quarter to ten. Why?"

"What time did they find Jackie?"

"Nine-fifteen," he said, and then he choked. "She had been stabbed and beaten. She wasn't dead until they got her to the hospital."

Nothing I could say seemed important but still I went on, "If that's true then I can prove that you didn't do it."

"Do you know who did?"

"I didn't sign up for that. But once the cops clear you then they'll probably find the man who did it. It's somebody she knows. It always is."

"So what do we do now?"

"Give me the name of your lawyer. I'll tell him what I found out."

Musa gave me a name, William Berg, and the number to call.

I told Rita that the lawyer would probably call but that it wouldn't be any trouble.

It was time for me to leave but I hesitated.

"He really fired you because of Jackie?" I asked.

"Yeah. I asked him for my last paycheck but he said that I didn't even deserve that. I can take him to court but my landlord'll have me on the street before he'll pay me."

"Can you do accounting work?"

"I learned a lot from Mr. Munson. I could do simple stuff. Preparin' and like that."

"I can probably get you a job. I know a guy runs a place that does unofficial accounting work. Over on Pico."

I gave her Anatole Zane's name and number. I told her to use my name and he'd probably hire her right off.

I keep a hundred dollar bill in my wallet at all times—in the *secret* fold. I gave it to the young siren.

"What's this for?" she asked. It was almost an accusation.

"To pay your rent until the next check comes through."

"Why?"

"How old are you, Rita?"

"Twenty."

"I'm forty-four. I went in there today and slapped your boss to the ground. That's why he fired you. At my age a man should take responsibility where he finds it. Take that money and use it. And remember, you didn't have to do anything for it except be on the right side of life."

❖   ❖   ❖

BONNIE AND I MADE LOVE that night. It wasn't the way we usually came together. Afterward she asked, "What is it, Easy?"

"What?"

"The way you touched me. It was so delicate, as if you thought you might hurt me, as if you didn't know my body."

"Do you love me, baby?" I asked her.

"Yes. You know I do."

"I'm not talkin' about in a perfect world," I said. "I'm not askin' do you love me lyin' here next to you. I don't mean do I measure up to other men you've known pound for pound. What I'm sayin' is that I'm just a janitor and a small-time property owner. I'm not ever gonna make a difference in the way you live or in the quality of your life."

"I don't understand, Easy."

"The only doors I can open are back doors," I said. "The only money I'll ever have is either small change or money that got blood on it, one way or the other it's not what a woman like you should expect."

"Is this about Jogaye again?"

"Not just him. There's other princes and bankers, generals and entrepreneurs you meet. Some of 'em are black but there's white ones too. What I'm sayin' Bonnie is that I can't do for you. I can only follow and hope you don't take off so far ahead that I won't even see your dust. I meet people every day that need my help. Kids at the school, people like Theodore Steinman. But you're in a whole other class. You in the sky half the time around men and women who wouldn't give me a second look."

"Does any of this has to do with what Mr. Steinman asked you to do for him?"

"There was girl a friend of his knew. She was murdered."

"That's terrible."

"It was. I met a friend of hers, another girl who needed help. I gave her a little information and a couple'a dollars. I helped her. I made a difference."

"And didn't you save me when I was in trouble?"

"You never needed me," I said, and I meant it. "You're every bit as tough as I am and smarter too."

Bonnie touched my cheek with her fingertips. "My father once told me that a great man walks the back roads. He does what's right every day and no one knows it but those lucky enough to be loved by him."

"He did, huh?"

"I love you, Easy Rawlins. No matter what happens with us or with how you feel about me. I have never known a better man than you."

I CALLED THEODORE the next morning and told him that Raymond would collect one pair of handmade shoes. Then I called Raymond and asked him to go over and talk to Jackie's mother.

"Explain to her that Musa did not kill Jackie and tell her that the police will be put on the right track. Also tell her that I'll be sending a gift that Jackie had been saving for her."

"Okay, Ease," Mouse said. "But you know you wastin' all that talent on these poor people. A dollar down here don't stay long, brother. And you know it's only a matter'a time for that poor woman lose her stupid son too."

AFTER WORK I drove out to the Pacific Palisades, to Musa Tanous's home.

It was a modest house compared to some of the mansions in that neighborhood. I doubted if he had more than five bedrooms on the three floors. Birds of paradise proliferated on either side of his front door.

He seated me in his den. There was the heavy odor of port wine and tobacco in there. He had a chess board set up for play.

"Do you play chess, Mr. Rawlins?"

"No sir. I do not."

He handed me an envelope. Inside was the key I expected but also a small stack of hundred dollar bills, ten by the feel of them.

"I didn't ask you for money," I said.

"The money you saved me in legal expenses alone is worth that," he said. "And I want you to have it. You proved I didn't kill Jackie and you never even saw the photograph of her."

"I saw one at the house of a friend of hers," I said, but he was already reaching for a something on the bookshelf behind him.

He took down a small picture and handed it to me.

All I saw was the polka dot scarf and the felt green derby with the yellow band and green feathers.

I WAS DOWN at the vacant lot across from Jackie's apartment in less than an hour. At the far corner was a cardboard lean-to that smelled of Harold.

There were twenty-three little girl's dolls lined up against the paper wall. Above them was a note written in red lipstick.

Little black girls mess with white men ain't worth the shit in they mamas toilets. They need to die. They going to die. Oh yes, dear lord.

By the time I had gotten to the police station and back again the fire engines were already there. The lean-to had burned up completely. The only thing left of the dolls was the smell of burnt rubber, a few charred limbs, and glass eyes.

I PUT UP A SIGN on my amber door. It reads:

EASY RAWLINS
RESEARCH AND DELIVERY

I spent over six months looking for Harold but he was nowhere among the poor street people of Watts. I couldn't convince the police to even mount a search. They decided that Musa Tanous had hired someone to kill his girlfriend. And even though they couldn't prove it they refused to believe that some tramp could be smart enough to leave no clues.

I figure that he saw me go into his cardboard teepee. He set fire to it when I went for the cops. Maybe he had searched Musa's car when he was in Jackie's house and knew where they went. Or maybe he followed her somehow. Manchester wasn't far from Musa's building.

I still work at Sojourner Truth Junior High School and see Raymond now and then. Bonnie and I are still together. I read the newspapers a little closer nowadays. Looking for the deaths of young black women and reading in between the lines.

Printed in the USA
CPSIA information can be obtained
at www.ICGtesting.com
CBHW010754200224
4502CB00005B/85